# CRAVING KARA

## THE ACES' SONS

# BY NICOLE JACQUELYN

# DEDICATION

*To Biz and Danielle,*
*My cousins and very first best friends.*
*I don't know how I would've ever done*
*this life without you.*

# PROLOGUE

# DRACO

CRACKED MY knuckles—the only show of nerves that I allowed myself anymore—as I watched the door across the room. It had been a month since I'd seen Kara and I didn't want to miss a second of being in her presence. I felt starved for her. It was pathetic, really, the way I used her visits to keep me going. It was also supremely fucking unfair to her, which was why I never let on how important her visits were. She was young, and since I'd been inside, the small age gap between us seemed to have widened exponentially. She was still going to school, getting yelled at by her parents, and figuring out where to send her college applications, while I... well, I spent the morning carrying around a contraband joint for a guy called Mutt because we'd heard that his cell was going to get tossed—and I owed him.

It was a whole different world inside, and I was trying to figure out the best way to navigate it. Sometimes, I felt like forgetting home was better. I'd spend the entire day refusing to think about life on the outside—our house, what my parents were doing, if Curt had completely trashed the media room now that I wasn't there to tell him to clean up his mess—but always, by the time I laid my head down at night, I'd put myself into a panic, forcing myself into remembering every miniscule thing I could, terrified that I'd forget what real life was like.

My pop had told me to keep my head down and do my time. The club had set up protection for me inside, which was a relief, but that protection didn't come without strings. Mutt was the main watchdog, which worked out pretty good for me because I actually liked the guy. He reminded me of my Uncle Grease a little. But there were others, too, men who made it known that they'd step in if anyone fucked with me. The consequence of being protected so I didn't get raped or stabbed in the shower? I had to run errands, pass messages, hold shit that could get me into serious trouble, and occasionally be a rat. It was a more than fair trade, but it still fucking sucked.

I hated it. I hated the way everything smelled. I hated being sur-rounded by men who would as easily stab me in the throat as look at me, I hated the isolation and my cell. I hated the food. I hated the fact that I couldn't go outside until my designated yard time. I hated the boredom and the tedium and the motherfucking fluorescent lighting that had started giving me migraines.

But what I hated most of all and could never tell anyone was the fact that I felt like I had a bullseye painted on my back and I was scared all the goddamn time. Wanted-my-fucking-mommy terrified. I'd had to teach myself to freeze instead of flinch anytime someone surprised me. Weakness, no matter how protected I was, could get me killed. I barely slept.

I held my breath as the door opened and the visitors filed in. My eyebrows rose in surprise as Charlie and Curt came walking through the door with my mom. The group always had to have an adult with them when they visited, which seemed incredibly ironic since Curt was my twin and I fucking lived in the prison—but whatever. Where was Kara?

"Hey!" Charlie said, dropping onto the bench across from me. "How you doin'? You okay?"

"Brother, dear," Curtis said dryly, shooting Charlie a *chill* look.

"Hey, baby," my mom said as she sat down last, her jaw tight. She took great pains to hide how much she hated that I was in there, but it was impossible for her to mask every expression. Her loathing for the guards that barked out orders any time she got too close to me was a palpable thing. If she could've carried a weapon inside the prison, I had a feeling she would've done something stupid.

I waited for a minute for them to tell me where she was, but finally spoke when no one else did.

"Not that I'm not happy to see ya," I said to the small group. I cleared my throat. "But I thought Kara was comin'?"

Jesus, it felt pathetic to even ask. I hated that, too.

"She called last night and told me she couldn't make it today," my mom said with a small shrug. "So, I let Charlie know, since it was her turn next."

"Why?" I asked, looking at Charlie. "She okay?"

"As far as I know," Charlie replied, nodding her head. "Maybe she just had family shit or something. I don't know. I haven't talked to her."

"You should make sure everything's okay," I said, the words tumbling out of my mouth before I could stop them. I couldn't believe that Kara had missed a visit unless something was wrong.

I knew what they saw when they looked at me. I knew that they could see right through the nonchalance and the cool expression. They saw the way I was desperate to see Kara, the way I worried about her and pined for her and couldn't seem to focus on anything but her. I couldn't imagine any reason that she would cancel a visit unless there was an emergency, but by the looks on my family's faces, they didn't see it the same way.

"She's fine," Curt said dryly. "But my baby isn't. Someone slashed poor Roxanne's tires." Roxanne was his fully restored Chevelle. I rolled my eyes, but followed along with his change of subject.

"You know who it was?" I asked, leaning forward on my elbows. We'd faced a lot of backlash since the day I'd beat the hell out of one of our classmates, but I'd hoped that me being inside would take some of the heat off my brother. I was already being punished, they didn't need to give him shit, too.

"Coulda been Caleb Carson," Curt said, rolling his lips inside his teeth in an effort to hold back his smile. "Actually, I'm pretty sure it was."

"Yeah, because you were parked outside his girlfriend's house while her parents were out of town," Charlie said in disgust.

"She was helpin' me study," Curt said to me, straight faced. "She's real smart."

I knew Caleb's girlfriend, April. Sweet, pretty, and fun described her. Smart did not. I snorted.

"You know," my mom said, rolling her eyes, "it's gonna be real nice when you two are old enough to visit without me. I love bein' here, but it goes against nature for me to hear this shit."

All of us paused for a moment, the reality of the situation dropping like a bomb in the middle of the room. Eventually, Curt and Charlie would be legal adults and able to visit me by themselves—and I'd still be in here.

Not for the first time, my mind circled around whether or not what I'd done was worth it. Inevitably, the look on Kara's face when she saw the video someone had taken of her half naked and vulnerable flashed through my memories. That memory always popped up when I was feeling sorry for myself and I always came to the same conclusion. If I could go back, I'd still beat the shit out of the asshole who'd taken that video—I just wouldn't have done it with so many witnesses.

# CHAPTER 1

# KARA

*Four years later*

"YOU WANT A bean?" I asked, leaning out of the window toward the large truck and the chubby old man inside.

"You know it, darlin'," he replied, grinning.

I gave him two, just because.

"Here you go," I said, handing over his coffee, the two little coffee beans rolling around on top. "Gimme one sec and I'll get your bride's."

"Thanks, honey," his wife called from the passenger seat. I couldn't see her face unless she ducked down, but I could picture her perfectly. She wore her hair in a long gray waterfall down her back, the top half pulled back and held with a barrette, and her eyes were permanently crinkled at the corners from laughter.

Bill and Hazel were two of my best regulars. I loved them, probably because they reminded me of my grandparents who I didn't see often enough.

As I placed the lid on Hazel's coffee, I cleared my throat and glanced at the clock. Only two more hours until I closed up the little coffee cart, but it felt like I still had two weeks to go.

"Here you go," I said, not bothering to add beans to Hazel's half-sweet mocha, since she thought they tasted like the bottom of a shoe.

"Don't tell anyone," Bill said as he took the coffee carefully from my hand, "but you're my favorite."

"You really are," Hazel said, ducking down to meet my gaze. "He always watches to see if your Jeep is out front!"

"Well," I replied, glancing sneakily from side to side before I continued, "you're my favorite, too."

Bill hooted, and put his hand dreamily over his heart, making me laugh.

"Now get outta here," I said, glancing toward the sky.

"You should be leavin', too," Bill said as he started up his truck. He had to practically yell over the sound of the diesel engine. "Can't be good for you to be workin' in this."

"I'll be alright," I assured him. "I'm almost done here and then headed home."

"You be safe," Hazel yelled.

"You, too," I replied.

I cleared my throat again as they pulled away from the window and suppressed a cough as I leaned toward the truck that had taken their spot.

"Hey, how's it going?" I said automatically.

"Better now," Draco replied.

I huffed and gave him a half smile, trying to hide how flustered I was. I'd known Draco for most of my life and we had a more dramatic history than most couples that had been married for fifty years, but things were beyond weird between us now. I tried to keep an eye out for him and I usually had a second to brace myself before he got to the window, but I'd been too distracted this time.

"You want the usual?" I asked, glancing behind him at the line of cars.

"Please," he confirmed, grinning. God. It should be against the laws of nature to be that good looking.

"I don't know why you come through here to get plain black coffee," I replied as I stepped back and got his drink ready. "You could make this at home."

"I could," he said easily as I handed him the plain drip coffee.

I waved him off as he tried to hand me money. Charlie and I never let our people pay. We told them it was the perk of knowing the barista. Truthfully, we just took it out of our tips at the end of each shift. We considered it an even trade since we got visits while we were working. Plus, they usually tipped really well even though they weren't paying, so they ended up paying anyhow.

So, when Draco leaned further out the truck window and stuffed a twenty into the tip jar, I wasn't surprised.

I sighed dramatically, not bothering to argue. He wasn't going to take that twenty back, even though it was way too much. "Thank you."

He sat there, looking at me as he took a sip of his coffee. "Way better than I could make at home," he said quietly. "You out of here soon?"

"Not too much longer," I replied, even though I had hours left.

"Good," he said, still holding eye contact. "It's getting nasty out here."

"I'll be alright."

"Let me know if you need anything."

I nodded and swallowed hard. We both knew the world would have to be ending before I asked him for help...probably not even then.

"See you later, sweetheart."

I nodded and gave an awkward wave as he put the truck into gear and pulled away. As soon as he was far enough away not to see me, I took a step back into the little trailer and shook out my hands and smoothed back my hair. It didn't matter how many times he showed up for coffee, it left me frazzled every time.

I cleared my throat and forced myself to lean toward the little window again and smiled, "Hey, what can I get ya?"

For the next hour, I kept a smile on my face as my eyes watered and the air grew even more difficult to deal with. By the time my boss showed up with her husband and turned the neon *Open* sign off, I was so congested, I sounded like a honking goose when I spoke.

"You head out," she said, rubbing my back briskly as she passed me in the small space. "We're gonna tow the whole cart outta here for now. Stash it somewhere I don't have to worry about it."

"Text me later?" I said, not bothering to ask any questions as I pulled off my apron.

"I'll send out a group text in a couple hours," Mallory replied, nodding as she quickly secured the supplies on the counters and in the sinks. "Go home." She raised her head to look at me. "Check in, alright? Let me know how you guys are doing."

"I will," I agreed as I turned toward the door with a wave. Less than a minute later, I was driving home. I probably should've offered to stay and help Mallory pack up, but I knew I'd just be in the way. Plus, I couldn't wait to take a shower. I smelled like an ashtray.

By the time I got to my front door, every thought of a shower had gone out the window and I felt like I was walking through mud. Damn, I was tired. After barely getting any sleep the night before and my four am shift at the coffee cart, I was beat. Thank God Mallory closed the cart early. I wasn't sure how I would've made it to the end of my shift.

"Honey, I'm home," I called out, opening the front door and tossing my purse onto the couch. "Are you?"

"Yep," my roommate and best friend replied, popping up from behind the kitchen counter. I yelped in surprise.

"Jesus, were you hiding?" I asked, kicking off my shoes.

"No, I was looking for that cheese grater I borrowed from my mother so I can return it."

"She's probably bought a new one by now," I said, walking past her toward my bedroom.

"Yeah, I know," Charlie replied, following me. "But if I go over there without it, she'll bug me about it the whole time."

"Probably," I agreed, pulling my phone out to check it for the tenth time that day. The news was saying that the wild fire in our area was getting closer. *Zero containment* were their exact words. *Unpredictable winds.* "Mallory closed up the shop," I told Charlie as I sat on the edge of the bed. "She was having it towed somewhere out of the danger zone."

"Sweet," Charlie replied. We both worked at the shop, but we rarely had the same shift—which, if I was being honest, was probably a good thing. We spent enough time together as it was.

"*Sweet* until it's time to pay rent," I replied, making a face.

"We'll be fine. We always are. They're saying to stay inside because the air is so bad," Charlie said, leaning against the doorframe. "Which means you should've gotten hazard pay for this morning. You smell like a campfire. Are you gonna go to your parents' to wait this shit out?"

"Yeah, right," I replied with a scoff. "I'm not getting stuck there. The boys would probably shave half of my head or something while I slept."

"You just stayed the night a couple of months ago," she pointed out dryly.

"That was then, this is now," I said, dropping onto my bed. "Are you going to stay with your parents?"

"Well, I was going to—that's why I was trying to find the cheese grater," she said, crossing her arms over her chest. "But I don't want to leave you here by yourself. That sucks."

I laughed. "I can stay at our apartment by myself."

"Yeah, right," she replied stubbornly.

"It's no big deal. I'll go to my parents' house if shit gets crazy."

"As if this isn't crazy enough?" Charlie grunted in annoyance. "Why don't you stay at my parents' house with me? It'll be like old times."

A dozen snapshots ran through my mind—memories of the times

I'd stayed the night at her house growing up and the person I was then—and I shook my head. I wasn't feeling like a trip down memory lane.

"I'll be fine," I replied, making a shooing motion with my hands. "I'll keep an eye on the news. It'll be a nice break. Like a vacation."

"A vacation where you're all alone and surrounded by fire," Charlie said, grimacing. "Sounds super fun."

"Would you get out of here already?" I said, tossing a throw pillow at her. "I'm serious. I'll be fine. If I'm not, I'll drive over to my parents' house. No big deal."

"If you're sure," she hedged.

"I know I haven't been clear," I replied sarcastically, "but you can *really* go."

"Fine," she said, standing up straight. "But if you change your mind, I'm sure the old man would come get you."

"I know," I said with a smile. "I'm your dad's favorite."

"That's because he thought you kept me out of trouble," Charlie said with a snicker as she walked away.

As soon as she was out of sight, my smile dropped. God, I couldn't believe what was happening. We'd never dealt with wild fires like the ones currently raging through the state. Sure, we'd had fires—we had them every year—but never so close to home. Thankfully, our apartment was pretty close to town and I was sure that whoever was in charge would move heaven and earth to try and keep the damage in town to a minimum.

My parents' house was also inside the city limits and probably safe, but a lot of people we knew weren't so lucky. Charlie's sisters and parents all had places on the outskirts. So did most of the people in our circle. Hell, even the Aces' clubhouse and garage where I'd spent half of my childhood were out in the woods.

Even though the whole situation sucked, I was still going to try and take advantage of the time away from work. Look on the bright side of things, right? I planned to sit my ass on the couch and spend my time reading or sleeping when I wasn't watching the news.

Of course, there was always the chance that the fire crews would get the wildfires in our area under control and then I'd be working like usual. I wrinkled my nose. That was really the best-case scenario, but I didn't see it happening. We'd never dealt with fires like these before. They were fast spreading and scary as hell.

Climbing off the bed, I moved around the room plugging in my phone, laptop and e-reader. I told myself it was because I was going to take full advantage of the quiet apartment while Charlie was gone and not because I was worried that my electronics would go dead and I'd have no contact with the outside world.

"Kara!" Charlie yelled gleefully from down the hall.

"Charles!" I yelled back as I headed toward her room.

"Dude," she said, tossing me a face mask as soon as I'd stepped inside the doorway.

I didn't catch it in time and it landed on the floor.

"I warned you," Charlie said in exasperation.

"You said, *dude*," I argued, leaning down to pick it up. "That's not a warning."

"I will never understand how horrendous your reflexes are."

"I'll never understand how you could catch a marble someone threw you from thirty feet away. It's not normal."

"I'm exceptional," she replied matter-of-factly. "But look—" she nodded at the mask in my hand. "Mark sent those home with me like a year ago. Wear it if you go outside."

I stared at her uncomprehendingly.

"My brother-in-law is practically a doomsday prepper. He's pre-pared for everything," she said slowly. "That'll help keep the junk out of your lungs."

"Cool?" I replied.

"Oh my God," she said, laughing. "Just wear the fucking mask, okay? Seriously. The little infographic on the news said our air is like, red status."

"Well, if the air is red," I joked, nodding.

"Use the freaking mask," she ordered, pointing at it.

"How do I look?" I asked, putting the mask over my mouth and nose.

"Like a goober," she replied, with a laugh. "But it should work. Mark knows his shit and he said these ones are the best if you don't have a gas mask."

"Well, I'm glad he sent these because I'm not wearing a goddamn gas mask to the grocery store," I said, shaking the mask by the little elastic straps.

"I have one for Rebel, too," she said. "I wonder if she'd be able to use it?"

Our other best friend, my cousin Rebel, had some sensory issues. "It wouldn't hurt to ask," I said with a shrug. "She'd probably like to match with us."

Charlie nodded and imitated the Darth Vader breathing sounds behind her hand. Leaning back into the closet, she started talking. "You know you're going to have visitors when they find out you're still here."

"Then lie if they ask," I replied. I knew she was right. I also knew what her reply to my order would be before she said it.

"Not happening," she said, as I mouthed the words silently along with her.

I watched in confusion as she pulled out a pair of riding goggles with a huff of satisfaction. I had no clue what she planned on doing with those when we weren't even supposed to be outside.

"I'm not playing into this whole thing you're doing with Draco," she said flatly, taking my attention away from the goggles in her hand.

"You two can deal with it on your own."

"I'm not sure how that's true, since none of you can seem to keep your noses out of it," I shot back, meeting her eyes.

We'd had the conversation a hundred times before, and like a hundred times before, I knew there would be no resolution, no matter how long we went in circles.

"When you're making everything awkward as hell in a group that you've grown up with," she snapped, "it's kind of hard to ignore."

"We're not making anything awkward," I said, trying hard to keep my voice level. "You guys constantly pushing us together does that!"

"If you think anyone but Draco is pushing, you're fucking blind," she replied. "We're just all trying to stay out of the blast zone."

"So, stay out of it," I said, throwing up one arm in exasperation. "I don't need your commentary about whether I'll have visitors or not, and I don't need you telling them where I am, even if they ask. I have a dad, I don't need another."

She stared at me. "Don't think *dad* is the role Draco wants to play."

"I don't know why it's 'they' anyway," I continued, ignoring her comment. "Curt didn't give a flying fuck where I was or what I was doing when Draco was gone, but now, all of a sudden, he cares? What the hell is that about?"

"You tell me," she said insinuatingly.

My mouth dropped open. "Fuck you," I shot back. "Don't act like you think there's something going on with me and Curtis when you know there's not."

Charlie sighed. "You're right. That was a shitty thing to say."

The room was silent for a long moment.

"Are you sure you don't want to come stay with us?" she asked again, the change of subject swift and easy. We'd been having the Draco argument for a long time—it didn't change our friendship and we didn't even get mad about it anymore. "You know Farrah always has the good snacks."

"No, thank you, and stop calling your mother Farrah," I said, shaking my head. "Bring me home some Cheetos, though."

"No way," she said, tossing her snow boots onto the middle of the floor. "You snooze, you loose, bro. And I'll call her Farrah if I want. I think she actually likes it."

I snorted. Charlie's mom definitely did *not* want her daughter to call her by her first name. I'd lost count of how many times Farrah had corrected her over the years.

"I'm going to run to the store and get some supplies so I don't have to leave later," I said, already dreading the walk to my car. "Will you be here when I get back?"

"No, I'm almost done packing," Charlie said as she got to her feet. "But text me when you get home, okay? People are going to be acting nuts."

"Yes, Mom," I joked as I stepped into the hallway. I fought and lost the urge to poke my head back into her room, knowing I was a complete hypocrite. "Text me when you get to your parents'."

"Yes, Mom," she replied.

I deserved that one.

★  ★  ★

THE TRIP TO the store was uneventful beyond the fact that people had cleared out some of the shelves in preparation of being stranded. It always made me laugh when I saw what folks considered necessary for survival during a natural disaster. I was no expert, but I was pretty sure that they would've survived without cleaning out the toilet paper, individual water bottles, cans of tuna, and bagels, of all things. I shook my head as I carried a couple of two-gallon jugs of water inside. There had been at least a hundred of them, sitting untouched in perfect rows above the empty shelves.

Water was water and people were dumb.

Locking the door behind me, I carried the jugs into the kitchen feeling pretty proud of myself. I had food for at least four days, water, and soda. I even had a few beers and a bottle of wine that someone had left in the fridge in case the mood struck. I'd probably feel like crap after eating nothing but junk food, but it was a chance I was willing to take. Besides, the wind could always shift and the fires change direction or something. Maybe things would go back to normal faster than everyone was expecting.

As I texted Charlie that I was home for the foreseeable future, my phone rang, startling me.

I answered it formally, "Hello, Father."

"Hello, daughter," he replied, his raspy, deep voice laced with amusement. "How's my favorite girl?"

"Better not let Rose hear you say that," I joked.

"Rose is all woman, honey," he replied.

"Don't be gross," I ordered easily. "What's up?"

"Just callin' to check in," he said. "Been watchin' the news. They're worried the fires are headed in our direction. You gonna come over here?"

"I think I'm just going to wait it out here," I replied.

"You're shittin' me, right?" he said in disbelief. "Why the hell would you do that?"

"Because I'm an adult and I have my own place?"

"Your *own place* doesn't have a generator if the power goes out," he replied. "Charlie with you?"

"She went to Casper and Farrah's."

"Oh, okay, so one of you is bein' rational. That's good," he grumbled. "Wouldn't have thought it would be the crazy one, but alright."

I couldn't help but laugh. "I'll be fine," I assured him as I started putting groceries away. "I've got food and drinks and Charlie even left me a mask in case I have to go outside for some reason. Plus, I can watch the news just as easily here as I could at your house."

"You're gonna make me come out in this bullshit and get you," he said, ignoring my assurance. "Soon as you get freaked out enough. And I'm gonna have to be out there with the idiots that don't know where they're going or what they're doin', runnin' around like chickens with their heads cut off." He scoffed.

"I won't ask you to come get me, I promise," I replied.

"Well, hell, don't say that," he snapped. "If you need me to come get ya, of course I'll come get ya."

I smiled.

"Okay, I promise to call you if I need you," I replied. "But honestly, Dad, I'm just going to lay around and read. We don't even know if the power is going to go out."

"It's not lookin' good, princess," he argued. "The power company is sayin' they might be shuttin' shit off just to be safe."

"Well, I'll be fine even if they do. It's not like I'm going to freeze."

"More likely, you'll pass out from the heat," he agreed. "Keep checkin' in, alright?"

"Of course."

"Love you, kiddo."

"Love you, too."

Not long after we'd gotten off the phone, my anxiety started to grow. As I sat on the couch with my bag of pretzels, I scrolled through the news stations on my phone, trying to find the most recent updates. Fortunately, nothing had changed since I'd checked my phone earlier. The fires were still raging outside of town and our apartment was still on evacuation level one, which meant we were just supposed to have our things ready to go.

I couldn't imagine that the fire would make it into town, but I still felt a small twinge of panic when I thought about my conversation with my dad. He hadn't come across as outwardly worried, but he'd definitely seemed concerned about the situation.

My dad didn't generally get *concerned.*

Dropping my phone on my chest, I leaned my head back against the edge of the couch and closed my eyes. I had a few free days where I didn't need to be anywhere and had the apartment to myself. I needed to take advantage of that and I was going to start by taking a nap.

Opening my eyes, I lifted my phone again to make sure the ringer was turned up—just in case.

Even though I was worried, I fell asleep within minutes.

I slept so hard that when I woke up a few hours later, I was disoriented. What was I doing on the couch? What time was it? Where was Charlie? Was I late for work? Thankfully, after less than a minute, I'd gotten my wits back. I checked my phone again to make sure I hadn't missed any calls and refreshed the local news page.

The apartment was still at level one, but something seemed different when I looked at the little red, yellow, and green areas of the map. Had the boundaries moved? I couldn't tell.

As I pushed myself up off the couch and headed to my room, I called Charlie.

"What's up?" she answered. "You coming over?"

"No," I said with a laugh. "We're still at level one, but I think I'm going to take that *be ready* to heart and pack up some stuff in case I need to bail."

"Good call," she replied. "Don't worry about my shit, I already grabbed anything I couldn't live without if our apartment went up in a fiery inferno."

"When?" I asked in surprise.

"When they made us level one."

"Why didn't I notice?"

"Probably because there isn't a ton of shit I can't live without,"

17

Charlie replied. "I got my electronics and important paperwork and some jewelry and shit. The rest was just clothes and toiletries to stay with my parents. No big deal."

I looked around my room. What couldn't I live without?

"I better get packing," I mumbled. "I don't even know where to start."

"Birth certificate, EpiPen, and bank shit," Charlie replied instantly. "Did you need help or something?"

"No," I said distractedly. "I was calling to see if I needed to grab anything of yours."

"Oh, thanks," she said, a smile in her voice. "I'm good. If I think of anything I forgot, I'll let you know."

"Alright."

"Let me know if you leave the apartment, okay?" she asked. "Just so I know where you are."

"Will do. Are you guys okay at your parents' place?"

"All good here," she assured me. "Level two still and the smoke is terrible, but no sign of fire."

"Jesus," I mumbled. "Please leave before you see fire."

"I'll do what I can," she said with a laugh before hanging up.

With a sigh, I looked around my room. I wasn't really sure what to take. There were a thousand little things that I'd prefer not to lose, but what was really important? Following Charlie's advice, I double checked that I had my EpiPen in my purse, then pulled out my birth certificate, passport, school and bank information and stacked them on my bed. Those would have to go with me, for sure. I also grabbed the little notebook I used to keep track of bills and added it to the pile.

Setting my hands on my hips, I looked around. Okay, clothes and shoes next. As I picked through the things I may need, I set them on the bed next to my important stuff pile. After a few minutes, the stacks had grown so much that I was grimacing. The idea of having to pick and choose what I wanted to leave behind was harder than I'd thought it would be. After a few minutes of arguing with myself about what I actually *needed*, I put about half of the clothes back into my dresser and decided I wouldn't open the drawers again for any reason. Toiletries were easier because I didn't have much. I used the fancy shampoo, conditioner, face wash and moisturizers that Charlie's mom, Farrah, recommended, but it was a pretty streamlined system. I hadn't really cared about that stuff in a long time, and it was nice having someone else just tell me what I should use.

A little less than an hour after I started gathering my stuff, I had everything packed into a large suitcase, a duffle bag, a small cardboard box, a milk crate, and a backpack that was only halfway filled.

I sat on the edge of my bed and looked at the top shelf my closet. Did I need anything in there? Would it really matter if I left it all behind? If I took it with me, what would that say?

The small box at the far left side of the shelf seemed to stand out like a beacon, even though I'd been successful at ignoring it since I'd stashed it there when we'd moved into our apartment.

"Fuck it," I mumbled, surging to my feet. I emptied the backpack and carried it over to the closet. The box was light, but I still put it into the bag as fast as I could. Even touching it seemed like a bad idea. Then I put the contents I'd poured out of the backpack back into it, successfully hiding the box.

After debating for a few minutes, I decided to put my packed belongings by the front door instead of in my car. If I had to leave, it would still be pretty easy to lug them down the stairs, but I didn't take the chance of all my stuff being stolen if someone noticed it outside.

"Done," I said out loud, proud of myself. Then I caught sight of the bottle opener shaped like a penis that my stepmom had given me for my twenty-first birthday. She'd told me, *The guys would rather use their teeth than this thing, so you'll always know where it is. Genius.* It was ridiculous and awesome and *so* Rose, a mix of practical and wild. I'd just throw it in my purse. No big deal.

But then, when I went to grab the bottle opener, I saw the picture of Charlie and I on the fridge and I wasn't sure if we had a digital copy of it. I couldn't even remember who'd printed it in the first place. There was a candle holder my baby brother Brody had made me in preschool out of a small glass baby food jar with colored tissue paper stuck to the outside. A vase that had been my Nana's and she'd handed down to me when I moved out. All irreplaceable.

Thirty minutes later I had another bag full of things that I couldn't stand to leave behind.

I had to stop looking around the house. How did people do this? How did you narrow it down? Maybe it was easier when the threat was imminent and you could only grab the absolute basics. I had too much time to worry about the things I'd leave behind.

Oh, shit. I strode over to the couch and grabbed the blanket I always slept with and rolled it into a ball, setting it on top of the milk crate. Who cared about the stupid birth certificate? If I accidentally left my blanket behind, I'd be devastated.

I was just about to reach for my phone to check the news again when someone started pounding on my front door.

# CHAPTER 2

# DRACO

"**Y**OU SURE YOU don't want to go somewhere else?" I asked my mom for the fifth time. She was sitting at the kitchen table with her hands wrapped so tightly around a coffee mug that her knuckles were white. Not exactly as calm as she'd like everyone to believe.

"We don't need to go anywhere," she replied, taking a sip of her coffee. "The fire won't get to us." The words were more of a mantra than a statement—as if she was willing the fire in a different direction.

I looked out the window behind her. The sky was so murky and thick that you couldn't see a hundred yards from the house, but the glow of the distant wildfires still shone through, orange and creepy as all hell.

"You packed up the important shit anyway, right?" my brother Curtis asked.

Mom nodded.

We'd been through a fire before. When Curt and I were young, we'd been caught in a house fire with our cousin Gray and Aunt Lily. There'd been a whole lot of shit surrounding that situation that went way over my head at the time—but what I remembered most was the smell of smoke and the way we hadn't been able to see anything.

The sky outside was a vivid reminder. It made me feel claustrophobic.

"It's fuckin' pea soup out there," my dad complained as he stepped inside the kitchen door, closing it quickly behind him. "Can't see shit."

"You should be wearing something over your face, Cam," my mom scolded.

"I was out there five minutes," he replied easily. "Don't need to cover my face."

"Going outside to smoke when the entire house already stinks seems kind of stupid," my mom mumbled, making dad laugh.

My phone vibrated in my pocket and I reached for it at the same time Curtis reached for his. I knew what the notification was before I even saw it.

"We're at level two now," Curtis told my parents, lifting his phone so they could see it.

"We're packed up," my dad said with a nod. "If we need to go, everything's in your mom's rig."

"You takin' the bike?" I asked.

"Better wear a mask," Curt joked.

"He'll wear the full helmet," my mom said, pointedly ignoring dad's disgusted expression. "Like he said, you can't see shit out there, which means people are going to be driving like idiots."

"Can't breathe in that fuckin' thing," my dad replied, but I knew he'd wear it anyway.

"What's the plan with the clubhouse?" I asked just as the power shut off.

"Dammit," my dad bitched. "Knew that was gonna happen."

"It's fine. The power company warned that they were going to be turning everything off," my mom said tightly, getting up from the table. "I'll put the coffee in a thermos so it stays hot."

"Couple of the boys went over last night and made sure everything was locked up tight at the clubhouse," my dad answered me as he stopped my mom with a hand on her hip. He leaned down and kissed her, instantly calming her frantic movement around the kitchen before looking back at me. "Dragon and Casper made sure anything that couldn't be lost was packed up and moved into town, but there's a ton of shit that couldn't exactly be transported or stored anywhere else. Dragon said they're gonna park the RV at Poet and Amy's for a few days while we see how this plays out. They left last night."

"Grandpa and Grandma are fucked if it comes this way," Curt said with a grimace. My mom's parents lived in a tiny house on the club's property. "But the clubhouse and garage are brick buildings," Curt said. "That should make a difference, right?"

"Sure," my dad replied. "It could."

"This is fuckin' weird," I mumbled shaking my head. It was so surreal.

We'd dealt with forest fires before. Wildfires on the west coast were actually pretty common—but there'd never been anything so close to home. The county was telling people that the firefighters were doing a good job at keeping the fires away from homes, but we knew a few people that had lost everything already, and the fires were moving quick. Truth was, firefighters couldn't be everywhere at once.

"What about Gramps Casper?" Curt asked my dad. "Do you know what his plan is?"

My dad's parents lived in an old farmhouse outside of town, about six or seven minutes from our place. It wasn't a straight shot there by any means, but the fire lines were so wide that their place was in just as much danger as my parents' house. More, maybe.

"Charlie's over there helpin' pack," my dad said, nodding. "Plus, they've got CeeCee and Woody next door."

"Saying next door sounds like they live fifty feet away," I said with a huff.

My dad laughed. "You know what I mean. Their place is close enough. If the oldies need help in a hurry, Woody's right there."

"Wait, *that* generation is considered the *oldies*?" Curt joked. "I've been using it for you guys."

"Watch it," my mom said, pointing at him as she tucked herself under my dad's armpit. "I'm not old yet."

"What about Aunt Lily and Leo?" I asked. "They good?"

"Their house should be fine," my dad said.

"We'll probably all end up there before this shit is over," my mom said with a sigh. "I'm sure as hell not staying in your apartment."

"I resent that," Curtis shot back.

"It's clean," I said with a shrug.

"It's tiny," my mom replied. "And smells like funk."

"It doesn't smell like funk," I argued. "I got rid of the funk smell when I moved in."

"He did," Curtis said with a nod. "Smells like lemon now."

"I mopped the floor." I chuckled. "It wasn't hard."

"I don't even understand what you're saying right now," Curtis replied. "Womp womp womp."

"Slob," I said, covering it with a fake cough.

"Priss," he replied, using the same cough trick.

"You're both right," my dad interrupted with a grin. "Two sides of the same damn coin."

"I need to find some flashlights before it gets really dark in here," my mom said, pulling away from my dad. "Are they still on the shelf in the garage?"

"Yeah, but half the batteries are dead," he said with a grimace. "I'll help ya. I stocked up a couple weeks ago."

"I'm gonna head to the grandparents' and make sure they don't need anything," Curtis announced. He looked at me. "You comin'?"

"Sure. Unless you were plannin' on walking?" I was the one who'd driven. Roxanne and Curt's motorcycle were already parked safely at our cousin Tommy's house in town.

"Let me know where you're at, alright?" my dad said.

"Bye, love you!" my mom called out over her shoulder.

With assurances that we'd text them, we left the house and climbed into my truck.

"It fuckin' stinks out here," I bitched.

"Like a campfire on crack," Curtis agreed. "Wonder how this shit started."

"Probably some idiot that didn't put out their campfire that they weren't even supposed to have," I grumbled.

"Or tossed their cigarette out the window," Curtis added.

"Haven't had any storms lately," I said as I turned around in the driveway and headed toward the road. "It wouldn't have been lightning."

"Maybe someone took out a power pole and it sparked," Curt said. "Who knows? I'm sure they'll figure it out eventually. Doubt they're too concerned with it at the moment."

We both stared at the road ahead of us, straining to see through the smoke. It was the strangest fucking thing. Like fog, almost, but thicker.

"If I get rear ended I'm gonna be pissed," I said, turning on my hazard lights to give anyone behind us more notice that we were there. "But I'm not goin' any faster."

"Yeah, I'd be just as pissed if you hit someone else," Curt said leaning forward a little. "I'm a delicate flower," he joked. "Probably your best bet to go slow."

It took us twice as long to get to my grandparents' house as it would've on a normal day, and I was oddly relieved to see that it was unscathed, even though I'd known that everything was fine before I'd left my parents' house.

"Gramps shouldn't be on the bike in this shit," I said to Curt as I shut off the pickup.

"I'll offer to move it if it comes to that," he agreed, nodding.

We hurried toward the house and I didn't even pause, knocking as I opened the front door.

"What are you guys doing here?" Charlie called from the top of the stairs. "Did your parents' power go out, too? Never mind, I don't care. Come help me."

"Yeah, power's out at their place, too. What are you doin'?" I asked as I took the stairs two at a time.

"The parents decided we're leaving. There's some stuff in the spare room that my mom wants to take with us," Charlie replied as she led us into a bedroom. "Old school shit and baby books and stuff. I brought your dad's down already—"

"Dad had one?" Curtis asked in surprise.

"Of course he did," my Gram replied, flipping her long hair over her shoulder as she came into the room. She was dressed in full out seventies gear with a bandana folded in half covering the top of her head like a kerchief, and I was pretty sure it was all vintage. God, I loved her. She was the coolest woman I'd ever known.

"I mean," she continued, "he didn't have a *baby* book for obvious reasons." My grandparents had adopted my dad when he was already half-grown. "But we kept all of his school stuff and birthday cards and shit."

"They had him for only half his childhood," Charlie said, raising her eyebrows. "Yet his box was the biggest."

"That's because he's my favorite," Gram replied instantly. "Obviously."

"Well, I'm Dad's favorite," Charlie huffed.

"Lily is your dad's favorite," the three of us replied at the same time.

"Nice," Charlie said, throwing a stuffed animal at me. "Thanks for having my back!"

"Lies don't make friends, Charlie," Curt reminded her, ducking as she threw something at him. "Hey, don't throw shit at me! It's not my fault that Lily is *everyone's* favorite!"

"You're not making it better," Charlie snapped, looking around for something else to throw.

"Knock it off and get this stuff packed into the car, would you?" Gram asked, giving my shoulder a squeeze as she turned to leave. "I'm going to pack the rest of my suitcase so we can get out of here."

"Where are you guys going?" I asked Charlie as we reached for the neatly stacked boxes against the wall.

"We're going to stay at Aunt Callie's in town," she replied with a grunt as she lifted a box.

"The people in town are the smart ones," Curtis said as we carried shit down the stairs. "Random houses in the middle of nowhere are no big deal, but they're not gonna let the fire get into the residential neighborhoods."

"I'd rather have the space outside of town for the ninety-nine percent of time that we don't have to worry about natural disasters," I countered. "Too many people in town."

"You live in our apartment complex," Charlie pointed out.

"That's not *town*," I argued as we stuffed boxes into the back of Gram's SUV. The smoke in the air was making my eyes and nose burn. "It's...town adjacent."

"I'll give you that one," Curtis said with a laugh as we rushed back into the house. "Definitely quieter than any of the other places I've lived."

"Whatever," Charlie said with a wave of her hand. "The apartments should still be out of the danger zone."

"Probably," Curtis agreed.

There was something in her voice that had me searching her face. "She's still there, isn't she?" I asked, cursing inwardly.

Charlie didn't insult either of our intelligence by pretending she didn't know who I was talking about.

"She'll go to her parents' house if it gets bad," she replied. "She wanted to stay at the apartment."

"Why?" Curtis asked.

"Would you want to spend an undetermined amount of time with your parents?" Charlie replied. "She'll go if things start going sideways. She's fine where she's at."

"Fuckin' stubborn," I muttered as my gramps came down the stairs with bags in each hand.

"I'll get those," I said, reaching for the bags.

Gramps scoffed. "I think I can manage," he said with a grin. "But you can head up and grab the rest from your gram." He raised his voice. "She packed the whole damn bathroom."

"I heard that," Gram screeched.

"Wasn't tryin' to hide it, Ladybug!" he called back.

"*Dad,*" Charlie scolded as he reached the front door. She hurried toward him and pulled the bandana tied around his neck up and over his mouth and nose.

"Thanks, baby girl," he said as she opened the front door for him. "You make sure you have everything you want to take?"

Charlie nodded. As soon as he was out the door she turned to us and rolled her eyes. "He's the sentimental one," she told us. "Me and mom would let it all burn."

I was seriously doubting her pronouncement a minute later as I carried one of Gram's heavy ass bags down the stairs.

"Jesus Christ," I said as I stumbled down a step. "What the hell did she pack?"

"You know that saying, *everything but the kitchen sink?*" Curt replied as he followed me. "I think she packed the kitchen sink."

"Quit your bitching," Gram said, passing us on the stairs. "It's not that bad."

My mouth snapped shut as Curt started to snicker.

"Is this a dead body?" Curt yelled after her. "Am I helping you hide a dead body?"

"If you were, you wouldn't be packing it into *my* car," Gram replied without missing a beat. She strode out of sight.

As soon as everything was packed and ready to go, we found ourselves sitting around the gloomy living room. Even with all of the curtains pulled wide, there was barely enough sunshine making it through the smoke to lighten the room.

"Your mom and dad still planning on waiting it out?" Gramps asked, patting Gram's thigh. She was sitting on his lap and I wasn't sure what it said about any of us that the scene was perfectly normal.

"That's what they're sayin'," I replied. "But Mom's strung tight as a wire."

"She's always been like that," Gram said with a grin. "If your dad is staying, she will, too."

"I'd stay here if it was just me," Gramps added. "But she'd insist on stayin', too, and drive me up the fuckin' wall with her worryin'."

"There's no reason to stay if we don't have to," Gram said easily, shaking her head. "There's nothing we can do if the fire gets close enough to burn our shit, and I don't want to get stuck in it."

"Are Aunt Cecilia and Mark stayin' home?" Curtis asked.

"I think they're just waiting for us to leave," Gram said with an indulgent smile. "They'll probably head down south for a little while and visit their people in San Diego until the smoke clears. You know how Olive's allergies are. She's miserable with this smoke. Poor thing."

As we sat around talking, the room grew darker and darker. No one said anything and I wasn't even sure if they noticed until my Gramps looked out the window and sighed. "Alright, Ladybug. We better get on the road."

"I'm going to look outside and see if I can see anything," Charlie said quietly to me.

"Like what?" I asked. "Flames?"

"The smoke is thick as fuck," she replied grimly. "It has to be getting closer."

I followed her outside and pulled my shirt up over my mouth and nose. The smoke *was* thicker.

"I don't see any flames or anything," I said, glancing her way. "Do you?"

"Nah," she shook her head but kept staring in the direction of the fire. "But it looks different, doesn't it?"

It did look different. Not brighter or darker, but maybe the color was off? I couldn't tell, but I agreed with her. Something was different.

As we went back inside, I got another notification on my phone.

"Is that the emergency notification thing?" Charlie asked, craning her neck to see the screen. "I haven't gotten any."

"Yeah," I replied. It was another message reminding us that we were in the level two evacuation zone. Be ready.

Charlie pulled out her phone. "I'm going to see if the zone lines have changed," she said, tapping at the screen. She was quiet for a few moments. "Oh, shit."

"What's up?" I asked peering over her shoulder.

"Look how much it's moved," she said quietly, scrolling to a screen-shot from earlier in the day. "Its way closer."

"And there's the fuckin' apartments," I said darkly, pointing at a spot just inside the red zone. "Motherfucker."

"She must be headed to her parents' house already," Charlie said as I strode toward the front door. "She wouldn't just stay there."

"You're not gettin' notifications?" I asked. "She might not be either. Try and call her."

"What's up?" Curt asked.

"You takin' Gramps' bike?" I asked him.

"Already took it over to Grease's," Gramps replied before Curt could.

"We moved the important stuff yesterday," Gram joked.

30

"As it should be," Curt said seriously, pointing his finger at our gram. He looked at me. "What's goin' on?"

"Looks like the apartments are level three," I told him. "You got anything you want to go grab?"

"If you're in level three, roads might be closed already," Gramps said with a grimace.

"We'll figure it out," I replied. "We know the back roads better than any of the out of towners. Curt?"

"I wanna grab a couple things," he replied with a nod. "You got everything you needed?" he asked Charlie.

"I brought all my stuff here," she said with a nod. "It's in my car. Kara's not answering."

"I'll check your place. Text if you need us to grab anything," I told her. "You guys all set?" I asked my grandparents.

"We're headin' out now," Gramps answered. "You go get done whatever you need to."

"Keep me posted," Charlie ordered as we all exited the house, heading for our vehicles.

"We will," Curt replied, pulling his shirt over his face. "Fuck, this is nasty."

"Gonna get worse before it's better," I replied as I hopped in the truck.

I wasn't sure how the apartments were part of the level three evacuation zone, since they were much closer to town, but I wasn't going to question it. If I'd learned anything in the past few days of watching the news, it was that fires were unpredictable as fuck, didn't care about what was in their path, and didn't move in any kind of a straight line.

"You're worried Kara's still at their place?" Curtis asked.

"Charlie said she stayed there."

"Doesn't mean she's still there now," he replied, pulling out his phone. He tapped the screen and put it to his ear. "That vein in your neck might be throbbing for no reason."

"She's still there," I replied through gritted teeth. I couldn't explain it, but I *knew* she was still at her apartment.

As we got closer to our apartment complex, I cursed as I realized that my gramps was right. They had closed off the main road.

"Go around," Curt said, jerking his head toward a side road.

I nodded and drove slowly down the street. It was eerie how empty the roads were. There were no cars in driveways, no kids playing, no lights shining. Everyone had already gone.

As we pulled in the back entrance of the complex, my hands tightened on the steering wheel. There were cops everywhere, knocking on doors. The sight made me vaguely nauseous.

# CHAPTER 3

# KARA

"**C**AN I HELP you?" I asked the police officer standing outside my door. My stomach rolled. I knew him.

His fist was still raised from knocking, and he looked startled that I'd answered. "Miss, this area is now in the level three evacuation area. We're asking all residents to evacuate now while they can do so safely." There was nothing wrong with his words, but there was something in his expression, or maybe his tone, that rubbed me the wrong way. Instantly, I remembered every other encounter I'd had with him. They played quickly through my mind in Technicolor. I couldn't stand him, I didn't want his help, and if I didn't know that it would make things worse and hadn't been taught since birth not to antagonize the police— I would've told him to fuck off.

"Thanks for the notification," I replied tightly, taking a step back so I could swing the door closed.

My mouth nearly dropped open in shock when the door stopped short, held in place by his boot. I shouldn't have been surprised.

"Did you need something else?" I asked, tilting my head as I double checked that my phone was in my pocket.

"You need to get your things together and evacuate," he said condescendingly.

"I heard you the first time," I replied calmly. I made a show of looking down at the floor. "Please move your foot."

When I glanced back up, his expression had changed from condescension to anger. He opened his mouth to reply, but I spoke first.

"Legally, I don't believe you can make me leave the premises," I said, straightening my spine, forcing my voice not to shake. "And I haven't let you in and you don't have a warrant, so please get your foot off of my carpet."

"Bitch," he said under his breath, not moving. Instead of making him angrier, he looked almost like he was enjoying the fact that he was making me nervous. The realization disgusted me.

"Kara," a voice called, the sound coming from behind the officer. "You almost ready to go?"

For the first time in years, the sound of Curt's voice made me sag in relief. The officer stepped back, nodded at Curt and Draco, and then strode down the breezeway. Of course he did. Bullies didn't stick around to face people as big as they were.

"I just have to pack my car," I told Curt as I swung the door to the apartment open. "I got everything together."

"Damn, woman," Draco said with a laugh, the sound shooting like electricity down my spine. "This all you're takin'?"

"Ha-ha," I replied dryly. "I know it's a lot, but I had too much time to worry about it and I just kept finding more stuff to take."

"No worries," Draco said as he moved toward the pile of stuff. "It'll take two minutes to load it up." He picked up the backpack and slung it over his shoulder, and it took everything in me not to pull it away from him.

"I'll grab the crate," I said lamely, as the guys loaded their arms with my things. I hadn't had to ask for Draco's help—he'd pitched in anyway, just like always.

"Just grab the keys, sweetheart," Draco said gently as he stepped toward the door. "I'm guessin' your Jeep's locked."

"Always," I said, rolling my eyes as I dug my keys out of my purse. There had been a string of car break-ins in our apartment complex and nothing had been done about it. Management refused to put up any cameras and the cops kind of just threw up their hands and said there was no way to find out who did it. We'd learned not to leave anything in our vehicles and always make sure they were locked.

Draco picked up the mask I'd left on the back of the couch earlier. "Good thinking," he muttered to himself. He held it out in my direction as he pulled a bandana up and over his nose. "Put this on, baby."

Jesus, he looked like some kind of romance novel anti-hero about to steal a damsel's virtue in that bandana. Was this what hot flashes felt like? I rolled my eyes, but took the mask from him and put in on anyway. I wasn't going to touch the *baby* comment with a ten-foot pole.

As I led the guys to my Jeep, I watched as a couple neighbors loaded up their own vehicles. Most people had already left—the smoke was so bad—but there had been a few holdouts like me who'd waited until the last possible moment. My eyes burned as I unlocked and opened up the hatch.

"Where are you goin'?" Draco asked me as he carefully loaded up the trunk area. "Your parents' house?"

"Either there or with Charles," I replied through my mask, pushing my purse higher on my shoulder.

I'd been in his presence more times than I could count since he'd gotten out. It was impossible to stay away when our families were so close—but I still hadn't found a way to be comfortable around him. It was my curse. No matter how hard I tried, I couldn't fit him into a little box. I couldn't force myself to see him as less than he was to me—even if I'd never admit it.

"The grandparents and Charlie evacuated," Curt said, closing trunk. "They went over to Aunt Callie's."

"Fuck," I mumbled under my breath.

I loved my parents so much, but I didn't want to be stuck at their house. The moment I got there, it would be like I was sixteen all over again, having to keep them updated on every phone call I had and every place I planned to go. I wouldn't even be able to run to get a milkshake without their input.

"You know that cop?" Draco asked me, jerking his head ever so slightly to the left. "The one who was at your door?"

"No," I replied quickly, coughing as I inhaled. Fuck. The air was so nasty.

"You sure?" Draco asked.

I nodded.

"Huh." He said calmly. He clearly didn't believe me. "Why don't I drive you over to your pop's? Or Callie's, if that's what you want."

"I can drive myself," I replied, rolling my eyes.

"Him or me," Curt shot back, his eyes shifting over Draco's shoulder.

"You're adorable," I said dryly. "Thanks for stopping by."

"You wanna get pulled over on your way home?" Curt asked, his voice soft. "Out here where everyone has evacuated and there ain't any cars on the road?"

I opened my mouth to argue and then snapped it shut again. That scenario didn't sound pleasant.

"I know cops," Draco said to me, resting his hand at the base of my back. "And that one doesn't stink like a regular cop. That one stinks like a cop that got bullied in high school and got himself a badge so he could even the score."

I stood so still that I must've looked like a statue. I wanted to reply, to say something downplaying the asshole cop—but I couldn't. Every molecule in my body was focused on the point of contact between Draco's long fingers and my back. Just as I started to panic that I must look like a complete nutjob, his hand slid away and I felt like I could breathe again.

"Run over to our place with us real quick," Curt said, starting toward their building. "We need to grab some sentimental shit in case the place goes up in flames."

"I really hope it doesn't," I replied, giving in and following behind him. I might be stubborn, but I wasn't stupid.

"Me, too," Draco said with a chuckle. "Any other place that cost this much would be a total heap. We got lucky as hell."

"Wasn't luck," Curtis said distractedly as he led us up the stairs. "Kara researched for like a month before we moved in. She found this place."

"Is that right?" Draco asked, glancing at me.

"Can't make any decisions without overthinking them," I said, shrugging.

"Truth," Curt said as he opened their front door. "Come on, let's get our shit and get the fuck out of here."

I didn't let my surprise show as I stepped inside the clean apartment, even though it barely resembled the apartment Curt had been living in alone. The carpet was freshly vacuumed, there weren't any food wrappers littering the couch, and most importantly, I couldn't detect any strange smells from behind my mask. It wasn't until that moment that I realized how long it had been since I'd been to their apartment. Draco had been out for months.

"We'll be right back," Draco said as he strode down the hallway. "Don't answer the door if someone comes knocking."

I nodded and stood in the middle of the room where they'd left me. I couldn't believe that I hadn't been in their apartment since Draco moved in. There wasn't anything special about it—it was the mirror image of me and Charlie's, but for some reason, it seemed incredibly foreign. Even when Curt had lived alone, I'd never wanted to be there.

Since no one could see me, I let my eyes roam around the room, taking in every little detail. The couch was old, leather, and looked like someone's cat had gotten to the arm of it at some point, but it looked crazy comfortable. The coffee table was one I recognized that Curt had made in woodshop in high school. There was a short bookshelf along the wall that was filled with paperbacks, but I couldn't see what the titles were from where I was standing. On top of that shelf was a picture of Curtis and Draco at around thirteen. They were standing, bare chested, on each side of their mom, and all three were laughing.

I looked away. I remembered them at that age far too well. It was something I tried not to think about.

"You got what you wanted?" Curtis asked Draco as they came back down the hallway.

"Yeah," he replied. "Wasn't much here to begin with."

My stomach twisted into a tight knot, and it took every ounce of willpower I had not to grimace. As the guys reached me, my eyes widened.

"Is that the ukulele that Amy got you when we were kids?" I asked Draco, blurting out the words without thinking. I hadn't seen the thing since we were young. Suddenly, a million memories crashed down around me.

I couldn't even hear Draco's reply as I pictured him at eleven, his hair falling into his eyes. Then at thirteen, pushing a dirt bike helmet onto his shaved head. At fourteen, playing catch with Curt in his backyard, barefoot and wearing a pair of swim trunks. At fifteen, laying on the floor in the movie room, his head propped against the side of my bean bag chair. In every memory, I could feel the familiar shape of the ukulele in my hands. I'd played it far more than he had, and I was pretty sure the only reason he hadn't given it to me was because he liked that it gave me an extra reason to come to him.

By the time I pulled myself together, Draco had finished talking and was looking at me curiously.

"Haven't seen that thing in years," I mumbled, turning toward the door. "Let's go."

As we walked back to my car, I dug my nails into my palms.

There was a reason I tried not to remember those memories. It was *necessary*.

"I'll drive," Draco said as he came up beside me. "Main road's closed."

"Fine," I replied, forcing up every barrier in my mind that I could. I wasn't going to argue about which one of us was driving as long as the trip was fast and I could get away from him as soon as possible. I couldn't handle being around him this way, not when it was just the two of us. I needed the buffer of other people.

"You want me to follow you to her parents' place?" Curt called out to Draco.

"Nah. I'll let you know where I end up," Draco replied, tossing Curt his keys, making Curt frown. "You can come get me if I need ya."

I knew exactly what Curt was thinking and I couldn't lie—a small part of me felt satisfaction at his worry.

As we reached my Jeep, I handed my keys to Draco and waited for him to get in and unlock the doors.

"I can't believe you drive Rose's old Jeep," he said as I climbed in beside him.

"It was free," I said, buckling up. "And it gets me from one place to the next."

"Hey, I wasn't making fun," he said in amusement, adjusting the seat. I watched as he slid it back as far as it would go. He looked at me. "Just brings back a lot of memories, that's all."

I took a deep breath and imagined a vault door slamming shut in my mind.

"They gave it to me when I started driving," I said, pulling my mask off. The car was marginally better air-wise, but even if we'd been outside, I would've taken the thing off. It was so hot outside, it made breathing through the mask feel like you were trying to exercise in a sauna. "Then they signed it over to me once I was eighteen."

"Nice of them," he said. "Your dad's a good guy."

"He said it wasn't worth much in trade," I replied, fidgeting a little as I tried to figure out what to do with my hands. We were leaving through the back entrance of the apartment complex and I couldn't believe how eerie everything looked. "And Rose needed something bigger anyway."

Draco scoffed good-naturedly. "Plus, your pop has always thought the sun shines out of your ass."

"That's a disturbing way of putting it."

"He adores you," Draco replied.

"Isn't he supposed to?" I asked.

"Of course," Draco said in surprise. He looked over at me. "I just meant that it's easy to see how much he thinks of you. Always has been."

I nodded.

"You remember when Rose brought us all down to the river?" Draco said after a couple minutes of silence. "We brought so much crap, coolers and towels and chairs and God knows what else, that whenever she'd hit the brakes, all of us would have to put our arms up so the shit in the back wouldn't slide forward onto us?"

"No," I said, looking out my window.

"You remember," he insisted, laughing. "Me and Curt had to share a seatbelt in the middle because we had Reb with us and there weren't enough to go around."

I didn't respond even though the scent of sunblock and the feel of the armrest on the door digging into my hip came back to me like a sledgehammer.

"And Charlie called dibs on the front seat and we were all pissed because she was by far the smallest of all of us and she had the most room?"

In my memory, I could see the back of Charlie's blonde head, bouncing along to the music.

I didn't engage.

"Curt swung out on that old rope swing and it busted halfway to the river and we thought he broke his arm?" he continued. "Remember?"

"I don't want to remember," I finally snapped. "Okay?"

"Ah, the truth. Finally," Draco said, glancing at me. "Maybe we should have this out. You finally ready to do that?"

"There's nothing to have out," I replied. "I don't want to go skipping down memory lane with you."

"You got a problem with me, Kara?" he asked, pushing. He was always pushing.

"Just because I don't want to remember some idyllic summer memory with you doesn't mean I have a problem."

"Seems like you do."

"I'm not doing this," I breathed, crossing my arms over my chest as I stared out the windshield.

It was quiet for a few minutes, the entire car filled with tension so thick it almost had a smell.

"At some point," Draco finally said, his voice calm and low, "you're gonna have to talk to me."

"No, I won't," I replied flatly.

"You will," he said, his voice still calm. "Because at some point, I'm gonna be done with this shit and I'm not gonna let you keep dodging it."

"Cool threat, bro," I muttered.

"Just a promise," he said, reaching over to lightly run his hand down my thigh.

I held my breath as I broke out in goosebumps.

"If you think I don't notice that shit," he said, putting both hands on the wheel, "you're an idiot."

41

# Chapter 4

# DRACO

THE REST OF the drive was silent. It wasn't really surprising.

Kara had been dodging me for almost a year, skittering away like a scared cat anytime I was near her. It was both infuriating and seriously fucking confusing. After the way she'd greeted me when I got out—holding onto me like she was never going to let go—she went in the complete opposite direction. All of a sudden, she didn't want to see me, didn't want to hear from me, wanted to act like she was completely indifferent.

And it *was* an act. I'd known her my entire life and been best friends with her for over half of it. She was dealing with some shit—that much was certain—but pretending that she didn't want to be around me was garbage. She couldn't stay away.

Kara had no idea how well I could read her. She had no clue that I could feel the way her eyes tracked me across a room or the fact that she did so, often. She watched me. If we were in the same place, it was a guarantee that Kara had her eyes on me. She never approached or tried to get my attention, but I sure as hell had hers.

I'd been playing the game by the rules she'd set. I didn't approach her, either, not more than I'd approach anyone else. But the minute we were within five feet of each other, the air went fucking electric.

"My parents aren't even here," she said with a sigh as we pulled up in front of Mack and Rose's house. "Rose's car's gone."

"Maybe she ran to the store," I said, following her as she climbed out of the car. "Wanna check if your dad's here?"

"Yeah, come on," she huffed, pulling on her mask. I pulled my bandana up and over my nose as we walked toward the house, smiling and waving at the camera that was hung on one of the porch posts. I probably looked like I was about to rob the place.

It only took seconds before Kara was letting us into the locked house. Just as I closed the door behind me, her phone rang.

"Where are you guys?" she asked as she put the phone to her ear. She paused. "Okay, it's creepy that you're watching us on the cameras."

I laughed and looked around the room, trying to find a camera inside the house.

"They only saw us on the porch," Kara said after a minute, putting the phone back into her pocket. "They don't have cameras inside."

"Wouldn't be surprised if they did," I said seriously. Once I had a house of my own, I was gonna put cameras all over. You never knew who'd come knocking or what kind of proof you'd need later.

"They went over to Grandma Callie's," Kara said, throwing her hands up like she didn't know what to do with her crazy parents. "So, I can just stay here if you want Curt to come get you?"

"Don't you wanna go to Callie's with everyone else?" I asked in surprise.

"Yeah," Kara replied with a laugh. "But I can drive myself there."

"Jesus." I gestured toward the door. "Come on, let's go."

"You don't need to drive me there."

"Curt's probably already over there," I replied, ushering her back toward the front door. I couldn't keep my eyes above her waist, but I felt like less of a creep by only glancing at her ass as she walked ahead of me—instead of staring like I wanted to. There wasn't as much there anymore. Kara had gotten very slender in the last few years, but it was still *her* ass. I didn't care what size it was—it was still hers and I still couldn't keep my eyes off it.

The drive between Kara's parents' place and her grandparents' was mostly silent, but only half as awkward, which I considered a win. As we parked outside, I grinned as Kara muttered, "Good grief," under her breath. There were so many cars parked out front that we had to park down the street.

"Is that Dragon's RV?" Kara asked as she got out of the car, pointing at the monstrosity parked in the driveway.

"I think technically it's my Grandma's," I replied with a laugh. "She drives that and he takes the bike. I thought they were parking it at the greats' house."

"Poet's probably here, too," she replied. "They seem to congregate, and this looks like it's the spot for now."

"Truth," I replied. With the clubhouse evacuated, I should have known they'd find somewhere else to gather.

"That's gonna be me," Kara replied, pointing at the RV. "My guy can ride his bike and I'll follow in the freaking tour bus."

"Your man's gonna be a biker, huh?" I asked, bending down a little as I tried to meet her gaze.

"Even if he isn't, I'm still going to have one of those," she replied quickly, jerking her head toward the RV as she sped up and weaved her way through the parked cars.

"I'll get you one," I said, catching her with one arm around her waist. Her body relaxed against me for a full moment before she stiffened.

First the genuine reaction, then the dishonest one. Always.

"I'll buy myself one," she said, pulling away.

"That works, too," I replied easily, letting her go. I lowered my voice. "Long as I get to ride in it."

Kara tripped at my words, but thankfully caught herself before she could face-plant on the pavement.

"You're here," Charlie yelled, coming out the front door to meet us.

"Finally!"

"You haven't even been here that long," Kara replied with a laugh. "And I just saw you a few hours ago."

"Well, it felt like goddamn forever," Charlie shot back. "Why the fuck did you stay at the apartment so long?"

"Because I didn't realize I was supposed to evacuate until some cop came to the door."

"Ew."

"Seriously, ew," Kara said, nodding. "He was a total asshole. He put his foot in the door so that I couldn't close it."

"He did what?" I asked, my hands involuntarily clenching at my sides.

Slowly, Kara turned her head so she could look me in the eye. By the expression on her face, she hadn't meant for me to hear that last part.

"It was no big deal," she said slowly.

"If it wasn't a big deal, you wouldn't have brought it up," I countered.

"Maybe he didn't do it on purpose," Kara replied with an unconvincing shrug.

I didn't even bother to respond to that, just continued to look at her. I knew that guy had given me a bad vibe and it had been impossible not to notice how he'd watched her from across the parking lot—but I hadn't realized he'd been harassing her before we got there. Was that the first time? She seemed pretty fucking calm about it.

"Ugh," Charlie said with a grimace, interrupting our stare-down. "Whatever, it's over now. Let's go inside—it stinks out here."

"Just drop it," Kara said quietly to me before turning away. She followed Charlie inside, her arms crossed over her chest.

Drop it, my ass. Kara was about as far from a troublemaker as someone could get—there was no reason whatsoever for her to be hassled by the cops. Hell, there hadn't even been any drama with the club lately that could've trickled down to her. It didn't make any sense that he'd fuck with her, and that got under my skin more than anything.

Four or five people called out greetings as we entered the house and I waved at the crowd gathered around the living room.

Kara was right, the greats *were* there. I made my way to Great Grandpa Poet first. I bent down to be level with his spot on the couch.

"Which one are you?" he joked, pulling me into a hug. "Handsome devil."

"Hey, Gramps," I said, taking my time with the hug. Gramps was older than dirt, and I had a feeling we didn't have much time left with him—which was the reason I made a point to have dinner with him and my nan at least once a week.

He knew exactly which twin I was.

"How ya doin'?" I asked, falling back onto my haunches so he didn't have to look up at me. "Surprised you guys aren't at home."

"Your grandmother wanted us to hit the road with her," he said with a smile. "And I couldn't pass up the chance to ride shotgun in that apartment on wheels."

"Don't get lost in there," I joked.

"Go to the John and end up in another state," Gramps cackled.

"You're on the state line," I said, shrugging my shoulders. "That could actually happen."

Gramps guffawed and I grinned at him. He had a past—hell, all of us did—but to me and Curt, he'd never been anything but the gruff, old great-grandpa that told shitty jokes and could stop bad behavior with a look. Getting a laugh out of him, or a look of pride, or even a pat on the back in passing had always been the highlight of my week.

"Where's your beautiful wife?" I asked, looking around.

"She's in the kitchen," he said, reaching out to pat my knee. "You go say hello."

"Alright," I said, standing up. Gramps coughed. "You need something to drink?"

"I'd take a bourbon," he replied, wiping his mouth with a handkerchief.

"I meant water," I said with a chuckle.

"*I* meant bourbon," he replied, waving his hand at me as if to shoo me away.

"Ah, my favorite grandson," Grandma Brenna said as she met me in the hallway. "When did you get here?"

I leaned down and kissed her cheek quickly since she'd already started moving again. "I just got here," I said as she walked away from me. "And don't think that I haven't heard you say that to every grandson you have!"

"And it makes every one of them feel special," she called back, grinning over her shoulder at me.

"I kind of love your other grandma," Charlie said, coming up behind me. Standing on tiptoe, she tried to throw her arm over my shoulder. It didn't work until I wrapped an arm around her waist and lifted her up so we were hip-to-hip.

"How did you stop growing at twelve?" I asked, walking us toward the kitchen while her legs dangled.

"I come from small people," she said easily. "But I don't mind. That just means I can date anyone because they're all taller than me."

"You don't care about a person's gender but you *do* care about their height?" I asked in surprise.

"Hey, man," she said, shaking her head with a sigh. "The heart wants what it wants, and I like my partners—man or woman or neither—taller than me."

"Maybe it's not that you want them taller," I said as I dropped her back on her feet. "Maybe you're just conditioned to be attracted to taller people *because* everyone is taller than you. You ever think of that?"

Charlie grimaced at me. "Well, now I will."

"Figure out that riddle," I said, pointing at her.

"Don't point at me."

"Why not?" I asked, still pointing. She'd always hated it. When we were kids, she lost her mind if someone pointed at her.

"Knock it off, ass," she said through her teeth.

"Really bothering you, huh?" I asked conversationally, trying my best not to smile.

"Draco," my nan called out in admonishment. "Stop poking the bear and get over here."

"Yes, ma'am," I said, dropping my hand.

"You're going to pay for that," Charlie said under her breath.

"You don't scare me," I whispered back.

"I should," she hissed.

I was laughing as I caught Nan around the waist from behind and hugged her, resting my chin on her shoulder. "Whatcha makin'?"

"Biscuits," she said, patting my arm at her waist with a hand dusted with flour. "Making about a million."

"I got here just in time," I said, giving her a squeeze before letting go.

"Hell," she said, looking at me as I rounded the counter and sat down across from her. "I'm going to be baking these all night at this rate. People just keep showing up."

"I get the first batch," I said, raising my hand.

Nan smiled. "Sometimes, I marvel at how much you've grown and sometimes, I look at you and you're eight years old again, raising your hand for a biscuit."

"Can't help it," I said, leaning my elbows on the counter. "I love your biscuits."

"Then you better learn how to make them," she replied dryly. "I won't be around forever, you know."

"Yes, you will," I shot back. "Quiet."

"Are you talking about dying again? Stop it," my gram Farrah said as she strode into the kitchen. She looked at me. "I see you picked Kara up."

"She was still at the apartments," I replied.

"And she needed you to save her," Gram said, reaching into the fridge. When she stood, she was holding an orange soda in her hand. She slid it across the counter to me. "Our boy's quite the hero," she said to Nan, bumping her gently with her hip.

"Ah, they always want to be the hero," Nan replied, winking at me. "He comes from a long line of 'em."

"On both sides," Gram said, nodding.

"If I wanted to get picked on by two out of three grandmothers, I would have—"

"Three out of three," my grandma Brenna said as she came into the kitchen. "Why are we picking on Draco?"

"He wants to be a hero," Gram Farrah said with a small laugh.

"Ah, the plight of every man."

"You three are the worst, you know that?" I asked.

"Oh, you haven't seen anything yet, boyo," Nan replied, her accent thickening to imitate Poet.

"Jesus," I muttered.

"We're just teasing you," Grandma Brenna said, sitting down on the bar stool next to me. "It was good of you to go pick up Kara. Mack was wearing a path in Callie's backyard trying to call her."

"Why didn't he just go pick her up?" I asked, opening my soda.

"Because you can get away with being heavy handed with Kara," Gram said. "Her dad can't."

"Bullshit," I replied.

"It's true," Nan said, still rolling and cutting out biscuits. "Throw

49

that pan in the oven for me, would you, sweetheart?" she asked Gram. Then she glanced at me. "Kara doesn't put up with much from Mack. Hasn't in years. There's never been any kind of blow up or anything of that nature—but if she thinks he's crossed the line, she just shuts down."

"And he doesn't see her for weeks," Grandma added.

"No drama and gets her point across," Gram said with a sigh.

"Still terrible for Mack, though," Nan said.

"How did I not know this?" I asked, looking around at the old women.

"How could you?" Nan asked. "It's not as if Kara talks about it."

"She won't even talk to Charlie about it," Gram said, shaking her head.

I sat there as the conversation moved on, drinking my soda and letting their familiar voices wash over me. I even added to the conversation once in a while—but my head was somewhere else. Because, if Kara was giving her dad the cold shoulder whenever he pissed her off, that meant it was a habit of hers. Kara loved her dad. She put him on a fucking pedestal. So instead of fighting with him, she ghosted him. *It was what she'd done to me.*

So, what in the hell had I done that pissed Kara off so much that she'd spent years avoiding me?

# CHAPTER 5

# KARA

"**I** WAS FINE," I said, letting my dad pull me in for a hug. "God, why are you standing out here?"

"You get used to it after a while," Grandpa Grease's gravelly voice replied in amusement.

"That's because you smoke like a chimney," I said through my mask as my dad let me go. "Those of us with healthy lungs don't enjoy breathing this shit in."

"You're wearin' a mask, ya big baby," Grandpa Grease joked.

"I can still smell it!"

"You get everything you need from the apartment?" my dad asked, cutting in to our argument. "I coulda helped ya pack up."

"Yeah, I did," I said, sitting down in an empty lawn chair. "I had way too much time to think about it, so I packed half the apartment."

The men laughed.

"Everythin' starts feelin' important, huh?" Dragon said from a couple chairs away. "You get caught in some shit and you grab the kids and the wife and fuck everythin' else. You actually have to think on it? Hell, you've had that damn cookie jar for thirty-five years and the ear is broken off from that time your son threw a ball in the house... gotta take that with ya."

I laughed along with everyone else. That was exactly how it had felt.

"We grabbed all the kids' keepsake boxes," Charlie's dad Casper said. "And Farrah packed up the entire fuckin' bathroom."

"Now *that* doesn't surprise me," I said, nodding.

"Kara!" my brother Brody yelled as he came running out of the house. "When did you get here?"

"Just a few minutes ago," I said with a grunt as his body hit me with full force. My chair would've tipped over backward if my dad hadn't caught it in time. "What are you doing outside, dude?"

"Mom said she could see your car."

"I don't know how," I complained. "We had to park down the street."

"She's got a sixth sense," my dad said with a laugh. "She knows if any of you are in the vicinity."

"Who's we?" Brody asked. "Who'd you bring?"

"Draco drove me," I replied, knowing that every man on that stupid back patio was now far more interested in the conversation.

"That's good," Brody said seriously. "There's a bunch of dumbasses on the road today."

"Brody Jacob," I scolded.

"That's what Dad said," he replied in exasperation. He deepened his voice. "*Bunch of dumbasses on the road today. Fuckin' idiots.*"

"Don't say *dumbass*," I said, pinching him in the side. "And don't say *fuck*, either, you little monster."

"I'm not little anymore."

"You're little enough to still be sitting on your sister's lap," I countered, digging the knuckle of my pointer finger into his ribs. "Like a *wittle baybay.*"

"You suck!" he said, hopping off my lap.

"Don't say *suck* either, dirtbag," I called as he ran back toward the house.

I couldn't help the laugh that fell out of my mouth when he flipped me off as he threw open the sliding glass door.

"Your kid is feral," I told my dad as I turned back toward the group.

"Which one?" my dad replied, deadpan.

"So, my grandson drove you over here?" Dragon asked nonchalantly.

I glared. He might be the president of the Aces and Eights Motorcycle Club, but he was also family and annoying as hell. Did I think I could rat on the club and get away with it? No. Did I think I could call him a dick and storm off? Also, probably no. But could I send lasers from my eyes and make sure he knew exactly how much I thought he was a nosy, gossiping pain in the ass? Yes.

"Yeah, Draco drove me over here," I said shortly. "He and Curtis were at the apartments getting some stuff since we're in the red zone now."

They all watched me.

"Any other questions?" I asked through gritted teeth.

"When you gonna give that boy a chance?" Casper said with a laugh, lifting a joint to his mouth. "Poor kid."

"When are you gonna stop smoking?" I shot back.

"Never," he replied with a grin.

I raised my eyebrows and tilted my head.

Casper laughed and then choked and then laughed again. "Bullshit," he said, pointing the joint in my direction. "I give it less than a year."

"Shit," Dragon added, drawing the word out. "Less than six months, if that."

The slider opened up again and my stepmom came outside, her hair in a high ponytail and wearing a pair of shorts that didn't belong on someone's mother. "What's happening in six months?" she asked as she strode toward us. She reached out and smoothed my hair before dropping down in the seat beside me. "Ugh. It's terrible out here."

"Nothing's happening in six months," I replied in exasperation. "And it *is*. It's like when you're sitting by a campfire and the wind is blowing the smoke straight at you."

"But you can't move away from this shit," Rose said with a scowl. "I hope they get these fires under control soon. The boys are going crazy cooped up inside."

"You should send them to Uncle Tommy's house," I said, leaning back in my chair. "The boys would keep them busy and they probably wouldn't even notice a couple more kids."

"That's actually a good idea," Rose said, nodding. "Maybe I'll just have a couple of Tommy and Heather's kids over to our house. Give poor Heather a break."

"You call her, you tell her we're makin' a big spread for dinner," Grandpa Grease said. "They can bring the kids over to eat and play with their cousins."

"I'll let her know, Pop," Rose replied. She leaned back toward me. "She'll probably come over and then sneak away and leave all the kids here," she said with a laugh. "That's what I'd do."

"You should," I replied with a grin. "Then we'd have the house all to ourselves."

"Oh," Rose murmured, her face falling dramatically. "I forgot you were home. Might as well bring the boys home, too, if me and Dad won't have the house to ourselves."

"I can stay with Charlie—"

"I'm teasing you," Rose said, swatting me with the back of her hand.

"You're staying with us," my dad said gruffly at the same time. "And so are the boys. We're all stayin' in one place until this shit is over."

"We're fine in town," Rose said to him quietly.

"Yeah, we'll see," my dad replied with a huff.

"Are Molly and Will coming over?" I asked Rose.

"No, I think they're sticking close to home," Rose replied. "Reb's pretty freaked out by the fires."

"I bet," I said with a grimace. Rebel still lived with her parents, but she usually came and hung out with us at least once a week. I hadn't seen or heard from her in a few days, which was out of the ordinary.

The men continued with a conversation about all the things the fire departments and county officials were doing wrong and all the things they were doing right, while me and Rose leaned toward each other to talk.

"You look so funny in that mask," Rose said, pulling a bandana out of her shirt pocket. She unfolded it with a flourish and tied it around her face. "But I understand the need for it." She rolled her eyes above the bandana.

"Charlie gave it to me," I said, adjusting the mask. "It's actually not that bad. Once I've had it on for a while, I kind of get used to it."

"Can you imagine if you had nasty breath, though?" Rose said jokingly. "Just huffing that shit back in."

"Ew!"

"No kidding," she said, nodding. "Good thing you have superior personal hygiene."

"I am remarkably clean," I laughed.

"I wish I could take credit for that," Rose said, reaching over to squeeze my knee. "But you already had most of your good habits before I started bossing you around." She looked over at my dad, her eyes crinkling at the corners.

"I got the good habits from my nana," I joked.

"I'm glad they're not here right now," Rose said with a sigh. "It's a relief to know that your other grandparents are in Montana *not* dealing with these fires and smoke and evacuations."

"Yeah, I was surprised that Nana hadn't called me yet—or started driving in our direction."

"Your dad talked her out of coming here," Rose said with a small chuckle. "But I'm sure she'll call you tonight. She's worried."

"I am, too," I confessed. "This feels like apocalypse shit."

"Right?" Rose said, nodding as she opened her eyes wide. "That's what I said to your dad earlier!"

"And I'm sure he gave some perfectly logical rebuttal," I grumbled.

"Of course he did. He said all we'd have to do is drive a hundred miles away and we'd barely even be able to see the smoke. It's just our little patch of ground that's burning—everyone else is fine."

I scoffed. "*That we know of.*"

Rose barked out a laugh, throwing her fists into the air. "You're *so* my kid. I said the same goddamn thing!"

"The world ain't ending and it ain't on fire," my dad said dryly, barely even glancing in our direction.

"How do you know?" Rose asked stubbornly.

"Not gettin' into this again," my dad replied.

"That's because you know I'm right," Rose shot back.

"It's because we're havin' a conversation, sweetheart," Grandpa Grease said, pointing his cigarette at Rose. "And you're interruptin' with your end of the world shit."

"You, my friend," Rose said, pointing back at her dad, "are butting in to a conversation that you were not invited to."

"You're invited," my dad said to Grandpa Grease. "Welcome to the shitshow."

"You're both the worst and I have no clue why I put up with either of you," Rose said, getting to her feet.

"Because you're stuck with us," Grandpa Grease said, grinning. "And you know it."

"Come on, Kara," Rose said, reaching out to grab my hand. "Let's leave these old men to scratch their balls and tell each other how—with no experience whatsoever—they'd be fighting and winning against the forest fires."

"Hey," Casper called out. "I didn't scratch my balls once since you came out here. I'm a fuckin' gentleman."

"Oh, my God," I said to her, gagging as we walked toward the house. "Please do not ever refer to any of their balls again."

"I won't," she said, squeezing my hand and shuddering. "I even grossed *myself* out with that one."

As we stepped inside the house, I pulled off my mask and took a deep breath of semi-fresh air. It sucked—there was really no way to get away from the smoke. Even inside the house, you could still smell and taste it, it just wasn't quite as thick.

"I wish they'd come inside," Rose's mom, Callie, said, wrinkling her nose at us. "The news said people should try and stay inside." She pulled me into a hug.

"Hey, Gram," I said, giving her a squeeze back.

"Your apartment's in the red zone?" she asked, pulling away. "Did you get everything you needed out of there?"

"Yeah," I replied, nodding. "Draco and Curt showed up and helped me get it all to my car."

"Those boys," Gram Callie said with a smile, wrapping her arm around my waist so she could tow me toward the kitchen. "They always go the extra mile to make sure everyone is taken care of."

"Especially Kara," Rose said insinuatingly from behind us.

"Shut it," I shot over my shoulder.

"You better be careful," Rose warned. "My mama doesn't put up with any back talk."

"Pfft," Gram said, tightening her arm around my waist. "You deserved that one."

"Yeah, you deserved it," I called happily, flipping Rose off behind Gram's back.

"Hey," Rose complained, laughing. "A little respect here."

"Be careful now," Amy warned as we came into the kitchen. "Those biscuits are hot!"

"That's how I like them," Draco countered, grinning as he tossed a biscuit from one hand to the other.

"So hot that they adhere to the roof of your mouth and burn off your tastebuds?" Rose asked with a laugh. She reached for a biscuit on the baking sheet. "Me, too."

"Suit yourselves," Amy said, throwing up her hands. "But don't come complaining to me."

"We won't," Rose said cheekily. "Ma, where's the butter?"

"I swear I taught you manners," Gram complained as she let go of me and moved toward the counter. "But you never seem to use them."

"Biscuits supersede manners," Rose replied. "Hot, hot, hot," she whispered as she pulled the biscuit apart with her fingers.

"You want one?" Draco asked me, smiling over his shoulder at me.

"I'll wait until they aren't as hot as the gates of hell," I replied. "But thanks."

"You're missin' out," he said with a shrug. "They're the best straight out of the oven."

"I think I'll wait a minute," I replied dryly.

"I can't believe that your apartments are in the red zone," Gram said, handing Rose a vintage butter dish. "How in the world did the fire get that close to town?"

"News is sayin' it came straight down the valley," Farrah replied. "Just bad fuckin' luck."

"Seriously," I mumbled.

"What are you complainin' about?" Draco teased. "You brought the entire damn apartment with you."

"That's my girl," Farrah said with a smile. "You know what to do."

"I didn't bring that much stuff," I said, glaring at Draco. "But I was at home for a while and I just kept noticing things that I wouldn't want to lose!"

"You don't have to explain yourself to us, honey," Amy said. "We've got twice the amount of junk that we wouldn't be able to live without."

"That's because we're three times her age," Callie joked.

Amy made a scoffing noise. "Three times? Sure, I'll go along with that."

Everyone in the kitchen laughed.

We were still laughing when the familiar sound of multiple sets of motorcycle boots thumping down the hallway caught my attention. Before I turned to see who was coming, I glanced up and caught the expression on Farrah's face as she looked over my shoulder.

"Who?" she said, hoarsely.

"Not a who, Ladybug," Casper replied as I spun to look at him. "A what."

"The house," she replied on a sigh.

"Fire's gettin' close," he told her, his eyes never leaving her face. "Hasn't taken it yet, but it's lookin' likely."

"Fuck," Farrah muttered.

"We were checkin' out the cameras on the house and garage," my dad said. "And there's definitely no one out there fightin' it."

"The fire departments are stretched so thin," Rose said with a grimace, wrapping her arm around my shoulders. "They can't be everywhere at once."

Dad nodded.

"But we can," Draco said, setting down the half eaten biscuit in his hand. "We can go out there, create a fire break."

"The hell do you know about creating a fuckin' fire break?" Farrah asked with a snort.

"Less than a firefighter, more than you," Draco said easily, making her laugh. "At the very least, we can water everything down."

"Not a bad idea," Grandpa Grease said.

"Or they could just let the place fuckin' burn," Rose said so quietly that I knew I was the only one who'd heard her. I laid my head on her shoulder.

Farrah and Casper's house had been the place where my stepmom's older brother Michael, her great grandmother and a couple others had died. Grandma Callie had almost died. Needless to say, Rose didn't have any fond feelings toward the house, even though she'd spent half of her life there with her best friend—Charlie's older sister Lily.

"We'll head over and get things in order," Casper told Farrah. "Alright, Ladybug?"

"You know you're goin' no matter what I say," she said in exasperation. "I'm just hoping your ass gets stopped on the road and they don't let you through."

"Chances of that happenin' are slim," he replied, his eyes crinkling at the corners as he smiled at her.

"Don't look at me like that," Farrah said, throwing a biscuit at him. "You're not going to charm me into agreeing with this bullshit."

Casper caught the biscuit. "Can I get another for the road?" he asked innocently.

Farrah's expression darkened and she reached for the pan in front of her.

"Ah," Amy said sharply, smacking at Farrah's hands. "I've got arthritis and I cut each of those by hand. Do not throw them."

The kitchen was quiet for a moment.

"That was a spectacular guilt trip," Farrah said to Amy, looking at her in admiration.

"I've had a lot of years to practice," Amy replied. "Now go kiss your man goodbye and bring him another biscuit for the road."

Draco stood from his seat and stretched his arms above his head.

"This is a stupid idea," I told him, my stomach beginning to twist with anxiety. "Let the professionals handle it."

"They aren't handling it," Draco said as Rose slipped away and moved toward my dad. "They've got their hands full."

"So let the place burn," I hissed quietly.

"I'm not gonna sit back if there's somethin' I can do, Kara," Draco said, reaching up to smooth my hair away from my face. For the first time in a long time, I didn't even startle at the touch. I was too focused on the fact that his stupid ass was planning on driving *toward* a wildfire.

"There isn't anything you can do," I argued.

"I can help wet down the house and the area around it," he said, leaning down so our faces were close together. "Maybe stop by Cecilia and Mark's and grab his tractor."

"This is fucking ridiculous," I ground out through my teeth.

"Like I said," Draco replied, dropping his hands away from my hair, "I'm not gonna sit back if there's somethin' I can do."

"Yeah," I snapped. "I'm aware."

"What's that mean?" he asked, his head jerking back at the venom in my words.

"Go," I said, ignoring his question. I made a shooing motion with my hands. "Go *save the day*."

"Kara," he said, his voice dropping as I stepped away from him.

I shook my head and walked away.

I was halfway up the stairs, heading toward the sound of my brothers' voices, when Charlie came bounding down them.

"Where are the guys going?" she asked. "I saw them out the window."

"They're going to wet down your parents' house to protect it from the fire," I replied, rolling my eyes. "Like that's going to help."

Charlie looked stricken and I immediately felt like a piece of complete garbage.

"Jesus, Charles," I said, reaching out to hug her. "I'm sorry. That was an asshole thing to say."

"It's okay," she replied, hugging me before pulling away. "You're probably right." She smiled and squeezed my shoulders with both hands before moving around me and jogging down the stairs.

"Where are you going?" I asked suspiciously as she turned at the bottom of the stairs.

"To help," she said with a shit-eating grin. "I'm not letting the dudes have all the fun."

"Oh, Christ," I spat, following her down the stairs. "That's so stupid."

"Probably." She paused. "But, you're coming with me, right?"

I stared at her as different terrible scenarios ran through my mind.

"Of course I'm going with you," I said begrudgingly. "It's not like I'd let you go by yourself."

We didn't say a word to anyone as we snuck out the front door and jogged to my car.

"You have the keys?" Charlie asked, coming to a stop in the middle of the sidewalk.

I lifted my hand and grinned, shaking the keys from side to side. "Draco put them on the counter."

"If he had any idea that we would follow, you know he would've taken them with him," she said with a laugh.

I grunted as I unlocked our doors, not nearly as amused.

"There's clothes in the back seat," I told her as I cranked the car and pulled a U-turn. "We both need some long pants."

"Good call," she replied, slapping my shoulder. "You're so smart."

"At least one of us is."

"Please," she said, the top half of her body disappearing out of view as she leaned between the seats. "If you were smart, you'd get your shit together and start school."

"I told you," I said, carefully turning a corner as Charlie's body swayed, "I'll start this winter."

"You should've started three years ago," she grumbled. "Got some!" She scooted back into the front seat and held up two pairs of pants.

"You had to grab my most expensive pair," I said in exasperation.

"They were the only ones I found," she replied with a laugh. "At least they'll cover our legs."

"Oh, hell no," I said, snatching my expensive jeans out of her hand. "You can wear the other ones."

"Aw, man. These are mom jeans!"

"They're not mom jeans. They're *work* jeans that I wear when I'm helping the oldies outside. You can roll them up easier."

"If you weren't such an Amazon," she muttered.

"If you weren't such a shrimp," I shot back. "Just be thankful that they'll fit."

"Oh, yeah," she said as she stripped out of her shorts. "I'm so glad that you're now skinny as a rail and I can wear your clothes. It's a fuckin' dream come true."

"Hey," I griped, coughing a little. "Fuck, where did I put that mask?" I searched my pockets, finally finding it under me. It was bent all to hell, but thankfully popped right back into shape when I put it on.

"I'm supposed to be this size," Charlie ranted, ignoring my search. "I come from small people. You are not. Your dad is a fucking monster and your mom had an ass for days. I've seen photos."

"I'm slender because I work out," I said, glancing at her as she bent over to roll my jeans up her ankles.

"You're slender because you don't eat enough and you run like you've got a wild animal chasing you."

"How else are you supposed to run?" I joked.

"I think what you never figured out," she said, leaning back and crossing her arms over her chest, "is that you don't have to sprint when you're running over five miles. It's just fuckin' weird, okay?"

"I like going fast," I replied.

"No, you don't," Charlie scoffed. "You're literally driving about twenty miles an hour right now. You're the least fast person I know."

"It's smoky!"

"You're an old lady."

"Okay, that, too," I conceded.

"And you need to start taking better care of yourself," she har-rumphed. "It was a whole thing while Draco was gone—but he's home now. There's no more need for the fuckin' hair shirt. Go back to school. Eat. Have fun."

"That's not even—" I sputtered, unsure how to even reply.

"It is," Charlie said, cutting me off. "He was in limbo, so you were in limbo. But he's not now, Kara. So move the fuck on."

"In a minute, I'm going to drop your ass on the side of the road and let you walk," I snapped. "Fuck you."

"You know I'm right," Charlie said, pointing at me. Oh, man, that irritated the shit out of me. She hated when people pointed at her, so I knew she was doing it just to be an asshole.

"I know that you have no fucking clue what you're talking about," I spat. "Stop trying to analyze me."

"I don't have to analyze you," she said, her voice a little lower as she leaned back in her seat. "Everyone can see it—not just me."

"Well, all of you can mind your own fucking business," I replied. "I didn't start school yet because I needed a goddamn break." Charlie made a noise of disbelief in her throat that I chose to ignore. "And my body changed because I got older, not because I'm starving myself or some shit."

"No one said you're starving yourself," Charlie replied instantly. "That's not what I meant."

"Well, that's what it sounded like."

"I just meant that you don't take care of yourself like you should,"

Charlie said, throwing her hands up in the air. "You don't. And also, I'd just like to point out that losing *baby fat* after high school is normal, *not* losing the glorious tits and ass God gave you."

"I still have tits and ass," I said distractedly as we came up on a makeshift roadblock.

"Just drive through the gap in the middle," Charlie said, leaning forward to stare through the windshield. "If we don't fit, I'll get out and move the signs."

I nodded as I threaded my car through the narrow opening.

"Fuck," Charlie said with a sigh, glancing behind us as we continued toward her parents' house. "Shit's getting real. That wasn't there when we left earlier."

"We're driving toward a fucking wildfire," I replied, turning my headlights on. They didn't do anything except illuminate the haze, so I turned them off again. "That's about as real as it gets."

We were quiet for the rest of the drive, both of us leaning forward, as if it would help us see through the haze of smoke. It wasn't so thick that it was impossible to see, more like a really foggy morning.

"God," I said as I turned on my blinker. "If I hadn't been here two million times, I wouldn't have even known where to turn. You can't even see the mailbox."

"I know," Charlie said. "Fuck, Kara." She turned to me. "How the fuck are we supposed to even know if the fire is close?"

"I'm sure we'll see it," I lied.

We crept up the road until I could see the back of Rose's SUV and Grandpa Grease's big pickup. Parking behind them, I braced for the inevitable what-do-you-think-you're-doing-here conversation.

"I'm going to change my pants real quick," I told Charlie, pushing my seat back. I slipped off my shoes. "Keep an eye out, would ya? I don't want to scar my dad."

"You're not wearing underwear?" Charlie asked with a mocking gasp.

"Yes, I'm wearing underwear," I shot back, pulling off my shorts. "But that's bad enough! He'd have a heart attack."

"We're all good," Charlie replied as I reached for my jeans and awkwardly put my feet in them. "The only person I see is Draco."

"What?" My head shot up as I struggled to yank my jeans up my legs.

"Oh, he looks pissed," Charlie said conversationally as I jerked my jeans over my hips. "I'll let you deal with that."

Without another word, she was out of the car and jogging in the opposite direction of Draco—and I was stuck in the car trying to get my shoes on.

"What the fuck are you doing here?" Draco asked as he yanked my door open. "Crank your car and drive your ass back to Callie's."

"I hesitate to say this for obvious reasons, but—" I shrugged as I got out of the car. I was really trying to ignore the way the black bandana covering the bottom half of his face made his eyes seem even more striking than they usually were. "You're not the boss of me."

"You just got done tellin' me that comin' out here was stupid and now you're here?"

"It's a woman's prerogative to change her mind," I replied airily. I refused to give him any indication of my real reaction—the way my toes curled at his tone or the way my heart raced at the thought of arguing with him.

I was clearly demented.

"Kara," he growled, his fingers wrapping around my bicep as I tried to move around him. "You need to go back."

"So, you can be out here but I can't?" I asked, raising my eyebrows. "Huh."

"There's no reason for you to be here," he replied, skirting around the question. "We've got it covered."

"Well, I'll pitch in where I can."

"You aren't needed."

"Oh, I don't know about that. I'm sure it's all hands on deck, right?"

"For fuck's sake," he ground out in frustration.

"Don't use that tone with me," I snapped back, yanking my arm out of his grip.

"I didn't use a tone," he replied in the same tone.

"So, only *you* can help out, right? Only *you* can step in when someone needs it. Only *you* can put yourself in danger. Right?"

"The fuck are you even talkin' about?" he shot back. "You know you don't wanna be here. Fuck, I don't even want to be here. It smells like shit and my goddamn eyes are burning."

"Then why don't you leave and let other people handle it for once," I replied, stalking off toward the house.

I was feeling pretty damn good about my parting shot. I mean, I'd really nailed the whole passive aggressive thing and I was hoping that he'd stand there for a few minutes trying to figure out what I'd been implying. Instead, I only made it about four steps before I was being lifted off the ground and carried toward the back of my Jeep.

"Draco," I said in warning as he dropped me back on my feet.

"You got somethin' you want to say to me?" he asked, leaning down until our faces were just inches apart.

"Pretty sure I already said it," I replied, glaring.

"No, you made some bullshit comment and then stomped off like a twelve year old."

"Right," I bit out.

"I've given you time," he said. "I've given you space. I've left you the fuck alone even though I—" He pointed his thumb at his chest. "—was never the one in the wrong. But I'm not gonna let you be a fuckin' idiot just to make some stupid point that no one understands but you."

I opened and closed my mouth twice, trying to figure out what I should reply to first. I couldn't even wrap my head around everything he'd said.

"You were never in the wrong?" I finally yelled. "You were never in the wrong?"

"The fuck did I ever do to you?" he asked incredulously, smacking his hand on the window behind me. "Be your friend? Support you? Stick up for you? Love your stupid ass?"

"I never asked you to stick up for me!"

"You didn't have to," he yelled in my face. "I fuckin' loved you! I couldn't have stopped it!"

"I didn't ask you to love me, either!" I yelled back.

"I know that," he replied derisively. "You were too busy tryin' to ride Curtis' dick."

I hit him. I slapped his face so hard that my palm stung and I felt the twang all the way to my elbow. For a second, I think we were both shocked into silence. I'd never hit anyone before. I'd never even had the urge.

"Fuck you," I rasped out. "Get the fuck away from me."

"Kara," he replied, his voice full of remorse as he reached for me.

I slapped at his hands, pushing them away from me. "Get away from me," I hissed. Furiously, I wiped at my face. I didn't want to fucking cry. I hated crying. Why the hell was I crying?

Shame and embarrassment burned the back of my throat until I felt like I was choking.

"Talk to me," Draco said, following me as I strode toward the house. "I don't wanna keep doin' this shit!"

"Then don't," I said tiredly, not bothering to look at him.

"Jesus Christ," Curtis called out as he rounded the house ahead of us. "The fuck could you two possibly be fightin' about when we're already dealin' with this shit?" He gestured around him.

It was the wrong thing to say and the wrong way to say it.

"Draco was just reminding me of how I wanted to ride your dick when we were teenagers," I replied conversationally. Curtis's mouth snapped shut as his eyes widened. "We should just do it now and get it over with, don't you think?" I asked. "I mean, everyone knows I had a thing for you—so if you're up for it?" I shrugged.

The venom pouring out of my mouth didn't even sound like me, but Jesus it felt good. It felt good to turn the tables. To be the person talking about the stupid crush I'd had on Curtis instead of the one trying to forget it. It felt good to throw it back into Draco's face. It felt spectacular to throw it back at Curtis. After all of the years of him acting like I was going to try to make a move on him, my mocking offer had frozen him in place. Like I'd *ever* touch him. The thought made me physically ill.

Draco made a sound from behind my shoulder but I ignored him, staring at Curtis like I was waiting for his answer.

"Kara," Draco said, his hand landing softly on the back of my neck. "Enough."

I firmed my jaw and straightened my shoulders, but I couldn't find the strength to jerk away from him again.

"You stay away from me and I'll stay away from you," I replied to Draco, my eyes still on Curtis. "We were friends when we were kids, we aren't now."

"Bullshit," Draco said.

"If you think you're ever going to have the opportunity to throw that shit in my face again," I said, finally pulling away so I could turn to look at him. "You're out of your mind. Yeah, I had a crush on your brother."

Draco jerked, as if the confession physically hurt him.

"Because you were out fucking and flirting with any person who had a vagina, while Curtis hid what a man-whore he was." I shook my head. "I thought he was fucking mysterious. I didn't know that he was a self-righteous prick."

"Kara," Charlie said in warning. I hadn't even realized that she'd come out of the house.

"Go ahead," I said, waving my arm out in front of me as I pulled off my mask. "Anything you want to add?"

"Let's just take care of the house and go," she replied. "We can deal with all of this later."

"Right," I laughed. "Later. Sounds good. I'll put it on my calendar."

"What did Curt do?" Draco asked quietly, stepping between me and Charlie. His eyes searched my face like he was trying to read the answer there.

"Ask him," I replied.

I followed Charlie up the porch steps and into the house, my hands shaking with leftover adrenalin.

"When I left you to deal with Draco, I didn't realize you'd start World War Three," she said, spinning to face me in the middle of the living room. "You okay?"

"I'm fine," I replied, using my shirt to wipe off my face.

"It's probably a good thing that you two are fighting," Charlie said with a sigh, striding toward the downstairs guest bedroom. "At least that means you're talking."

"We aren't fighting," I countered. "He was being an asshole."

"Well, either way, at least you're talking."

"No, we're not," I argued, putting my arms out in front of me so she could stack a pail of quilts on them. "Seriously, don't get your hopes up. I'm done."

"You can't be done," she said, shaking her head. "You never even started."

"Why would I need to? I didn't see him for over three years and now we're different people. It's not a big deal. I don't hang with Curtis either."

"Don't think you're going to get away with that shit either," she said, glancing at me over her shoulder. "You're gonna tell me what the fuck Curtis did. I thought you just didn't want to hang with him because of Draco, but after that shit out there, something tells me there was a different reason."

"Just drop it," I grumbled.

"Yeah, that's not gonna happen," she replied. "Help me bring these to the car. My mom texted and asked me to bring them to Aunt Callie's. I can't believe she fuckin' forgot them."

"The original Rose made these, right?" I asked as we carried the quilts outside.

"Yep. Gram and her sister, too," Charlie said with a smile. "They were gone before I was born."

"What the fuck are you two doin' here?" my dad practically yelled as he caught sight of us in the driveway.

"We've been here a while," I replied, strolling toward my Jeep. Dammit, I should've put my mask back on. "Where have you been?"

"We went over to Mark and CeeCee's and grabbed their excavator," he said, hurrying forward to open the back door of the Jeep. "Gonna clear some brush and get it moved away from the house."

"That's a good idea," I said, putting the quilts on top of the stuff I'd packed earlier.

"I know it's a good idea," he said dryly. "Now, what the fuck are you doing here? Did Rose know you were comin' here?"

"Nope," I replied, popping the p. "But somehow, Farrah knew where we'd gone, so I'm sure Rose knows now."

"She's gonna skin you," he said, his lips twitching. "And I would, too, if I wasn't here lookin' at how far away the fire actually is. Those fire maps are a bit deceivin.'"

"Charlie wanted to come help you guys," I said as we moved out of the way so Charlie could add her quilts to the pile.

"And you had to come with her," my dad grumbled.

"You're surprised by this?" I put my mask back on, but it didn't seem to make that much difference.

"Nope," Dad said, copying the way I'd popped the p. "But I don't know that there's anything you can help with, sweetheart. There're already too many people here as it is. We only got so many hoses."

"We can go back," Charlie said, shrugging as she shut the Jeep's door. "I got Gram's quilts and you're right—there's not a lot for us to do."

"Seriously?" I asked incredulously.

"I just wanted to make sure," Charlie said, unrepentant. "But it seems they've got it under control."

"Thanks for the confidence," my dad replied in amusement.

"Anytime, Mack Truck," Charlie said, happily giving my dad a quick hug.

"You two let me know when you get back to town, alright?" Dad said, ruffling Charlie's hair.

"We will," I replied, glaring at Charlie as I gave my dad a hug.

"Oh, stop," she said, waving me off. "You know you didn't want to come out here in the first place."

"And I wouldn't have if you hadn't been so hell-bent on it," I replied as my frustration boiled over. "And I hate this fucking smoke!"

My dad laughed.

"Tell me how you really feel," Charlie said in mock sympathy.

"This shit's gotta end at some point," my dad said in real sympathy as he opened my door. "It won't be long."

"I should've hitched a ride to California with Cecilia's family," I said, hopping into the Jeep.

"I doubt that would've been any fun," Charlie called out as she rounded the hood. "That's a long ass time in the car with all her kids."

"If it don't get handled pretty quick, we'll head out and spend time with your grandparents, alright?" my dad said, leaning in to kiss the side of my head. "Now go back to Callie's and let me know when you get there. Drive careful."

"I will," I said as he closed my door.

"Sometimes, I feel the urge to throat punch you," I said to Charlie as I turned around in the driveway. "Like, I wouldn't actually do it—but I fantasize about it."

"Sometimes, I fantasize about making you go out on the town with me and then holding you down and making you eat carbs and drink tequila," Charlie replied, not looking at me. "But I haven't done that either, so I guess we both deserve a gold star."

We were silent for the rest of the ride back to my grandma's house.

# CHAPTER 6

# DRACO

"**I** RECOGNIZE THAT look on your face," my gramps Casper said as he strode toward me. "And I'm sure your brother deserves whatever ass whoopin' you're about to dish out, but put it on hold, would ya? I need ya to get the roof watered down."

I stared at Curtis, who still hadn't said a fucking word.

"Fine," I said finally, turning toward Gramps. "Where should I start?"

I followed him around the side of the house, nodding as he handed me the hose and pointed at where I should start the process. Thankfully, he was pretty good about keeping gutters clean and shit, so we didn't have to worry about any embers starting a fire that way. Still, though, if it made its way to the house, I wasn't sure anything we did would stop it.

"Just do what you can, bud," Gramps said, patting my back. "We're fightin' a losin' battle here."

"If you think that, then why are we even here?" I asked curiously as I pulled the trigger on the hose nozzle, making it spray twenty feet into the air.

"'Cause I couldn't let your grandmother's house burn without at least tryin' to save it," he said with a rueful smile. "Without knowin' that I did what I could."

"Alright," I said.

"You're a good boy," he said softly, reaching up to cuff the side of my head lightly. "Mostly a man, now, I guess. Can't really think of ya that way, no matter how hard I try."

"Mom can't either," I joked as he started walking away.

He turned around to look at me and kept walking backward. "My gram lived with my woman and almost grown kids, and she still felt the need to remind me to shower after work," he said, his eyebrows high on his forehead. "I don't think mama's ever see their kids as adults." He laughed to himself. "And big sisters ain't no better. Callie still reminds me to buy your gram her birthday gift, like I'd forget all these years later." He shrugged, then spun and rounded the corner and strode out of sight.

Turning back toward the house, I focused on methodically wetting every single inch of roof I could see. Maybe, just maybe, it would be enough to keep embers from lighting the place up. Gramps was right—trying was better than not doing anything.

I tried to keep my thoughts on the house in front of me, but they strayed back over and over to Kara calling Curtis a self-righteous prick. It wasn't so much the words she'd said as how she'd said them that set off warning bells in the back of my mind. He'd done something or said something, and I didn't think it had been recent. The pain in Kara's voice hadn't been new and sharp. It was old and dull. A memory. Something she'd lived with for a while.

I'd just reached the edge of the roof when Kara and Charlie came out of the house, carrying a bunch of blankets. I acted like I didn't notice them as Kara's dad, Mack, intercepted them and they stopped to talk with him. If I was being honest, I was trying not to call any attention to myself. I wasn't ready to go rounds with Kara again. Not yet. Not until I knew what my twin had done.

No, first I'd talk to Curtis.

"Those two have given me every gray hair on my fuckin' head," Mack said as he strode toward me a few minutes later. "My boys are wild, but Jesus, Kara and Charlie scare the shit out of me."

"Are they headed back to town?" I asked as Kara spun the Jeep around.

"Yeah," Mack replied. "Charlie decided we had it handled, so they could go."

I laughed. "Typical."

"You know why Kara was all wound up?" he asked me, crouching down to untangle the hose at our feet.

"I told her to go back to town and we got into it," I replied, giving him the most simplified version I could think of.

"That'd do it," he said, nodding. "That girl doesn't like bein' told what to do. Independent to a fault."

"She wasn't like that when we were kids," I replied, stepping to the side a little once I had more hose to work with. "Independent, yeah, but not stubborn like that."

"Nope, she wasn't," Mack said with a small smile as he rose back to standing. "I just figured it was part of her growin' up. She started wantin' to make her own decisions and fight her own battles and she was the devil incarnate if someone got in the way of that."

"It drives me nuts," I muttered. "Everyone needs help once in a while."

"Of course it drives you nuts," Mack replied, chuckling. "Kid, you're a born fixer. You see somethin' wrong, you pitch in to help. Doesn't matter if you're asked to or not."

"That's not a bad thing."

"It sure as hell isn't," Mack agreed. "But when you put those two personalities together? The super-independent type and the fixer? Shit. *Fireworks.*"

"Is this your way of saying I should just keep my distance?" I asked, only half joking.

Mack looked at me with no trace of the previous amusement in his expression. "Now, why the hell would I say that to the kid who loved my daughter so much that he went to jail for her?"

"I was a stupid kid," I countered.

"Oh, yeah," Mack huffed, nodding. "It was stupid as hell. But you did it for the right reasons. No one can fault your reasonin.'" He paused. "Just the execution."

"Hey, Mack," my grandpa Dragon called from further out in the yard. "Ya lazy fuck, come help!"

"I should be doin' that," I said, jerking my head toward the branches and brush they were clearing. "And you should be doing this."

"Ah, give the old farts this," Mack said, smiling as he moved past me. "A little physical labor makes us feel like we're twenty-five again…at least until we're finished and can hardly bend down to take our boots off."

I worked on wetting down the house as far as I could reach with the front porch hose and then worked my way back over it for good measure. I could hear someone else on the opposite side of the house doing the same thing, but I wasn't sure who it was. Eventually, I shut off the water and stored the hose before rounding the house.

The back yard was pretty much deserted, no one really went back there on a good day—but further out, I could see the men working. I couldn't tell who was in Mark's excavator, but whoever it was knew what they were doing. Slowly and methodically, they picked up huge piles of downed branches and moved them further from the house.

It was surprisingly noisy outside, which is the only reason I could think of that I didn't hear anyone pull up or see the men that had rounded the opposite side of the house and were striding toward the excavator and the guys working around it. I knew instantly who they were, or at least where they'd come from.

As I headed in their direction, both my grandpas stopped to talk to the older of the three, a grizzled man who looked like he'd been working for the past week with no breaks. They were all wearing heavy work pants and t-shirts and they were filthy from head to toe.

"What's goin' on?" I asked as I reached them.

Gramps looked at me and ran a hand down his face in defeat. "Looks like it's time to head out," he said, reaching out to squeeze my shoulder.

"Can't make ya go," the old timer said sympathetically. "But there's a good chance if you don't go soon, road is gonna be blocked and you'll be stuck here."

"You don't wanna get stuck here," one of the younger men muttered.

"Fuck," Curtis said as he walked up.

"We'll head out," my grandpa Dragon said. "Thanks for the heads up."

"We'll do what we can," the old timer told him, reaching out to shake his hand. "The rest of the crew will be here shortly."

After that, we hurried around, double checking that we'd done everything we could to protect the house. Within minutes, we were back in our vehicles and headed toward town.

Curtis was silent beside me as we stared out the front windshield of my truck, watching for brake lights so we didn't accidentally run into Rose's SUV ahead of us. I looked in the rearview mirror just as a water truck turned down my grandparents' driveway.

As soon as we'd driven through the signs blocking the road to my grandparents' house and sped up a little, I glanced at Curtis.

"You wanna tell me what the fuck you did to Kara?"

"Nothin' to tell," Curtis said, sitting back in his seat as he crossed his arms over his chest. "Don't know what the hell her problem is."

"Bullshit," I spat. I knew that he was lying and honestly, I was surprised he thought he could get away with it. We'd never been able to lie to each other. Between sharing a womb and spending most of our lives connected at the hip, there wasn't a single tone of voice or facial expression of his that I didn't recognize.

"I'm serious," he replied defensively. "She's been weird as fuck for years. Didn't have anythin' to do with me."

"Gonna have to disagree with you after that scene at the house."

"After you went in, she started keepin' to herself," he said, dropping his arms to swipe one hand through his hair. The other curled into a fist on his lap. "It wasn't long before she stopped goin' to see you and stopped comin' around the house at all."

"And you didn't have anythin' to do with that?" I asked incredulously.

"Hell, I don't know," he replied. "All that shit was years ago."

"She obviously remembers."

"I don't know what she thinks she remembers," he said dismissively. "But I didn't do shit to Kara."

"You watch out for her?" I asked quietly, realization dawning.

"She didn't want me to watch out for her," he said with a huff. "She didn't want anythin' to do with me. What part aren't you understandin' here?"

"So when I was inside, and I was askin' you to make sure she was okay?" I asked, my stomach churning.

"I told you what you wanted to hear," he confessed. "But I wasn't hearin' any different. She was fine and you had enough on your plate, brother. You didn't need to be worryin' about Kara. She's got a family to take care of her. Wasn't your responsibility or mine."

"We're her fuckin' family," I yelled, a sense of foreboding settling under my skin like fire.

"No, we're not," Curtis yelled back. "And maybe if you'd realized that a little sooner, you wouldn't have spent four years inside."

I couldn't even respond. I had nothing for him. The years since I'd gotten locked up became so much clearer now that I was getting a full picture of what things had been like outside. The way Kara had been acting, the animosity between her and Curt that I'd written off as a consequence of her avoiding me, the way Charlie was always trying to smooth shit over—all of it was beginning to make some kind of sense.

"It wasn't her fault," I finally said, my voice hoarse. "Goddamn it, Curtis."

"Drop it," he replied through his teeth.

"You stupid motherfucker," I mumbled under my breath.

If we hadn't been in the middle of nowhere in the midst of a fucking wildfire, I would have left his ass beaten and bloody on the side of the road. As it was, I still had to drive him into town. I'd deal with his ass then.

It took everything inside me not to pass the cars ahead of us so we could make it back to Callie and Grease's faster.

# CHAPTER 7

# KARA

"HOW LATE ARE you planning on staying here?" I asked my stepmom as we sat curled up on my grandma's couch.

"Well, at least until your dad gets back. He's got my car," she replied, stretching out until her legs were slung over my lap. "Why, you got somewhere to be?"

"No." I glanced out the front window at the haze outside. "But I might go back to the house, if that's cool with you."

"You can't avoid him forever, you know," she said knowingly. "Not only because I didn't raise you to be a fucking coward, but also because you know he's not gonna let you."

"I'm not avoiding him," I replied dryly. "You should've seen how much I didn't avoid him at Farrah's."

"Ooh," she said, wiggling her eyebrows. "Tell me."

I huffed out a laugh and pinched her leg. "Nothing like that, sicko."

"Uh huh," she replied, unconvinced.

"I bitched him out," I said with a sigh, leaning my head back. "Him and Curtis both."

"They probably deserved it," she replied loyally.

"Oh, they definitely deserved it."

"It's been a long time coming," she said quietly, watching me. "You think we don't see shit, but we do. Just because we're your parents doesn't mean that we missed how things went down, you know. If anything, it made us notice it more."

"It's not that big of deal."

"Yeah," she said, bumping me with her legs. "Yeah, it was."

"I'm here, bitches!" Heather yelled out as she came through the front door, her kids swarming around her. "Now someone take these kids before I lose my effing mind."

"Let 'em roam," Rose replied, laughing as she sat up. "There's enough eyes here to make sure they don't get into too much trouble."

"Go find your grandma and say hello before you trash her house," Heather instructed the kids, giving her youngest daughter a light slap on the tush. She rounded the couch and dropped down on Grandpa Grease's recliner. "Jesus, can you believe this shit?"

"Where's Tommy?" Rose asked.

"He's outside," Heather replied. "Poor guy is moving slowly these days."

"He finally did it?"

"Yep," Heather said in satisfaction. "No more babies for me. He got snipped a couple days ago."

"It's about time," I muttered.

"You know, you could have waited for me," Tommy griped as he swung open the front door.

"I'm not moving like a snail because you can't suck it up," Heather replied.

"Where's my mom?" he asked, moving through the room. "She'll give me some sympathy."

"Probably in the kitchen," Rose replied. "If you ask her, she probably has some frozen peas for your balls."

Tommy flipped her off over his shoulder as he shuffled away.

"I swear," Heather said, rolling her eyes. "He's such a baby."

I laughed. The two of them were hilarious. Between the loud arguing and the constant quiet bickering, you'd think the two of them hated each other until the very public displays of affection proved that to be a lie.

"I'm going to head out," I said, pushing up off the couch. "You want me to do anything before I go?"

"Nah," Rose said, waving me off. "Enjoy having the house to yourself for a bit. I'm sure we'll be here for a while."

"Is it me?" Heather asked jokingly, smelling her armpit as I left the room.

All the older ladies were still in the kitchen visiting when I made the rounds and told everyone goodbye.

"You sure you don't want to stay?" Farrah asked, giving me a hug. "It's gonna be boring at home all by yourself."

"It's going to be quiet," I corrected, making her laugh as I pulled away. "I'll come back tomorrow. You know everyone will show up for breakfast."

"Hell," Grandma Callie said from her spot across the island. "That's assuming anyone actually leaves tonight."

"Good luck with that," I called, waving as I headed toward the stairs.

The kids were all on the second floor, wrestling and playing and watching a movie, and I picked my way through the chaos to tell my brothers goodbye.

I found Charlie laying on my grandparents' bed, staring at the ceiling.

"What are you doing in here?" I asked, sitting down next to her. "You want to go back to my parents' house with me?"

"No, I'm gonna stay here tonight," she replied with a small smile. "I like the noise."

"You're crazy."

"It sounds like home," she said with a shrug. "Plus, you know everyone's gonna be drinking and playing cards later. I'm gonna make some money to recoup our lost wages from this week."

"Yeah, right," I scoffed.

"Hey, you don't know," she said, turning toward me. "I think I'm getting better at finding the old timers' tells."

"Are we talking about the same old timers that sit with zero expression on their faces unless they're laughing at your frustration?" I asked.

"Shit, maybe they'll feel sorry and let me win," she replied. "You don't know."

"Good luck and Godspeed," I said with mock seriousness.

"You're really going back to your parents'?"

"Yeah." I stretched my arms above me. "If I get bored, I can always come back."

"See you in a couple hours," Charlie replied knowingly.

"I'm going to be nose deep in a book, so probably not," I sang as I moved toward the door. "Text me later?"

"Yep."

Pulling my mask out of my pocket, I jogged down the stairs and out the front door. As soon as I was outside and confirmed that I really did still need the stupid thing, I put it back on. I'd just gotten into my car as Rose's car pulled into a spot up the street. I waved at my dad as I drove away.

I'd left just in time because a few seconds later, I drove past Draco's truck going in the opposite direction.

I couldn't believe that I'd actually said everything I had. It wasn't me. I didn't get into arguments. I didn't cause drama. I'd done enough of that in high school to last the rest of my life. I'd avoided it at all costs since.

So, why the hell had I decided to go off the rails all of a sudden? I had to assume it was just a response to everything happening around me. Having to pack all my important stuff up, being in forced proximity to Draco, seeing that fucking cop again, the fires and the possibility of Charlie's childhood home being destroyed, all of it was just too much. I was smart to go back to my parents' house and disconnect for a little while. I needed it.

I was patting myself on the back as I waved to the security camera and let myself into my parents' house. A little time in the quiet, in my old bedroom, surrounded by books and the familiar scent of home was just what I needed. Dropping my bag of clothes and toiletries on the floor, I strode across the room and flopped down onto the bed.

Brody wanted my room so bad, and I was suddenly really glad that my dad and Rose hadn't let him move in there yet. He and Jamison shared the only other bedroom besides the master, but Rose had been adamant that they didn't get to have their own rooms yet. She said it was because it forced them to share and get along, but I was pretty sure she just wanted to make sure that I knew I still had a place in their house. She'd even bought me a new bed for my apartment so that I could leave my old twin bed in my room at home.

Closing my eyes, I tried to relax, but it wasn't working. Memories that I willed away on a normal day kept forcing themselves forward. The look on Draco's face when we discovered a boy at school had taken a video of me topless. The tense set of his shoulders as he led me and Charlie out of school. The way he'd beaten the boy who'd taken the video, no hesitation or remorse, even after he was through.

How protected I'd felt. How guilty. How scared I'd been later.

Sitting up, I kicked off my shoes and let out a long breath, but I couldn't stop the memories.

The police showing up at Draco's house to arrest him. The look of relief on his face when he was let out on bail. The tense months that followed, waiting for his court date. Pacing the house because my parents wouldn't allow me to go to court. The minute my dad had walked in the door, the look on his face as he'd given me the news.

"Nope," I said out loud, refusing to allow the trip down memory lane to go a single step further.

Grabbing my toiletry bag, I pulled a random book off my shelf and stomped across the hall to the bathroom. The house was silent and I was going to take a bath with the lavender Epsom salts that smelled like heaven and my stepmom always kept stocked. I was going to read and relax and escape my own goddamn mind.

Fifteen minutes later, I'd succeeded. The good thing about being such a bookworm was that I'd read so many books that when I did a re-read, if it had been a few years, it was almost like reading a story for the first time. Even if I remembered the basic plot points, I never remembered the small things. It was enough to keep me distracted from what was happening outside the humid bathroom and inside my own memories.

A noise from the front of the house made me pause and look up from my book. Was someone knocking? I froze, listening. After a minute of no other sounds, I fell back into the story.

I nearly jumped out of my skin a few minutes later when someone knocked on the bathroom door.

"Kara," Draco called.

He didn't say anything else. Just my name.

As I scrambled out of the tub, I accidentally knocked my book into the water and slipped, hitting my elbow hard on the toilet lid. It didn't even slow me down as I practically dove for a towel.

"What are you doing here?" I asked once I'd securely wrapped it around myself.

"Open the door."

My eyes widened at his tone. "Give me a second," I called back, pulling my clothes on. I was still damp and it took me twice as long because everything stuck to me.

"What?" I asked, flinging open the door. My mouth dropped open. "What the fuck happened?"

His hair was a mess. He had a black eye and a busted lip. There was a long scratch along his jaw and the neck of his t-shirt was so stretched out I was pretty sure it was ruined. As I took stock, I glanced at his hands. The knuckles were swollen and bloody.

"What did you do?" I asked through the lump in my throat. My heart began to beat so loud in my ears that I wouldn't have heard him if he'd responded. Every emotion and memory that I'd been trying so hard to ignore came flooding back, leaving me on the edge of some kind of panic attack.

"Kara," Draco said, reaching for me.

I stumbled back, bumping my hip hard against the doorframe.

"What did you do?" I asked again.

All I could think was that I'd done it again. It had been five years since the first time, and I'd been so careful since then. One slip, that was all it had taken.

"Oh God," I murmured. "Oh, God. What did you *do?*"

"What?" Draco asked in confusion, reaching for me again. "Kara, *what?*"

I stared at him, a million things racing through my mind. Whatever it was, we'd take care of it. I wasn't a kid anymore. We'd run if we had to. We'd go somewhere far away. We could hide. People did that all the time. The club would help, wouldn't they? They'd help this time. They had to.

"Baby," he said, pulling me against his chest. "*Breathe.*"

One arm banded around my back while the other hand cupped the back of my head, pushing my face against his neck.

"Breathe, Kara," He said against my hair. "It's okay, baby. What's wrong? Whatever it is, I'll fix it."

My hands shook as I lifted them to the small of his back.

"Shh," he said, holding me tighter. "You're okay. It's okay."

It wasn't. I knew that it wasn't. What had he done? What secret had he unearthed? I pressed my hands against his back harder, curling my fingers into his t-shirt.

"We have to go," I said, almost in a daze as I pulled back a little. "It's okay. We've already packed the important stuff. Let's just go."

"What the hell are you talking about?" he asked in confusion, jerking his head back to look at me.

"We can just go," I said, pulling away completely. I turned and swiped my toiletry bag off the counter, ignoring the still full bathtub. "Come on. We can just go now."

Later, much later, it would be almost funny when I remembered the look of absolute confusion on his face as I'd hurried past him to grab my bag from my room.

"I'm ready," I said, turning to face him with my bag slung over my shoulder.

"Ready for what?" he asked, stopping me in the doorway. "What the fuck are you talking about?"

"Let's go," I said, nodding. "We can figure it out later, okay? Whatever it was, we can figure it out later. Let's just go *now*." My words were frantic. Why wasn't he moving? We needed to *go*. I wiped at the tears of frustration running down my face. When had I started crying?

"Baby, I'll go anywhere with you," he said soothingly, his hands out in front of him, palms up. "But you gotta tell me what the fuck is happenin' right now."

I stopped, staring up at his battered face.

"We have to go before the cops come," I replied as calmly as I could, my voice wobbling. "Hurry."

Draco's expression moved from surprise to shock, and as his eyes closed, to understanding. When he opened them again, I had to force myself not to look away.

"Cops aren't comin', sweetheart," he said softly.

"You—" I looked at his hands again. "You—"

"Curtis," he explained, making my shoulders droop in relief. "No one's callin' the cops."

"Oh," I said, my voice barely a whisper.

"Jesus, Kara," he replied.

"Okay," I said, slowly setting my bag down on the ground. "That's okay, then."

My voice hitched, and I slapped my hand over my mouth to hold the noise inside.

"Come here," he said, his hands hanging at his sides.

I shook my head.

"Come here, baby."

I shook my head again as a sob escaped through my fingers. I couldn't. I couldn't move. Relief and fear and embarrassment had me frozen to the spot.

"Goddamn it," he breathed, striding toward me.

The toiletry bag dropped from my fingers as he lifted me off my feet, turning to sit on the edge of the bed with me in his lap. I sobbed into his neck and wrapped myself around him, clutching at his back and shoulders.

"Fuck, Kara," he said, one hand around my waist. He threaded the fingers of his other hand through my hair, holding me just as tightly as I was holding him.

"You have to be careful," I cried against his neck. "You have to—"

"Shh," he soothed. "I'm not goin' anywhere."

"I can't—"

"Calm down, sweetheart," he said, pulling my face away from his neck. "*I'm not goin' anywhere.*"

I knew he believed it, but I didn't. Because if the day had proven anything, it had proven that I wasn't as good at keeping secrets as I thought I was. If something as simple as an argument had me flying off the handle at Curtis, then a fight had the chance of bringing everything I'd hidden to the surface.

And if he knew even half of the secrets I'd been keeping, there was a good chance he'd end up back in prison.

With that thought, the damn completely broke. I leaned forward and pressed my lips to his for the first time in five years.

He sat completely still for a few seconds and my heart felt like it fell to the bottom of my stomach.

My breath hitched.

Then he moved.

His hand tightened painfully in my hair as he tilted my head for a better angle and bit my bottom lip. Then it was me who sat frozen.

"You're not takin' this back later," he said against my mouth.

His chest rose and fell as fast and as hard as mine as we looked at each other, just inches apart.

Finally, I nodded.

The world shifted as he stood with me in his arms and slammed my bedroom door shut. Then I was on my back in bed with Draco's lips against mine, his tongue sliding against the roof of my mouth. I shuddered.

He hadn't forgotten.

Neither had I.

As our mouths broke contact, I arched my neck and sucked his bottom lip between my teeth, lightly running my tongue across it the way I knew drove him crazy.

He gripped my jaw in his hand.

I lightly scratched the back of his neck.

He rolled his hips against the notch between my thighs.

I wrapped my legs around his waist.

He groaned.

I sighed.

His mouth went to my throat and I saw stars.

My hands slid under his t-shirt and he shivered as my fingers brushed his ribs.

He leaned up to tear the t-shirt over his head and I stared.

The body I'd once known almost as well as my own had changed. The shoulders were unbelievably broader. The muscles thicker.

"What?" he asked hoarsely.

"Mine, too," I replied without thought, lifting my arms above my head.

As he helped me pull the shirt off, the only thing I could focus on was the way his skin would feel against mine once the barriers were gone. So I was surprised when he paused, braced above me, his eyes hooded.

It was then that I realized my body had changed, too. Where there had once been roundness and softness, there were now valleys and angles. I swallowed hard, forcing myself not to cover myself with my arms.

"You have abs," he said, his voice almost teasing. "There are actual abs down here."

"Shut up," I breathed as he dropped down, his mouth opening against the space between my breasts.

We didn't speak as we slowly undressed each other, taking stock of the things that had changed and all of the things that were remarkably the same about our bodies. He still loved it when I scratched his back and reached between us to run my hand down his stomach. It still drove me crazy when he gripped the back of my thigh to position me just right and slid his thumb into my mouth, his eyes focused on the way my lips wrapped around it.

We both held our breath as he slid inside me, and I waited for the proclamations of love that had spilled from his mouth in the past, but they never came. He was different now. More reserved, maybe. More focused.

By the time I came, both of our bodies were slippery with sweat and the room was filled with a scent I never thought I'd experience again. Draco's face was buried in the crook of my neck as he suddenly pulled out and came on my stomach, his entire body shuddering.

"Goddamn," he breathed, pausing, his body braced above mine.

"Now's probably not the best time to ask, but you're clean, right?" I said softly.

He tensed and then laughed humorlessly against my neck.

"Way to ruin a moment," he said, rolling to his side.

I shrugged. Now that it was over and the aftermath was upon us, I was feeling very exposed.

"Haven't been with anyone in years," he said, not meeting my gaze. "Not since before I went in."

"Seriously?" I asked in surprise. That was a long ass time, especially for someone that had whored his way through high school.

"I should be the one askin' you," he said bluntly.

"I'm clean," I said quickly.

"You been with anyone else?" he asked nonchalantly.

My jaw snapped shut. "None of your business," I replied tightly.

He huffed and sat up, swinging his legs over the side of the bed.

"Don't get all pissy," I ordered, reaching for the t-shirt by my feet so I could slip it on. "And don't act like I'm the one who gets around."

"That's not what I said and not what I implied," he shot back, standing up to gather his own clothes.

"Whatever."

"I've been in love with you since we were kids," he said, angrily yanking on his clothes. "So, no, haven't been with anyone else. Can't say the same about you."

I inhaled sharply. "That's a low blow."

"Truth, though," he replied.

I scoffed. "It's also the truth that you were fucking your way through Eugene while you were supposedly in love with me."

"Not since you," he said firmly, his eyes on me.

I nodded, looking away.

"I was gone a long time," he said with a sigh, running his hands through his hair. "Didn't expect you to wait. Don't worry about it."

I didn't reply. It was stupid, but I didn't want him to know that I hadn't been with anyone else. It felt... telling, somehow. Like I'd been waiting for him, when I hadn't—at least, not on purpose. I'd spent the last four years focused on surviving, on living. I hadn't had the time or inclination to date.

"Can we rewind?" he asked, stepping back to the bed so he could lean down over me. As I dropped back down against the mattress, I sighed.

"Yeah, we can rewind," I replied.

"Good." Our lips met softly, his nose brushing against the side of mine. "I feel like I got run over by a truck. Take a nap with me?"

Suddenly, a nap sounded like a very good idea.

"Let me get dressed first," I replied.

Draco laughed. "What?"

"If my parents come home while we're asleep, I don't want them coming in here and seeing us all—you know," I gestured wildly with my hands.

"All, *you know?*" he asked in amusement, leaning back so I could get up.

"Half naked and debauched," I replied, grabbing my underwear and jeans.

"You've been readin'," he said, laying down on the bed.

"Historical romance is my jam," I said easily as I finished getting dressed.

"Well, no worries about your parents finding us half naked and debauched," he said as I climbed back in bed and curled up against him. "Though, too bad we can't open a window. Smells like sex in here."

I snorted, and Draco chuckled and tightened his arm around me. "Relax," he said against my hair. "My truck's out front. Your dad is gonna know better than to open your bedroom door."

"If you think that'll stop Rose, you don't know her very well," I grumbled against his chest.

I pushed away my instincts that were screaming at me to run as far and fast as I could and let my body relax against his. I'd have plenty of time to call myself every kind of idiot later. What was that saying, in for a penny in for a pound? I might as well enjoy my terrible decision for a little while longer. Within minutes, I was asleep.

*"Everything's gonna be fine," Draco said, his hands meeting my back as he pushed me higher on the swing. "They're probably gonna just offer me a deal. Probation or something."*

*"You don't know that," I said worriedly, my shoulders slumped and my hair whipping around my face.*

*He was trying to cheer me up, but I wasn't having it. Even swinging at the old playground wasn't enough to snap me out of my funk.*

*It was just the two of us again. More and more often since he'd been arrested, Draco and I found ourselves together without the others. We still hung out as a group all the time, trying and failing to pretend everything was normal, but there was something about being alone together that both of us gravitated toward.*

*We preferred it, actually. I liked having all of his attention centered on me and I thought he did, too. We could be ourselves when we were alone, with all of our doubts and fears and anxieties. Alone, we could be in a funk, without Curtis brushing off our fears or Charlie acting crazy to distract us.*

*"You shouldn't have done it," I said, dragging my feet through the bark chips to stop the swing. I looked over my shoulder. It was the first time I'd said the words out loud and somehow they felt like a betrayal, like I wasn't*

*thankful he'd stuck up for me.*

*"Kara," he said, shaking his head.*

*I swallowed against the lump in my throat. The guilt felt like it was going to choke me sometimes.*

*Draco walked around the swing until he stood in front of me. His hands wrapped around the chains and he held them as he walked forward, lifting me from the ground until our faces were just inches apart.*

*"You're right," he said, his expression darkening. "I shouldn't have. I'm going to end up in prison and it's all your fucking fault. All of this is because of you."*

I gasped as I woke up, my heart racing. The dream was familiar. I couldn't count how many times I'd woken up sobbing—but I hadn't had it in over a year. In real life, Draco had comforted me and assured me that he'd do it all over again, a thousand times, that he loved me and there wasn't anything he wouldn't do. It had been the first time we'd kissed.

It had also been the first time I'd realized that he was the other half of me. The first time I'd realized just how blind I'd been. That I'd held tight to my crush on Curtis because he'd felt safer. Curtis would never look at me that way. He'd never reciprocate anything and if he had, I'd have lost all interest.

Draco was scarier. He'd had the power to devastate me and the chance of him doing so had been so high. By focusing on Curtis, I'd been able to ignore the way my chest felt like it was going to cave in every time Draco had detailed one of his exploits.

I looked up at the sleeping face just inches from mine. New bruises were darkening his cheeks and jaw.

Draco still had the power to bring my world crashing down around me.

# CHAPTER 8

# DRACO

"**W**AKE UP," KARA said, her elbow digging into my stomach as she rolled away from me.

"I'm awake," I replied groggily. I'd slept surprisingly well, considering I was in an unfamiliar twin sized bed.

People lied when they said size didn't matter. I'd promised myself when I got out of prison, I'd never again sleep in a bed the size of a coffin—and I hadn't. The first purchase I'd made was one of those king sized mattress that they shipped to your house in a box.

"My parents are home," Kara said, gesturing at me to get my ass up.

"My truck's out front, baby," I said as I sat up, gingerly rubbing my eyes. Fuck that hurt. "They know I'm here."

"Well, they don't know you're in my bed," she hissed. "Get up."

"We're home," Rose called gleefully from somewhere outside the bedroom.

"Jesus," Kara moaned, covering her face. "This is going to be painful."

I laughed. Kara's stepmom was my cousin, or maybe second cousin? Something like that. Her aunt and uncle were my grandparents. So I knew as well as Kara just how the next few minutes were going to go. There'd never been a situation that Rose didn't want to make more awkward than anyone thought was possible.

"Let's get it over with," I said, getting to my feet. I rounded the bed and reached for Kara, which had her skittering away nervously.

"Hands to yourself," she mumbled, making me grin. "Oh, God, does it still smell like sex in here?"

"No, we're good," I lied.

I followed her out of the bedroom, shutting the door behind me when she glared over her shoulder.

"Relax," I said quietly as we headed down the hallway.

"You relax," she snapped back, her shoulders perfectly straight.

"Well, *hello*, Draco," Rose said, rounding the corner from the kitchen. "Fancy meeting you here."

"For fuck's sake," Kara said under her breath.

"Hey, Rose," I replied.

"We brought you guys dinner," she said with a smile.

So she'd known I'd be headed to her house after Grease and my dad had broken up the fight at Callie's.

"Thanks," Kara said, moving toward the kitchen. "Where's Dad?"

"Right here," Mack said from the kitchen table. His eyes met mine and I felt myself straightening my shoulders. Shit.

He'd practically given me a green light when we'd spoken at my grandparents' house earlier in the day, but apparently, he was seeing things a bit differently now that he'd found me at his house, alone with his daughter.

Mack's lips quirked when he realized his stare had the intended effect.

"Where are the boys?" Kara asked as she walked toward the pile of to-go containers on the counter.

"Heather took them to her house," Rose replied as she followed. "It was pretty much a cluster as everyone was leaving. This kid wanted to go to this kid's house, that kid wanted to go there, on and on. Your dad eventually caved and we ended up with no kids."

"Except your favorite," Kara replied.

"You wipe your own ass," Rose said, grabbing a couple of plates out of the cupboard. "You're automatically the favorite."

"Brody wipes his own ass," Kara said, laughing.

"True," Rose replied. "But try getting his stinky ass to shower."

"How you feelin'?" Mack asked.

I stopped, standing in the middle of the kitchen like an asshole before sitting down across from him at the table. "Sore as fuck."

"I bet," he laughed. "Strange seein' a fight so perfectly matched."

I scoffed.

"It was like watchin' a man fight himself," he joked some more.

"Yeah, yeah."

"Between you and me?" he said, tilting his head a little. "You were wailin' on him. I'd never call your brother soft, but—" He shrugged.

"There's a difference between learnin' to fight against people not tryin' to hurt ya, and learnin' to fight with people who do," I said quietly, glancing at the women, who were having their own conversation.

"Ain't that the truth," Mack said knowingly. "Also helps that he was defendin' himself and you were tryin to beat the shit out of him."

"He got some of his own in," I said, moving my jaw from side to side.

"Hell yeah, he did," Mack replied. "If it helps, he looks far worse."

"It helps," I said darkly.

"You ready to say what all of that was about?"

"Nope."

"Figured," he replied, nodding.

"Curt knows," I said, meeting his eyes.

He nodded again.

"You got lucky," Rose said as she carried me over a plate of food. "I grabbed you and Kara food before everyone could jump in."

"Thanks," I said, glancing down at the heaping plate in front of me.

"Figured you'd be hungry after expending all that energy."

I jerked my head up and met her eyes.

"Fighting with your brother," she clarified, widening her eyes at me in warning.

Jesus Christ. I couldn't even glance at Mack to see if he'd caught my reaction. What, was I fourteen?

"Did anyone end up staying at Grandma's?" Kara asked as she sat down.

"Dragon and Brenna were staying in the house," Rose answered. "Baby, you want coffee?" she asked Mack. At his nod, she went back toward the counter, still talking. "Poet and Amy were going to stay in the RV in the driveway."

"Leo and Lily showed up," Mack said. "Farrah and Casper went back to their place with 'em."

"I think Charlie was going to stay at Callie's, too," Rose added. She looked at me. "Curtis headed back to stay with your parents."

"That's good," I replied. "One more set of eyes to stay up—just in case."

"These fires are fuckin' nasty," Mack said, shaking his head. "Can't believe they still haven't gotten a handle on 'em."

"They're so big," Kara said as she started eating. "I don't know how they'll get them under control."

I watched her. I couldn't help myself. There'd been plenty of times since I'd been out that we'd sat down at the same table to eat, and it shouldn't have been a big thing, but it still was. I'd spent so many hours, laying in my bed, picturing how it would be when I got out. I'd pictured little things, like driving with her next to me or laying on the couch watching a movie together or sitting down to a meal. Part of me still couldn't believe that it was finally happening. I was finally done.

"Eat," Rose said to me quietly as she leaned over the table to hand Mack his cup of coffee. As she leaned back, she gave my shoulder a squeeze.

"Thanks," Mack said to Rose. He looked at Kara. "Your apartments still okay?"

"I think so," she replied with a shrug. "I haven't looked at my phone in a while. They wouldn't really say, though, would they?"

"I'll check the map," I said, pulling out my phone.

"Your place will be fine," Rose said, finally sitting down with her own cup of coffee. "They wouldn't let it burn. Too many people live there. It's Casper and Farrah's place that'll burn."

"It wasn't lookin' good when we left," Mack said, leaning back in his chair.

We all sat quietly for a moment. It was weird to think about my grandparents' place no longer being there, but I had a feeling that it wouldn't be considered a loss to some of the people in our circle. The shooting that happened there when my mom was pregnant with me and Curtis had pretty much ruined the place for most of our close family. If I had to guess, pure stubbornness was the only thing that had kept my grandparents there after it happened.

I looked back at my phone. "Our place is still in the red," I told Kara. "But there's no little fire icon, so hopefully, it's not burning."

We sat around the table, visiting while Kara and I ate, but as soon as we were done, her parents were, too.

"I have a feeling it's going to be another long day tomorrow," Rose said, standing up and stretching her arms above her head. "And that coffee didn't do shit to wake me up."

"Ready for bed?" Mack asked as he got to his feet.

Rose nodded as she grabbed my plate and brought it to the sink.

"Thanks," I said, looking in her direction.

"You're welcome," she said, turning toward me. "Don't expect me to do it again. This is the first time in a while you've eaten with us and you're kind of a guest. Next time, you can take care of your own shit."

I laughed. "Alright."

As Kara took her plate to the sink, Mack looked at me.

"You're sleepin' on the couch," he said flatly.

"Right," I said quickly.

"I'd offer you one of the boys' beds," Rose said, making Mack glare at her. Apparently, that side of the house was off limits to me. I couldn't really blame him. "But they're little boys and they stink and I'm not changing the sheets for you. The couch is probably safer."

"The couch works fine," I replied. "Thanks for lettin' me stay."

"As if we had a choice," Rose said, rolling her eyes. She looked over at Kara, who was surprisingly silent. "Night, kiddo. Love you."

"Love you, too," Kara said as Mack walked over to give her a hug and kiss the top of her head.

"I better not find you on the fuckin' couch," he said as he let her go.

Rose laughed, loud and hard.

"Thought you were goin' to bed," Mack snapped at her, making her laugh harder.

We watched as he moved toward her and she cackled, racing toward the hallway he chased her. Just as they were almost out of sight, Rose yelped, and I was pretty sure Mack had reached under her very short shorts and pinched her ass.

"I know I should be used to it," Kara said dryly. "But watching my own parents flirt is disgusting as hell."

"Looks like I'm sleepin' on the couch," I said, turning to face her.

"Did you think he'd let you sleep in my room?" she asked, raising her eyebrows.

"Nope." I reached for her, and something settled inside me as she walked into my arms. "But I didn't realize he'd be so adamant about it."

"Adamant's a good word," she said with a laugh. "You've been reading, too, huh?"

"What else would you call it?" I asked.

"Unbending?" she asked, her lips twitching. "Resolute?"

"I don't know, but he *sure as fuck* does not want me near your room," I replied, leaning down to kiss her. I lowered my voice. "Little does he know, I was already in there."

"Why the fuck is there a book floating in this full bathtub?" Rose called, startling us apart.

"Shit," Kara said, grimacing. She walked toward the stair that separated the family room from the hallway. "I forgot to drain the tub!" she called.

"And you decided to give the beautiful man on the cover of this book a Viking funeral?" Rose called back incredulously.

"It was an accident!"

"Well, this poor guy can't be saved," Rose yelled.

"Just throw it away!"

"Are you sure?"

"Yes, I'm sure," Kara yelled in exasperation.

"Well, you're weird about your books," Rose shot back.

Kara shook her head as she turned toward me. "I better go clean up the bathroom. Do you need a blanket or anything?"

I looked at the couch. "No, there's one in here."

"Okay, I'll see you in the morning."

"Just like that?"

"What?" she asked.

"Kiss me goodnight," I ordered.

Her surprise was a little annoying, but she still stepped forward and up onto her toes to reach me.

"Sleep good," I said against her mouth. I was trying to be respectful of her dad and his ability to hide my body where no one would ever find it, but I couldn't stop my hands from wandering to her ass.

"You, too," she said, pulling away.

I watched her as she strode out of sight.

As I shut off all the lights and settled in on the couch, my thoughts ran in a circle of surprise, relief, and worry. I was seriously fucking happy that things had played out the way they had. Finally, it felt like Kara and I were getting somewhere, and I didn't even mean the sex. She'd seemed comfortable around me for the first time since I got home. The constant jumping and moving away and distance that she'd put between us had suddenly vanished.

But something in the back of my mind reminded me over and over on a loop that it couldn't be that fucking easy. Her feelings and whatever the fuck had her acting like I had the plague hadn't disappeared.

Once the house was completely quiet, I stared up at the ceiling and let myself remember the way she'd looked, her eyes unfocused as she clutched at me, and the way she'd felt—familiar but also, not.

We'd only had sex once before, right before I'd gone inside. We'd done plenty before that, but neither of us had pushed for sex. I wasn't sure what her reasoning had been—maybe just because it had been her first time. For me, I'd been hesitant to go that far when I knew, deep in my gut, that I was going to have to leave her. I'd made the decision before we'd ever even kissed that I wasn't going to put any label on what we were doing because while I'd spent months assuring her that everything would be okay, I'd known it wouldn't. Then, with the court date looming, my reasons hadn't felt so important. The only thing that mattered had been binding her to me as tight as I could before I couldn't anymore. I'd told myself that it was okay, because I hadn't asked her to wait for me or promised anything in the future.

Jesus, I'd been such a selfish little prick.

I'd known it was selfish when it happened and I'd felt so shitty about it that when she'd stopped coming to visit me, I'd kind of just figured it was what I got for doing something I'd known wasn't right.

Not right, but I'd never call it wrong. Saying it was wrong cheapened it somehow, and I wasn't about to do that. Not when it was *Kara*.

Taking a deep breath, I tried to shut down my thoughts. Overthinking shit in the middle of the night was never a good idea—I'd learned that. I'd spent too much time doing it already.

Eventually, I must have fallen asleep, because I woke up the next morning to Mack standing across the room.

"Draco," he called. When I opened my eyes, it took me a minute to find him. He shot me a half-smile. "Didn't know if you woke up swingin', so I figured I'd keep my distance."

"Good call," I said, sitting up. I glanced at the window.

"It's early still," he said. He reached up to scratch his jaw and sighed. "Casper and Farrah's place—"

"Gone?" I asked, my stomach sinking.

"Mostly," he replied with a nod. "Got a call this mornin'."

"Fuck," I muttered. I reached up to rub my eyes and stopped a centimeter from my face. Not a good idea. One of my eyes was barely open, it was so swollen.

"Should've iced it," Mack said. "Probably a good idea to do it now. I'll get ya somethin'."

"Thanks," I said, following him into the kitchen. Someone was moving around at the other end of the house and I wondered if it was Kara.

"They're gettin' dressed so we can head over to Callie's," he said, gesturing with his chin toward the bedrooms. He grabbed a frozen bag of corn out of the freezer and tossed it to me. "You want coffee?"

"Yeah, thanks," I said, putting the corn against my eye. Fuck, that hurt. Everything hurt. I had a feeling that my clothes were covering a shitload of bruises that hadn't been there yesterday.

Mack had just handed me a mug and I was pouring my coffee when Rose and Kara came down the hallway together.

"I won't be an asshole about it," Rose was saying. "But I can feel how I wanna feel."

"I'm just saying, it would probably be better if you didn't say good riddance to anyone but me," Kara replied. "That's their home."

"I know," Rose snapped.

"You don't have to bite my head off," Kara grumbled, stomping toward me.

"Everyone's strung tight," Mack said, his voice low.

"I can't be sorry that fucking house is gone," Rose said, looking at Mack. "I'm sorry, but I can't. Yes, it's Aunt Farrah and Uncle Casper's house. Yeah, the kids grew up there. But I was there when everything went down, okay? None of you were. And if I never have to see that fucking place again, I'm not fucking sorry about it, okay?"

I felt seriously out of place as Rose stood in the middle of the kitchen, her entire body tense as she spoke. I wasn't a mind reader, and I'd never pretend to know what someone else was thinking, but I had a pretty good feeling that Rose was a lot more upset about my grandparents' house burning down than she was letting on.

"Nobody's arguing that," Kara said, her voice wobbling as she slammed a mug down on the counter. "I just said—"

"Enough," Mack ordered.

"I just—"

"Kara," he growled.

I moved closer to Kara. Rose clearly wasn't the only one upset about the house.

"I'll get coffee at my parents' place," Rose said after a moment. "You ready?"

Mack nodded. "You'll bring Kara over?" he asked me.

"I can drive myself," Kara replied.

"I'll bring her," I said at the same time.

We were quiet as Mack ushered Rose out of the house.

"You wanna finish your coffee here or bring it with us?" I asked Kara after the front door had closed behind them.

"I can drive myself," she said, not bothering to turn and face me.

"You got a problem ridin' with me?" I asked. I reached out and wrapped my fingers around her hip, my stomach churning as she tensed up. Shit.

"No, it's fine," she said, setting down her mug. "I'll just leave the coffee. It tastes like shit anyway."

She gave me an unconvincing smile as she moved away.

"You gonna kiss me good morning?" I asked, testing the waters.

I couldn't complain about the quick kiss she gave me. On the surface, it was fine. But something was off and we both knew it.

The drive was quiet and I braced for the moment we were surrounded with people. There'd been so much talk about me and Kara, I knew that even with the worry about my grandparents' place, all the eyes were going to be on us.

"Poor Charlie," Kara said as we pulled up outside Callie's. "Rose is right, we weren't there. Neither was Charles. It's just her *home*."

"She'll be alright," I said, turning the truck off. "It sucks, but they got the important stuff out. Everybody's okay. It's just a house."

I knew it better than anyone after the house fire we'd had when I was a kid. It was overwhelming and seriously fucking sad when it happened, but eventually, just like everything else, it got easier.

"You okay?" I asked Kara as she sat, not getting out of the truck.

"I—yeah." She stared out the windshield. "It's weird to think that it's gone. I spent half of my childhood there." She laughed humorlessly. "You know that. You were there."

"Yeah."

"We better get inside," she said, unbuckling her seatbelt as she threw open the door.

"You should be wearing your mask," I said as I followed her out.

"It's like fifty feet to the front door," she argued.

"Fifty feet of smoke," I replied, resting my hand at the small of her back. "You got it with you?"

"It's in my pocket," she said, glancing up at me. "I'll put it on if we come back out."

I didn't bother arguing since we were already climbing the front steps. When we got inside, the familiar sound of people talking over each other surrounded us. Pretty much everyone had congregated at Callie's, but the usual sound of kids running wild was absent.

They'd circled the wagons. I wasn't surprised.

"I'm going to find Charlie," Kara told me over her shoulder.

"I'll find you in a bit," I replied, kissing her head as we parted.

I went looking for my gram and found her standing in the kitchen, a cup of coffee in her hand. Anyone else and I would've expected them to look haggard, but not Farrah. She was dolled up to the point of looking like she was headed for a night on the town, not an eyelash out of place.

"How you doin'?" I asked as I walked over to give her a hug.

"Hey, sweetheart," she replied, sighing. She rubbed my back as she returned the hug. "I'm alright. It's just a house, right?"

"Still sucks," I replied.

"It really does," she said with a huff. She smiled as I pulled away.

"Have you guys seen it?"

"No," she replied, shaking her head. "Cody got a call from one of the guys you met at the house yesterday? I guess he gave him his number. We haven't been out there yet."

She got pulled into a conversation with someone else, so I made my way through the house, saying hello to people as I passed them. Surprisingly, my parents hadn't shown up yet.

"Hey, Muhammed Ali," Gramps Casper said as I reached him. "You look like shit."

"I feel like shit," I replied. "How're you doin'?"

"Pissed," he said with a huff. "But it is what it is."

"We did what we could," I reminded him.

"Yeah, we did," he replied. "Thanks for helpin' with that."

"Of course."

"I think we're gonna head over there in a bit. Get a look at the place," he said, glancing toward my gram. "Not sure it's sunk in yet. Might as well rip off the Band-Aid."

"Is it safe?" I asked.

"Safe enough. Sounds like the fire burned through and moved on down the road."

"Jesus," I muttered.

"Cecilia and Mark's place is fine," Gramps said, shaking his head. "Isn't that some shit?"

"Some people have all the luck," I joked.

Gramps smiled. "I'm seriously fuckin' glad for it." He paused. "We probably should've driven Mark's excavator back to their place yesterday."

"Oh, shit," I replied as realization dawned.

Gramps laughed. "Fuck it. I'm sure he had insurance."

"You better hope to God he did," I replied, imagining the cost of replacing that piece of equipment.

"Hell, I'll just blame it on you," he joked. He looked at my gram again. "I better go check on your grandmother."

"You know where Charlie is?" I asked.

"Upstairs, I think," he said, patting me on the shoulder as he moved past me.

I found Charlie and Kara sitting on the floor of one of the bedrooms with their backs resting against an old set of bunkbeds.

"Hey," Charlie said as I walked in, her face blotchy with tears. "If the apartments burn, too, I'm going to be seriously pissed."

"I bet," I said, sitting down with them on the floor. I leaned back gingerly against a dresser. My back definitely had some gnarly bruises. I could feel them every time I moved. I was almost nervous to take a piss. If there was blood in it, I was going to find Curtis again. The fucker.

"You look like you were put through a meat grinder," Charlie said, looking at my face.

"You should see the other guy," I replied dryly.

"I have," she said with a watery laugh. "Never a quiet moment around here, huh?"

"Hey, I'm here to entertain," I said with a shrug.

Kara was suspiciously quiet. When I looked over, she was staring at the carpet. When she finally looked up at me, I could see a hint of the panic she'd been in the day before.

We needed to talk about that. Soon.

"You two fucked like bunnies!" Charlie blurted, her eyes wide as she looked back and forth between us.

"Shut up," Kara hissed, glancing at the doorway.

"You did," Charlie said, barely lowering her voice. "I knew when you did it before, and I know it now! You look exactly the same."

"Oh, for fuck's sake," Kara said under her breath.

"You did," Charlie insisted. "You're all, *I can't meet anyone's eyes* and Draco's over there mooning over you."

That description was a little insulting.

"Well, it's about time," Charlie said in satisfaction.

"Drop it," Kara said, elbowing Charlie in the side.

Charlie ignored her and looked at me. "Nothing to say?"

"How old are you again?" I asked flatly.

"Nice dodge," Charlie said, rolling her eyes. She looked just like her mom when she did that. "Well, well, well, this just made my fucked up day a little bit better."

"I don't know why," Kara snapped. "You didn't get laid."

Charlie whooped. "Confirmation!"

"I hate you sometimes," Kara bitched.

"You love me," Charlie said, slinging her arms around Kara and tackling her sideways. As Kara squirmed to get away, Charlie's legs wrapped around hers. "You love me so much. I'm your bestest friend in the entire world," she sang. "You couldn't live without me and you'll never have to because we're going to be friends forever!"

"I'm seriously reconsidering that," Kara grunted as she tried to pry Charlie's arms away.

"Well, I'm glad you're not crying anymore," Callie said as she stared at them from the doorway. "We're going to run over and check out your parents' place. You coming?"

It was probably the only thing that would've made Charlie let go of Kara before she was ready.

"We're coming," Charlie said, kneeling above Kara's prone body. She looked down. "You love me," she said one more time before getting to her feet.

"You're a fucking lunatic," Kara replied. She still allowed Charlie to help her up.

I held back a groan as I got to my feet.

"You alright, there, Turbo?" Charlie asked as we left the room.

"I'm fine."

"Good, then I'm riding with you."

"You're riding bitch," Kara said, pointing.

"The hell I am," Charlie replied with a laugh, smacking Kara's hand down. "You're banging the driver, you can ride in the middle."

"Charlie," Kara hissed.

We'd reached the bottom of the stairs, and the people around us laughed.

"Who won the pool?" Grandpa Dragon asked dryly as the crowd moved toward the front door.

"I think I wrote the guesses down," my gram replied. "It's in my purse."

Kara turned about fifty shades of red and I stared at my feet, hoping to God that Mack was already outside and hadn't heard the conversation. I was too much of a coward to look around and be sure.

I let Kara into my side of the truck and waited for her to slide into the middle seat before climbing in behind her. She was refusing to even look in Charlie's direction. The cab wasn't very big though, and I wondered how she expected to maintain the distance when we were all shoulder-to-shoulder.

"We're all gonna drive out there and they're not even gonna let us through," I said as the tension in the truck mounted. "Just watch."

"Then we'll take a different road," Charlie said determinedly, her arms crossed. "I want to see what's left."

"I'm not drivin' you guys over there if it isn't safe," I replied.

"Then I'll catch a ride with someone else," Charlie replied easily.

Kara huffed in annoyance so I rested my hand on her thigh, giving her a squeeze. She must have interpreted my warning, because she didn't say a word.

Actually, none of us spoke the rest of the drive. Not far from my grandparents' driveway, the effects of the fire became glaringly obvious. Trees on one side of the road were charred black. The sight was eerie as hell.

"Holy shit," Charlie breathed as the sight of their charred mailbox came into view. The little metal box was lying on its side, the wood post that held it completely gone.

Seconds after that, we could see what was left of the house. It wasn't much.

Kara reached over and clasped Charlie's hand.

"It really is gone," Charlie said, her tone almost surprised. "Good thing we went back for those quilts, huh?"

"You guys got the important stuff," Kara replied soothingly.

We parked behind the other vehicles and got out, staring at the scene around us. It was the weirdest fucking thing. There were patches of grass that were completely untouched by fire, sprouting green and cheerful out of the ground, and five feet away, bushes that had burned to a crisp. There didn't seem to be any rhyme or reason to the path of the fire.

"Nobody get too close," Grandpa Dragon ordered, looking toward the house. "Who the fuck knows what kind of shit the fire caused."

I stared at a little metal garden decoration still standing proudly where the edge of the porch should've been.

"What does he mean?" Kara asked, walking over to my side.

"All sorts of shit you're not supposed to burn, burned," I replied, wrapping my arm around her shoulders. "Until the fire department checks it out, it's not safe. Could still be hot, too."

"I can't believe they let us back here," she said, leaning against me. She seemed shell shocked. Hell, I guess we all were to some degree.

"They don't know," I replied. "Someone comes, I'm sure they'll tell us to get the fuck outta here."

There were charred trees for as far as the eye could see, but only on the back and left sides of the house. The excavator, parked near the woods on the right side of the house, was completely untouched. It was almost as if the fire had turned a corner, and right at the corner had stood my grandparents' home.

Bad fucking luck.

I looked up just as my parents pulled in behind the rest of the cars and parked.

"My parents are here," I told Kara.

"Good," she said, glancing over her shoulder. "Your grandparents need them."

I nodded.

"Oh, Curt's with them," she said as my brother climbed out of the back seat.

"Fantastic," I muttered as she tensed. "He'll keep his distance," I assured her.

I said it, but I wasn't sure that he would. In Curt's mind, we'd probably settled the issue and now things would go back to the way they'd always been.

Except, I reminded myself, things weren't *the way they'd always been*. They hadn't been since I'd gone inside—I'd just been too stupid and too wrapped up in my own shit to realize it.

"Goddamn it, Draco," my mom said as she reached us. She lifted a hand to brush it against my face. "It wasn't the fucking time."

"No, it was years too late," I replied through my teeth.

Mom jerked in surprise.

"Keep him away from me."

"Grow the fuck up," she snapped. "Today clearly isn't about you."

"Draco," Kara said softly, putting her hand softly on the small of my back. I looked down at her and nodded, keeping my mouth shut as my mom turned and walked away.

"Come by the house later," my dad said as he passed us.

"I might have shit goin' on tonight," I replied.

"It wasn't a question," he said, not looking back.

I didn't realize that Curtis was walking up more slowly until he was directly behind us.

"Oh good," he said with a chuckle. "All it took was a little fight in her honor and she let you back...*in*."

I told myself I'd heard him wrong as I slowly turned to face him.

# CHAPTER 9

# KARA

"**D**ON'T FUCKING DO it," I snapped, holding the back of Draco's shirt in a death grip. "Not right now."

Curtis laughed humorlessly as he moved around us, walking toward the house.

My stomach churned with anxiety and my skin felt hot as Draco watched his twin join the crowd of people standing closer to what used to be the house. Curtis's words had stung. No, that didn't even describe it. They burned all the way down to the bone.

They affected me so much, in fact, that I felt naked. I wasn't sure what to do with my hands, so I dropped them down at my sides. Draco's presence loomed huge beside me and all I wanted to do was escape. Just for a minute. Just to get my shit together.

I searched for my parents in the crowd and let out a small breath of relief that they weren't anywhere near where Curtis had gone.

"I'm going to go talk to my parents," I said to Draco. Even I could tell that something in my voice was all wrong.

"Kara—"

"Just stay away from him," I said, cutting Draco off. "Don't let him goad you."

"I think I can control myself," Draco replied tightly.

"Good," I said, only realizing after I'd replied that he was being sarcastic.

I walked away quickly, scanning the yard for Charlie. She was standing with her arm around her mom's shoulders while they stared of what was left of their house.

I didn't want to leave her behind, but I wasn't sure I could stay, either. I had to get out of there.

"What's wrong?" Rose asked the second I'd reached her side, our earlier argument already forgotten. "You okay?"

"I'm fine," I said, waving off her concern. "Are you guys going to stay long?"

"I'm not sure anyone's plannin' on stickin' around," my dad replied. "Why?"

"I'm just ready to go," I answered with a shrug. My palms were sweating.

"Thought you rode with—" my dad stopped talking when Rose shook her head at him.

"I'm ready," Rose said. "Let me say goodbye to Lil, though."

I nodded as my dad dropped his arm over my shoulders.

"I need to kill him?" he asked, leaning down to whisper in my ear.

I couldn't help the small laugh that spilled from my lips. "No."

"Alright," he said with a sigh, straightening up. "If you're sure."

"I'm sure."

"You gonna tell me what's goin' on?"

"Nothing," I replied stubbornly. "This is just depressing."

"Did you think it would be a party?" he asked in disbelief.

"No, I just—I don't know what I thought."

"It is pretty shockin' to look at," he said with a sigh, leading me over to where Lily and Rose stood talking to Charlie and Farrah. "Even if you know it's gone, it's still hard to see the wreckage."

"We'll have dinner at our house tonight," Lily was telling Rose. "You guys come over later?"

"We'll be there," Rose said. "And Mack's driving, so we can get hammered."

"I'm looking forward to that," Farrah replied.

"Not you," Rose said, giving Farrah a hug. "You're nuts when you drink. Me and Lily will get hammered."

"Me, too," Charlie said. "I'm only a half crazy drunk."

All the women laughed.

"No strippin', no fightin', no Jaeger," my dad announced. "Or I'm leavin' your ass for Leo to deal with."

"No Jaeger?" Rose gasped theatrically.

"You're fuckin' mean when you drink that shit," my dad grumbled.

"Huh," Charlie said, looking at me. "You are, too."

I flipped her off behind my dad's back, making her laugh.

"Let Draco know I left?" I asked her.

"You tell him," she replied, frowning at me.

"Tell him I'll call him later."

"Oh, for God's sake," she said in exasperation. "Really?"

"Love you," I said as Rose and my dad started walking away. "See you in a few hours."

I jogged to catch up with my parents, feeling like I had a bull's-eye on my back and Draco was going to stop me until I'd climbed into the back of Rose's SUV. I didn't want to get into it with him, not then. I needed a little space.

I needed a lot of space, if I was being honest. Too much was happening too fast. It was as if now that the seal was broken, suddenly, I was expected to be with him. Ride with him, spend the day with him, be his fucking old lady. Everyone expected it, I could tell by their comments and the way they'd just accepted that we were suddenly together.

No one would understand why the thought of that made me feel like the world was going to implode.

Pulling out my phone, I checked the little fire map again. I must have made a noise when I saw that our apartment was back in the level two evacuation zone because Rose turned to look at me.

"What?" she asked.

"I can go back to the apartment," I replied, showing her the phone.

"Just stay with us," she said, leaning forward to look at it. "Better safe than sorry."

"No, I'll probably head home."

"What, our home isn't home anymore?"

"You know what I mean," I said, putting the phone away. "I'm going to shower in my own shower and stuff."

"Our bath was good enough for you yesterday. Why you always tryin' to leave us?" she fake wailed.

"Because you raised me to be an independent adult?" I asked, ignoring her theatrics.

"We shouldn't have done that," my dad told Rose like I wasn't right there. "We shoulda kept her afraid of everything. Shouldn't have taught her how to pay her bills."

"Pretty sure math class taught me that," I said.

They ignored me.

"Why'd you teach her how to drive?" Rose asked pathetically. "Now she can drive away from us."

"You shouldn't have told her all that feminist shit," he shot back. "If she'd kept believin' I was in charge, none of this woulda happened."

"You guys are hilarious," I said, deadpan. "Abbott and Costello."

It didn't take long before we were home, and by then they'd pretty much accepted that I wasn't going to stay with them. I could tell that they weren't happy about it, but they wouldn't push it, either. We'd come to a sort of understanding since I'd become an adult—I'd respect what they said and always take it under consideration, but I was going to do my own thing. Sometimes, but not always, that meant ignoring what they thought the right choice was.

I hadn't unpacked anything from my bag except the clothes I was wearing, so it only took a couple minutes to get my stuff together.

"You could just go home after we have dinner at Lily's," Rose said from the doorway.

I glanced at my bed, and in an instant, memories of naked Draco flashed through my mind.

"No, I'm going to go home for a few hours," I replied, smiling at her as I strode her way. "You act like I live in another country."

"It's nice having you home," she said with a sigh. "I like having all my chicks in one nest and I didn't even get that because your brothers weren't home last night."

"When are you going to pick them up?" I asked as we headed toward the front of the house.

"I don't know. I texted Heather and she said they're keeping her monsters occupied, so no rush."

"Poor thing. You should bring a couple extra home with you."

"You know, having kids isn't quite as terrible as you think it is," she joked, bumping me with her hip. "They keep things from getting boring."

"I like being boring," I told her. "Dad, I'm leaving!"

"Text me when you get there," he called back from somewhere down the hallway we'd just left.

"You better get used to less boring," Rose said as she opened the front door for me. "I have a feeling things are going to be exciting for you for a while."

"What does that mean?" I asked, turning my head to meet her eyes.

She didn't answer, just jerked her head to the driveway where Draco was getting out of his truck.

"Goddamn it," I muttered, stopping abruptly on the porch.

"Have fun," she sang, closing the door behind her.

I cursed under my breath as I heard the deadbolt lock.

"I have a key!" I yelled through it.

"Good luck unlocking it before he gets to the porch, ya coward!" she yelled back with a cackle.

I'd barely made it to the bottom of the steps before Draco's angry voice reached me.

"You fuckin' kiddin' me?" he asked, coming to a stop a few feet away. "What the fuck, Kara?"

"I rode home with my parents," I answered, walking toward my car.

"I see that," he replied. "I'm not fuckin' chasin' you."

"I don't want you to chase me," I said, turning to face him as I walked backward. "The apartments are level two again, so I'm going home."

"You plan on tellin' me that?"

"I asked Charlie to tell you I'd call," I said defensively.

"Right," he spat, shaking his head.

I threw my bag on the front seat, and turned to face him again. He hadn't moved from his spot near the porch steps, obviously serious about the whole *not chasing* thing.

He was clearly angry, but something in the way he stood and the expression on his face—it was like he'd known that I was going to run. Like he'd expected it. Like it was inevitable.

It shook me.

"Follow me back?" I asked, my voice small.

God, I was all over the place. I wouldn't have blamed him if he'd told me to go fuck myself.

"I need to stop by my parents' place first," he said gruffly.

"Okay," I said, nodding.

"I'll let you know when I'm on my way." He still hadn't moved.

"Sounds good," I replied, crossing my arms over my chest.

We stared at each other.

"Not gonna keep runnin' after you," he said finally. "You wanna kiss goodbye, you're gonna have to come get it."

"Right in front of the window?" I asked stubbornly.

"It's where you left me, baby. Take it or leave it," he replied just as stubbornly.

I wasn't sure I liked this new version of the boy who used to give me anything I wanted. I stomped toward him anyway.

"Whatever point you're trying to make is stupid," I said as I reached him.

The words were barely out of my mouth before he was pulling me against him, his hands on my ass.

"There she is," he said against my mouth. "I wondered when she'd come back."

"What the hell are you talking about?" I asked, leaning my head away to look at him as he lifted me off my feet.

"You've been running like a scared rabbit for months," he said, leaning forward, trying to catch my lips with his. "You're not a rabbit, baby. You're a cat. You scratch when you're cornered, you don't run."

"That's the dumbest analogy I've ever heard," I replied. "And I've read a lot of terrible books."

"Just fuckin' kiss me goodbye."

I gave in and leaned forward but I let him control the kiss.

"Get off my lawn," Rose yelled like an old man from inside the house.

I flipped her off as Draco put me back on my feet.

"I'll see you soon," he said, smacking my ass lightly. "Shouldn't take long at my parents' place."

We separated and I called myself every kind of stupid as I drove away. There were reasons why I hadn't started shit up with Draco again, solid reasons, and they hadn't gone away.

I wasn't some overly dramatic woman who thought she was poison to anyone she loved or anything stupid like that. I had close relationships with my parents and sibling and extended family and friends—I loved them all and they loved me. But, when it came right down to it, I was poison to Draco and I'd known it since I was sixteen years old—younger, if I went back to the very beginning. I didn't try to be—if anything, I'd gone to great lengths since then to make sure that nothing about my life touched him in any way. But getting closer to him, letting him in, was going to demolish all that I'd done to protect him.

I drove home on autopilot, wondering what the hell I was supposed to do now. Trying to find any way at all that I could have Draco and still maintain the distance that I'd cultivated over years of keeping to myself.

Damn it, I wanted to go for a run. It cleared my head in a way that nothing else had, and I'd tried nearly everything—reading, sleep, alcohol, even knitting. After Draco was gone, I'd been rudderless. I'd ached for him and school had been a nightmare, even with Charlie there. It's why I'd started running in the first place—for some quiet. When I ran, it was just me and the sound of my footsteps hitting the ground. No one was trying to talk to me, no one was staring, no one was checking up on me every five minutes to make sure I was okay. It was peaceful.

I needed some of that.

Unfortunately, the air was still disgusting and I had a feeling trying to run in it would be like trying to exercise with a cigarette in my mouth.

The parking lot at the apartments was nearly deserted as I pulled in and got a parking spot. There were a few cars here and there—people that must have had the same itch to go home as I did—but the normal hustle and bustle was absent. It was kind of creepy as I climbed out and grabbed my bag off the front seat.

I waved to one of my neighbors who was sitting on a lawn chair outside his sliding glass door and headed inside. It felt good to be home. It felt good to still have a home. I couldn't believe all that had happened in the last twenty-four hours. It was like some kind of alternate reality.

I went through the apartment, turning on lights and ceiling fans. The place smelled musty from the smoke outside. When I was done, I stood in the middle of the living room, not really sure what to do with myself. I wanted to take a shower before Draco showed up, but I also didn't want to leave my stuff in the car too long and risk it being stolen.

After letting my dad know that I'd made it home safely, I decided to grab my stuff first, since going out into the gross air after my shower seemed a little counterproductive. The guys had packed it all out in one trip, but it took me three.

I was just grabbing the last of it, the milk crate and backpack, when a familiar voice said something behind me and I turned, my stomach sinking.

"Level two means you're supposed to have your stuff packed up and ready to go." God, I hated him.

I always acted like I didn't know this particular police officer. That I hadn't dealt with him at least ten times in the last five years. It was the only way to deal with him without giving him a reason to hassle me further. It was a little dance we did.

I pretended to respect his authority and he pretended that he hadn't been harassing me since the day he'd stood beside his police car and watched the cops in the other car take Draco away in handcuffs. He'd been a rookie then. Baby faced.

"I'm keeping it packed," I said, closing the back of my Jeep. "Just taking it inside."

"Let me help you," he said, stepping forward.

I hated that he only bothered me when he was working. It was as if the uniform and badge made him feel brave. It gave him a veneer of respectability and command. If he'd been in jeans and a t-shirt, he would've just been another regular shithead and I could've told him to go fuck himself.

"I've got it," I said, taking a couple steps backward. I glanced over at my neighbor, still sitting in his lawn chair.

"You know, it seems like you'd be a little more appreciative of my help," Officer Dickface said, walking with me toward the building.

"My dad says I'm independent to a fault," I replied, laughing a little like it was a joke. I stopped on the sidewalk.

I didn't want to stand there talking to him, but I also knew that letting him walk me all the way to my door was a seriously bad idea. Being out in the open where anyone could see us seemed safer.

"I see you've hooked back up with the Harrison boys," he said, bracing his hands on his belt.

I wished I could tell him that when he stood like that, he looked like a little bantam rooster.

"They're family friends," I replied.

"Spending time with men like that's a bad idea," he said softly. "Wouldn't want to get wrapped up in something that was going to get you into trouble."

My stomach sank as the phone in my pocket vibrated. I couldn't be sure, but if I had to guess, Draco was on his way to my place. I looked toward the entrance to the parking lot. If he saw us, I wasn't sure how I was going to explain it.

"Curtis and Draco aren't into anything that's going to get me into trouble," I replied, looking back at him.

"That you know of," Officer Asshole said condescendingly. "Take my word for it—it's only a matter of time before one or both are back in prison."

I wanted to slap the smug look off his face. Silently, I just stared at him. It felt wrong to discuss the guys with him, dangerous, like anything I said could be twisted just enough for him to start hassling them, too.

My heart started racing as Draco's truck pulled into the parking lot.

"I better get back to catching bad guys," Officer Smalldick said, obviously noticing Draco, too. "Stay out of trouble."

I nodded. We both knew that I was about the last person in the town that was going to get into any kind of trouble that involved the police.

As he turned to walk away, I hurried toward my apartment. I wanted to get inside before Draco reached me. He was going to have questions that I didn't want to answer and I didn't want to get into an argument on the sidewalk.

I also didn't want Officer Jackass to see us together, not when I knew Draco would kiss me hello the moment he reached me.

I'd just put my stuff down by the front door when Draco walked in behind me and I braced for the inevitable round of questions. He didn't disappoint.

"That the same cop that was hasslin' you yesterday?" he asked, closing and locking the door behind me.

"Yeah," I replied. It was best to keep things as close to the truth as possible. Besides, he knew the answer before he'd asked.

"Why the fuck is he botherin' you?" He half turned to face the door, like he was trying to decide whether or not to go back outside.

"I think he was just making the rounds," I said, trying to keep my voice even as I wrapped my arms around his waist. "Did you come here to talk about Officer Asshole or—"

"Officer Asshole?" he asked, his lips twitching.

"It's actually Officer Park," I replied with a shrug. "But Asshole suits him better, I think."

"You need to tell me if he comes around again," Draco said, his body relaxing a fraction.

"He won't," I assured him. "Why would he? It's not like I'm selling drugs from the coffee shop or something."

"Jesus," he said with a laugh. "Don't even joke about that shit."

"You worry too much."

"Yeah, well, I've seen the way people get railroaded by the cops." He shook his head. "Better to just steer clear of the fuckers."

"I will."

"I don't get why he's messin' with—"

His words cut off as I leaned up on my toes and kissed the side of his neck to distract him.

I wasn't proud of myself, but it worked.

"You shoulda let me help you carry the stuff inside," he said as he gripped my ass and hoisted me up to wrap my legs around his waist.

"I wasn't sure when you'd get here," I replied as he walked to the couch and sat down. "I figured you'd be at your parents' house for a while."

"Thankfully, not long," he said shortly.

"You want to talk about it?" I asked, running my fingers through his hair. He kept it cut short on the sides, but the top was getting pretty long. When he'd first gotten home, his hair had been shaved. I was glad he was letting it grow—he looked more like himself now.

"Not really," he said with a sigh. "They're pissed that Curt and I got into it, and pissed at the timing, and pissed that I wouldn't explain myself, and pissed that I wasn't gonna let it go. You get the idea."

"You shouldn't fight with him anymore," I said, leaning back to sit on his knees.

Draco huffed. "You're seriously sayin' that shit to me?"

"He's your brother," I replied, running my fingers softly across the scratch on his jaw. "You're a matching set."

"He's a fuckin' cunt and he's lucky I didn't beat him worse than I did."

"Draco," I scolded.

"Kara," he replied in the same tone. "He had one fuckin' job while I was inside, and he fuckin' lied and said he was doin' it, that he was lookin' out for you—and we both know he wasn't."

"It wasn't his responsibility."

"The hell it wasn't," Draco snapped. His hands tightened on my thighs. "I asked one thing from that motherfucker. One thing."

"Well, you can't blame him," I said in exasperation. "He didn't want anything to do with me, how the hell was he supposed to look after me? If it wasn't for me, you wouldn't have gotten into trouble in the first place. He and your mom knew that, and they made it clear." I scoffed. "It's not like I was going to let him look after *anything.*"

"What?" Draco asked, his voice low. "What did you just say?"

I froze.

"What?" I asked, confused about his reaction.

"How exactly did he and *my mom* make that clear to you?" he asked, watching me closely.

I didn't reply. When he said he'd gotten into a fight with Curtis, I'd assumed that he knew everything that had happened, at least with his family. If Curtis hadn't told him, then why had they fought?

"Why did you and Curtis fight?" I asked slowly.

"Answer me."

"You first," I said, dropping my hands to my lap.

"We fought because the piece of shit didn't look after you while I was away," he replied. "Now answer the question."

"It was no big deal," I said, gesturing lamely. "I just knew after you went in that they didn't want me hanging around. It was okay. I understood."

"It wasn't fuckin' okay," Draco replied, "or you wouldn't have tore him a new one yesterday. What the fuck did they say to you?"

"It was years ago," I sidestepped. "I don't even remember."

"Bullshit."

"Can you just drop it?" I asked, getting angry. "Why are we even talking about this? It's over. You're home. I'm sitting on your fucking lap, for God's sake."

"Tell me," he ordered. When I moved to climb off his lap, he stopped me.

"It wasn't some big thing," I said defensively, through my teeth.

"Tell me."

"Curtis said that it didn't matter how much I wanted to suck his dick, *he* wasn't going to fuckin' prison for me," I ground out between my teeth.

Draco moved so fast, standing from the couch and setting me on my feet, that I almost didn't catch him before he was out the front door.

"He was drunk," I said desperately, locking my arms around Draco's waist, my body between him and the door. "It was right after you left and he was a mess."

"There's no excuse for that shit," he replied in disbelief.

He was practically vibrating with rage, but his hands were still gentle as they pulled at my arms. Unfortunately for him, he wasn't succeeding because I wasn't being gentle, and I wasn't going to let him leave my house.

"Charlie hear him say that?" Draco asked.

"Of course not," I replied automatically. Charlie would've ripped him apart.

Draco let out a long breath. "What about my mom?" he asked.

I tilted my head like I wasn't sure what he was talking about.

"What did she say to you?"

"Why are you doing this?" I asked. "Just leave it."

"What did she say to you?" he asked again, tenderly wrapping his hand around my jaw.

"She said that I'd already gotten one son locked up, so to stay away from her other one," I replied in defeat.

"Jesus Christ," he said with a huff of disbelief.

"It's okay," I replied, loosening my grip on his waist. "Really. It was a long time ago."

"You don't get it," he said, dropping his head back to look at the ceiling as he shook it slowly from side to side.

"Then explain it to me," I replied. "Come away from the door."

"I spent every day inside worryin' about you," he said, not moving, his head still tilted back. "I knew that Curtis and Charlie were gettin' hassled a bit at school because of all that shit, but they were takin' care of it." He finally looked at me. "But you stopped comin' to see me, so I couldn't get a read on you. So I'm askin' 'em, right? How's she doin'? Is anyone botherin' her? You'll take care of it, right? And the whole time, they're sayin' that they've got it covered. That you're fine. That they haven't noticed you gettin' messed with. Seems like everyone's leavin' you alone."

I nodded. He leaned forward so our faces were inches apart.

"But they weren't takin' care of it, were they?"

"I had Charles," I replied quietly. "She's like a one man army."

"Charlie's five feet tall and a hundred pounds soakin' wet," he replied just as quietly.

"I'm okay," I said, lifting my arms out to my sides. "You're looking at me. I'm fine."

Draco stared at me.

"Sweetheart, when did they say all that shit to you?"

I didn't answer, because we both knew. It was right before I'd stopped going to see him.

"You can't really blame them," I said reasonably, giving him a small smile. "I *was* the reason you went to prison. If he hadn't taken that video of me, you wouldn't have beat him up."

"You take your top off on purpose?"

"You know I didn't."

"You take a video of it?"

"No," I snapped.

"You send it to the whole school?"

I didn't reply.

"You ask me to beat his ass? You force me to grab that bat?"

"You did it for me," I said, pushing at his chest.

"I did it because I fuckin' love you and that motherfucker deserved everythin' he got," Draco shot back.

"Then maybe you shouldn't have loved me," I yelled.

"It's not exactly somethin' I could fuckin' control," he yelled back.

"Then you could've controlled yourself, at *least*!" I shouted, immediately slapping my hand over my mouth in horror.

"You angry about that?" he asked, no longer yelling.

"No."

"Sounds like you are," he replied.

I took a step backward.

"Don't walk away from me."

I paused.

"You angry that I beat that little piece of shit?"

"Of course not," I replied, crossing my arms. What exactly did he expect me to say?

I was expected to feel thankful for what he'd done. Everyone we knew felt like the fact that he'd stuck up for me and damned the consequences was some kind of declaration of love or something. So how was I supposed to explain how fucking guilty I'd felt? How was I supposed to tell him that I was angry at the decision he'd made that had changed all of our lives forever—especially when I hadn't stopped him from beating Travis Sholes up in the first place?

"There will never be a time when I let someone treat you like trash," Draco said, lifting his hands, palms up. "It's not the way I'm built, Kara."

That was exactly what terrified me. It was the entire reason that I'd kept my distance for as long as I had.

"I don't need you to fight my battles," I replied.

"You're missin' the point," he said stubbornly.

"I don't think I am."

"If someone was goin' after me," he said, throwing his hands in the air with irritation, "you sayin' you wouldn't do anythin' about it?"

"That's different," I snapped. "I'm not six-foot-five of solid muscle."

"So you wouldn't be able to physically stop someone," he said, his lips twitching. "But there's plenty of ways for you to use your brain. You sayin' you wouldn't?"

I didn't reply.

"Fuck," he said with a sigh, running his hands trough his hair. "You know you would, Kara."

"Did you know that he got in trouble?" I asked. "You can't distribute naked photos of a minor, even if you are a minor."

"Yeah, I heard about it," Draco replied.

"He was arrested and everything," I said. "You didn't *have* to do anything. He got into trouble."

"That motherfucker got probation," he scoffed. "And had to clean up garbage on the side of the road."

"Can we just *please* stop talking about this?" I asked in frustration. "It was years ago. Do we really have to go over it all again?"

Draco's shoulders dropped. "Yeah, baby," he said, pulling me toward him. "You keep sayin' it was years ago, but I'm just findin' this shit out for the first time."

"I'm fine," I replied, leaning against him. "It all worked out in the end, right?"

Draco nodded, kissing the top of my head. "Thank Christ, you didn't have any problems while I was inside. Curtis would have a real hard time ridin' his bike with a coupla broken legs."

I closed my eyes and forced myself not to react to his words. If he had any idea what I'd gone through, I was afraid that his relationship with his brother would be broken forever. I wouldn't let myself be the reason for that.

For what had to be the millionth time, I told myself to forget it all, to push it down so deep that it never came up again. I was fine. I no longer had to see anyone I didn't want to see. I no longer had to endure situations where I was uncomfortable. If that made me look boring, or weird, well, I was okay with that.

# CHAPTER 10

# DRACO

A S I RAN my fingers through Kara's hair, I tried not to focus on anything but her. I was there, in her apartment, with her arms around me, *finally*, and I was fucking it up because I was so livid with my family.

I wasn't sure how Kara expected me to just ignore the fact that they'd treated her like shit while I was gone. Even if I hadn't asked them to watch out for her, they'd still known how I felt about her and they'd cut her out. Had they thought that I wouldn't find out? What had their long-term goal been? They'd known that eventually I'd be out, and if I was lucky, we'd start back where we left off.

"I need a shower," Kara grumbled. She tipped her head back to look at me. "You can watch TV or something?"

"Sure," I said. I wondered how pissed she'd be if I left while she was in the bathroom. I could take care of shit quickly, but there was no way I could be back before she got out of the shower.

"You'll wait?" she asked suspiciously. "It'll only take me a couple minutes."

I sighed. She knew me too well.

"Yeah, I'll wait."

"You can take one when I'm done," she said as she pulled away.

"You sayin' I stink?" I asked, smiling as she immediately started shaking her head.

Kara rolled her eyes. "You know what?" she said, putting her hands

132

on her hips when she realized I was teasing. "You do stink. I mean, I wasn't going to say anything, but whew." She fanned her hand in front of her nose. "Ripe."

She screeched as I lunged for her.

"You better grab some clean clothes," she yelled, racing for the bathroom.

"Why don't I just shower with you?" I asked, lifting her from the floor with one arm around her waist.

"No," she said, laughing as I nipped at her throat. "I'm trying to get clean, not dirty."

"We gonna get dirty after you get clean?" I asked, setting her back on her feet.

"If you play your cards right," she joked. "And, you know, get rid of that stank."

My mouth dropped open in surprise and she laughed as she bolted for the bathroom.

"I thought you were joking," I called through the door, sniffing under my arm.

"Everyone stinks like smoke, you big baby!" she called back. "Go grab some clean clothes. I'll even let you use my fancy shampoo."

I left the hallway and moved back to the living room. I had a bag of shit in the back of my truck, but I wasn't sure if those clothes would smell any better than what I was wearing. Debating whether I should just run over to my apartment building, I looked over in surprise as Kara tiptoed out of the bathroom in nothing but a towel.

"You change your mind on the joint shower?" I asked, reaching for the hem of my shirt.

"Just forgot all my stuff was packed," she replied sheepishly, awkwardly bending down to grab her bag off the floor. "Be out in a few minutes!"

I laughed as her towel slipped and she yelped, trying to carry the bag and hold the towel up at the same time.

God, she was sweet. She'd always been sweet.

Making a decision, I grabbed her keys off the top of the backpack she'd left by the doorway and let myself out of her apartment, locking the door behind me. It would only take a couple of minutes to run home and get some clothes, but I wasn't about to leave her apartment unlocked.

Kara meant it when she'd said she could fight her own battles, and I respected her for it, but I also knew that she wasn't *hard* like the rest of us—for lack of a better word. Get her with Charlie and the two of them were crazy, but Kara alone? She'd rather run than stand her ground. Confrontation had never been something she was comfortable with, and while that wasn't a bad thing, I knew from experience that it gave others the impression that they could do whatever they wanted and get away with it.

I glanced around the parking lot as I strode toward my building. It was still pretty empty, but it looked like people were slowly making their way back home. There wasn't any sign of Officer Asshole, though, which was good. I didn't have any idea why he was bothering Kara, but I was going to put a stop to it if it happened again.

Trying to figure out where I'd seen the guy before, I let myself into my apartment. Something about the cop was familiar, but I couldn't quite place it. I had to have met him before or at least seen him around. I had a feeling once I figured that out, I'd know why he was being a dick.

As I was grabbing what I needed in the bedroom, the front door opened and I paused. I wasn't sure if I was relieved or not that it wasn't someone trying to rob us—just my dickhead brother coming home. I straightened, ready to go out and confront him when I thought of Kara, sheepishly smiling at me in nothing but a towel.

I'd deal with Curtis later—when she wasn't waiting for me, all wet and sweet smelling from her shower.

Thankfully, he didn't say a word as he passed my doorway and I completely ignored him as he went into his room and shut the door. I guessed he wasn't anxious for round two as I was.

By the time I got back to Kara and Charlie's apartment, Kara was out of the shower and sitting with Charlie at their kitchen table.

Well... fuck.

"Well, hello there," Charlie said, grinning. "I see you have a key."

"Took Kara's," I replied, lifting the keys up to show her. "Glad you're home."

"You sound very excited to see me," Charlie replied drolly. "Sorry to rain on your sex parade."

"Oh, shut up," Kara said, reaching over to flick her.

"What?" Charlie replied. "He even brought clothes!"

"I was gonna take a shower," I said.

"And you couldn't have showered at your own apartment?" Charlie asked in amusement. "Less than a block away?"

Huh. Now I kind of felt like an idiot.

"I told him he could shower here," Kara said, getting up from the table. "He wants to use my nice soaps."

"Is that right?" Charlie asked, trying to hold back a smile.

"I can go back," I said with a shrug. I'd been in such a hurry to get back to Kara, I hadn't even stopped to think I could shower at home. It wasn't really a big deal for me to shower at my place real quick. Of course, there was a good chance Curtis wouldn't be able to keep his mouth shut long enough for me to get cleaned up—but I wasn't real worried about that. It was going to happen sooner or later.

"No," Kara said, coming toward me. "Just take a shower here."

She towed me to the bathroom as Charlie snickered.

"She gave Curtis a ride home," Kara said as we reached the bathroom. She grimaced, looking me over. "I guess he didn't want to take

Roxanne out in this. Did you see him?"

"Heard him come in," I replied. "Didn't talk to him."

"I thought you wouldn't be coming back," she said, grabbing a towel from under the sink.

"Told you I'd be back."

"I know," she replied, shrugging. "But probably better if you just avoid him for a bit."

I wasn't sure how to respond. I sure as hell wasn't going to promise not to get into it with my brother.

"So the bottles are labeled," she said jokingly as she gestured to the shower. "I think you've got it from here."

"You know," I said, reaching out to cup the back of her head. "I could really use some help in here. I'm real sore—"

"That's your own damn fault," she replied with a chuckle.

"Let's watch a movie," Charlie called down the hall. "I'll make popcorn."

I groaned.

"Take your shower," Kara said, scooting around me. "I'll make sure Charlie doesn't pick a shit movie."

It didn't take me long to get cleaned up. By the time I was dressed and carrying my dirty clothes out of the bathroom, Kara and Charlie were parked on the couch with pillows and snacks.

"You got a bag I can put these in?" I asked, gesturing with my handful of clothing.

"Under the kitchen sink," Kara said, turning her head to look at me. "You want me to get one?"

"I can grab it."

"Doc Holliday is hot," Charlie said as I was bagging up my clothes.

"Tuberculosis really does it for you, huh?" Kara joked.

"Guess so." Charlie shrugged. "Actually, I think it's the mustache."

"Only place you'll find that mustache is on a fuckin' hipster," I said, sitting down between them on the couch. "You into that now?"

"I don't have a type," Charlie replied, kicking her feet up onto the coffee table.

"She does like hipsters," Kara whispered.

"I do not," Charlie shot back.

"I got a friend you'd be into," I said, grinning as she scowled at me.

"I know all your friends," Charlie replied.

"Not all of 'em. I know a guy that was with me inside—"

"Let me stop you there," Charlie said, putting her hand up. "I'm not going for a guy you met in the joint."

"The joint?" I asked with a laugh. Was she sixty years old?

"Prison," she shot back, waving her hand around. "You know."

"Why not?" I asked. It was a surprising thing for her to say. We knew more men that had been in prison than ones who hadn't. It was just a part of life, honestly. A few of the old timers had made it without doing any long stints, but not many.

She wrinkled her nose.

"Charles," Kara scolded, staring at Charlie like she had two heads.

"I'm not making that face at *you*," Charlie clarified, bumping her shoulder against mine. "The only reason you went to prison is because that judge was a motherfucker."

"Sure."

"Oh, please," Charlie replied with a scoff. "Don't act like you're offended. You know I love you."

"Bishop's not a repeat," I said, circling back to the friend I was talking about. "He's in for some stupid shit. Should be gettin' out here soon."

"Are you trying to hook me up with your friend?" Charlie asked suspiciously. "Because I do okay on my own."

"More than okay," Kara mumbled.

"I have an active—"

"And loud," Kara mumbled again.

"—sex life," Charlie finished, glaring at Kara. "And I'm not that loud."

"Some of your dates *are*," Kara said in disgust.

"Well, excuse the fuck outta me," Charlie said, laughing. "I'm good at what I do."

"Change of subject," I said quickly. The conversation was going down a road I never wanted to be on. Ever.

"Let's just watch the movie," Kara said. The familiar intro to *Tombstone* started playing and I relaxed back into the couch, wrapping my arm around Kara's shoulders. No wonder they'd been talking about Doc Holliday. We'd seen the movie at least a hundred times because there was something in it for every one of us. Me and Curt liked the action, Charlie dug the history, Kara got all teary eyed at the love story, and Reb loved anything with Sam Elliot.

God, it was good to be home. It had been nine months since I'd gotten out and I still had moments when I couldn't quite believe that it was finally over. That I no longer had to watch my back constantly. That I could drive over to see my parents or walk outside any time I wanted. I was crazy thankful for shit that I'd taken for granted before, like sitting down in the middle of the day to watch a movie, lounging on the couch with my two best friends.

"Ah, there he is," Charlie said happily when Doc came on the screen. "Yum."

"You do realize they rarely bathed," Kara replied, tipping her head to look around me at Charlie. "His balls haven't seen soap in months."

"Just let me have this, okay?" Charlie joked. "I know all about their bathing habits. I'm choosing to ignore that little reality."

"Fine," Kara replied. "I'm more into Wyatt."

"I'm sittin' right here," I said gruffly.

"He's been dead for a hundred years," Kara replied, patting my chest. "Don't be jealous."

"The actor who played him isn't," I muttered.

"The actor who played him now plays Santa Claus," Charlie said.

"No shit?" I looked at her in surprise.

"No shit," she confirmed. "We'll watch that one when it's not hot as balls."

"You need blankets and hot cocoa with those movies," Kara agreed.

Charlie smiled and looked back and forth between us. "I like this," she announced, gesturing. "This is good."

I chuckled.

We didn't talk much for the rest of the movie, all of us finally relaxing after the shit day we'd had. It was only the afternoon, but I found myself nodding off. Some time later, I woke up to both of them leaning against me, completely passed out. It reminded me of when we were kids, and I would've stayed like that until they woke up, but it was too fucking hot. Everywhere they pressed against me was sweaty.

Gingerly, I pressed Charlie toward the arm of the couch. She grumbled a little in her sleep but didn't wake up as she settled back in.

Kara woke up instantly as I lifted her.

"Whoa," she said, instantly wrapping her arms around my shoulders.

"Figured we could sleep in a bed," I replied softly.

"If we take a nap, we'll be up all night," she said with a sigh, resting her head on my shoulder.

"You got some place to be tomorrow?" I asked.

"Not unless these fires magically disappear."

"Then who cares if we're up all night?" I replied setting her on her feet next to the bed. "I can think of some shit to keep us occupied."

"I bet you can," she replied with a smile.

I watched as she stripped out of her shorts and then reached for the bedding.

"It's too hot," I groaned.

"I just want the sheet," she replied, letting the quilt fall to the floor. "I like having something covering me."

"Too hot for a sheet," I said, but I didn't complain as I pulled my shirt off.

The bed at her apartment was nearly twice the size of the one at her parents' house, so we at least had a little more room and my feet weren't hanging off the edge. It wasn't as big as mine was, though, and I was looking forward to being able to sprawl out a little with her tucked into my side.

"I don't know why I'm so tired," she said, her head on my chest.

"It's been a long coupla days," I replied with a sigh.

I stared at the ceiling, rubbing her back. Now that I was awake, I wasn't sure if I was going to be able to fall back asleep again. I swept my hand down her back and on the next move upward, slid my hand under the back of her tank top.

Her skin was so smooth. She shivered as I tickled the tips of my fingers up her spine.

"That feels good," she whispered, arching into me a little.

"You feel good," I whispered back.

When she tipped her head back to look at me, I took the opportunity to kiss her. It was slow and leisurely, unlike the last time we'd been in bed together. Yesterday, we'd been almost frantic, using all the tools in our toolbox to keep the other person right there with us. This time, though, we both knew that it was happening. I was pretty sure it would take an act of God to get either of us out of that bed, especially when she climbed on top of me, her knees tucked into my sides.

"You're fuckin' beautiful," I said, in awe of her as she brushed her hair back from her face.

"I'm already a sure thing," she joked.

"Take the compliment," I replied, running my thumb down her

jaw.

"You're beautiful, too," she said, her eyes crinkling at the corners. "Usually."

I laughed, making her bounce on my stomach. "It's the eye, huh?" I asked. It was still swollen mostly shut and my face was mottled with bruises.

"And all of these," she said, running her hands all over my chest and belly, tracing the bruises there. "The neighbors probably thought you were trying to kill each other."

"Callie and Grease have sons and grandsons," I replied, enjoying the touch. "Probably wasn't the first fight they'd seen."

"They should've stopped you guys," she said, meeting my gaze. "They shouldn't have let it get this far."

"Took a minute for anyone to realize we were still outside," I admitted. "They broke it up pretty quick."

"I don't like seeing you hurt."

"Ditto," I replied.

She leaned down, her hair forming a curtain around our faces, and kissed me gently, her tongue running lightly over the scab on my lip.

"Sorry," I said hoarsely.

"They're still your lips," she said easily against my mouth. "I'm not worried about a little blood."

I gripped her ass as she continued to kiss me, learning her new shape. It wasn't better or worse than before, just different. Looking at her for the last nine months and not being able to touch her, I'd wondered if she'd feel fragile when I eventually got to hold her the way I wanted to. She was so slender now. But, as I ran my hands over her, I didn't get the impression of fragility at all. Her body was firm with muscle.

Pulling her tank top over her head, I leaned up and pulled one of her nipples into my mouth, ignoring the way my body protested as she moaned. She tasted so good, a mixture of salt and Kara.

We undressed each other slowly, letting the anticipation build. Kara smoothed her lips over my chest and belly. I pinched her nipples until she gasped and then soothed them with my mouth. By the time she pulled off my shorts, I was so hard I was afraid that any touch at all would set me off.

I was wrong about that, because I somehow held it together as she wrapped her hand around my cock and took it into her mouth. My vision went black for a second as I let out a shuddering breath.

"Stop," I stuttered, tightening my hand in her hair. "You gotta stop, baby."

"Why?" she asked with a small laugh.

"Because I've been imaginin' you ridin' me for at least the last ten minutes," I said as she crawled up my body. "And that's not gonna happen if you finish me off with your mouth."

"I liked you in my mouth," she replied wickedly, making me groan.

"You're gonna kill me," I said as her pussy slid over my cock. "But what a way to go."

She laughed as I rolled us until she was under me.

She stopped laughing when I returned the favor and slid between her legs, holding her thighs open so I could taste her.

It didn't take long before she was gasping my name and pulling at my shoulders. I took my time moving back up her body, and when I'd reached her mouth, I let her roll me to my back. She took the lead then, reaching between us to position me before sliding down my length.

Perfection.

It didn't take long for her to come and I was really fucking proud of myself that I held back a bit longer before I did, too.

We fit. In this way and a thousand others. I just hoped she remembered that the next time she thought about bailing—because even though I wanted to give her the benefit of the doubt, I knew there would be a next time. No matter how present she seemed, there was always something just around the corner that was going to make her want to run again—real or imagined.

"Where you goin'?" I asked as she moved away from me.

"I'm going to clean up," she said, kissing my shoulder as she got off the bed. "If I don't do it now, I'm going to fall asleep."

I enjoyed the view as she slid her tank top and shorts on, not bothering with underwear. She left the room quietly, shutting the door behind her, and I attempted to fix the top sheet that we'd pretty much torn off the bed.

I was grumbling under my breath, still messing with it, when she came back.

"I don't know why you use a top sheet," I said, realizing that I'd put the stupid thing on sideways.

"You don't?"

"Why the hell would you need two sheets?"

"Were you raised by wolves?" she joked, helping me set the sheet right. "You use a top sheet because you clean the sheets a lot more often than you clean the quilt."

I looked at her in confusion.

"That's why you have a top sheet," she said, laughing a little. "Because you clean the sheets like once a week or more, and quilts or comforters are a pain in the ass to wash, so those are cleaned less often."

"Huh," I said, looking down at the bed.

"The top sheet protects your quilt from the funk," she said, getting undressed.

I was instantly distracted from the conversation. I shook my head. "Sorry, I'm not followin'."

She grinned and shook her hips a little before climbing back into bed with me.

"You wanna try and sleep for a while?" I asked as she notched her leg over mine, her body nearly on top of me.

"If you don't care?" she said with a yawn. "Just for a little while."

"Fine with me," I said, spreading my fingers wide over her hip. Shit, I'd lay in bed for the next week if we were going to do it naked.

As Kara fell asleep, my mind wandered to the conversation I'd had with my parents earlier. It had pretty much been a shit show after I'd walked into the house.

*My parents were in the living room when I'd let myself into the house. The power was still out, but it was bright enough inside that my mom was looking over some kind of paperwork while my dad cleaned an old revolver that I'd never seen him carry, but he babied like a third child.*

*"You showed up," my dad remarked, looking up from the pistol. "Good. You wanna explain what that shit was about last night?"*

*"Not especially," I replied, leaning my hip against the couch. "It's between me and Curt."*

*"Well, it didn't stay between you and Curt," my mom said sharply, "when you brought it over to Callie and Grease's for everyone to witness."*

*"You embarrassed?" I shot back.*

*"Watch yourself," my dad ordered.*

*"Sorry," I said to my mom, the word coming out instantly.*

*"That wasn't a fuckin' tussle between brothers," my dad said, setting down the rag and pistol. "You were lookin' to cause damage. So, again, I'm askin' what it was about."*

*"And again, I'm sayin' it was between me and Curt."*

*"Yeah, your brother's sayin' the same thing," my dad said in annoyance.*

*"I bet he is," I muttered.*

*"What was that?"*

*"Is that all you needed to talk to me about?" I asked.*

*"You in a hurry?" my dad raised his eyebrows.*

*"I'm headed over to Kara's."*

*"Of course you are,"* my mom said, *shuffling through her papers.*

*Before I could ask her what she meant by that, my dad spoke again.*

*"You only got one brother,"* he said. *"Whatever shit you got goin' on, fix it."*

*"Not as easy as that,"* I replied.

*"Well, make it that fuckin' easy,"* Dad replied derisively. *"You're not gonna be fightin' like a couple of twelve year olds when we head back into the shop. It's a fuckin' business."*

*"Like no one has ever fought in the forecourt?"* I shot back. I'd been working at the Aces garage since I got out. It was a solid paycheck and I couldn't complain—but I didn't plan on staying there forever. It was still up in the air whether or not I'd patch in. The guys all figured I would, I was a legacy—both of my parents were kids of Aces MC members. My grandpa was the fucking president and my dad wore a patch, but I still wasn't sure. I was good at working on cars, but it bored the hell out of me. Plus, Curt had been a prospect for almost a year already, and I wasn't real sure that I'd want to prospect after my twin had already patched in. It just rubbed me the wrong way—especially since he'd been living easy while I'd been actually doing work for the club while I was inside.

*"My sons haven't had little bitchfits in the forecourt,"* my dad responded. *"And that's not gonna start now."*

*"Roger that,"* I said sarcastically.

*"Boy—"* my dad said in warning, almost rising out of his chair.

*"Is this about Kara?"* my mom asked, setting her papers down to look at me. *"Because if it is—"*

*"It's about Curt bein' a fuck,"* I replied, cutting her off. No way were they going to bring Kara into it when it sure as shit wasn't her fault.

*"Figure it out,"* my dad ordered.

I gave a short nod. I was ready to get the fuck out of there. *"I'm gonna head out. You guys need anything before I go?"*

*"We're good,"* my dad said.

*I kissed the top of my mom's head as I left the house.*

I was startled out of the memory when Kara jerked against me. She was frowning in her sleep, her entire body tense. She must've been having a bad dream. As she started to shake her head, mumbling something, I ran my hand down her back, trying to soothe her, but the motion didn't help—if anything, she seemed to tense up even further.

"Kara," I said quietly, pulling her closer. "Wake up, baby."

My words had no effect and I wasn't sure what to do. Were you supposed to let someone sleep when they were having a nightmare or wake them up? I couldn't remember—but I sure as hell didn't want her to have to go through it if I could help.

"Hey, sweetheart," I said, kissing her forehead. "Hey, wake up."

As she started to whimper, my stomach clenched. What the fuck was she dreaming about?

# CHAPTER 11

# KARA

*I* KNEW IT *was a dream, but I couldn't escape it. I'd never been able to wake myself up when the dreams happened, I just had to relive them until they came to a natural end. I hated it. They always followed a similar path, the good memories turning into nightmares and the bad memories playing out with stunning clarity.*

*I stood in the hallway after school, grabbing stuff from my locker. I tried not to ever have to stay after school, but I'd bombed a test in World History and the teacher had let me make it up. Unfortunately, that meant that I was still around when football practice ended. I froze as voices came from around the corner. As I hurried to pack up, they grew closer.*

*"Hey Kara," one of the guys sang, striding down the hallway toward me. "Lookin' good."*

*"Real good," another one said. "You feel like gettin' out of here?"*

*He stood right behind me and I wished the ground would swallow me whole. It didn't happen every day, but more often than not, one of the group would find a way to corner me.*

*"No, thanks," I replied, shutting my locker.*

*I froze as his hand smoothed down my back, coming to rest right above my ass.*

*"You sure?" I could feel his breath against the back of my neck as he leaned in. "It'll be fun."*

*"I'm sure," I said firmly, scooting around him.*

*"Hey, where you goin'?" he asked, his hand reaching out to grip my*

ponytail. *The hold was light enough that it didn't hurt, but firm enough to scare me shitless.*

*"I need to get home," I said, not making eye contact.*

*I'd learned over the last year that eye contact just made them bolder. It was like the moment I looked them in the face, they took it as a challenge. I fisted my hands in the straps of my backpack to keep them from shaking, sure at any moment that things would escalate.*

*"Nah, you don't need to get home yet," he said. "Come hang out with us."*

*"We're closin' up the school," the janitor said as she came out of a classroom. "You all need to head out."*

*"We're going," another one of the group said as the boys snickered.*

*"Then go," the janitor ordered.*

*I stayed in place until the boys had moved further down the hall and banged open the front door, then jostled and pushed each other through it.*

*"Thanks," I said, looking over at the janitor. Her name was Marie and I'd seen her around, but we'd never had an actual conversation before.*

*"You give me a minute and I'll walk you out," she replied, watching the boys go. "You got a ride home?"*

*"I drove," I said, walking with her as she put away her vacuum in a closet.*

*"I'll walk you to your car then," she said, glancing at me. "I might be small, but boys like that don't mess with old ladies like me."*

*"Lucky," I murmured.*

*"They're little shits," she said, surprising me. "Every school has 'em, going back to the beginning of time."*

*I nodded.*

*"You be careful," she said.*

*That night, I had Rose cut my hair to my chin. It didn't change anything, really. The harassment didn't stop until I'd graduated and didn't have to encounter any of them at school anymore. But no one ever grabbed me by the ponytail again.*

I gasped as I woke up. My first thought was that I needed to go for a run, the second was that I had a very large, very concerned Draco in my bed, and we were naked.

"You alright?" he asked, brushing away the hair that had gotten tangled around my face. "You had a nightmare."

"Yeah, I know," I said with a grunt. I relaxed into his body, even though every molecule in mine was urging me to get up and get dressed. "I'm okay."

"You get those a lot?" He was looking at me intently and I hoped he couldn't tell I was lying my ass off when I answered.

"Not really," I said with a shrug. "Every once in a while."

"I get 'em, too," he confessed with an embarrassed smile. "What are yours about?"

"They're generic," I replied, keeping the lie as close to the truth as I could. "You know, someone's chasing me or whatever. Sometimes it's just pitch black and I'm in a room and I can't find a door."

A month later, I'd been locked in that same janitor's closet until Marie let me out. After that, she'd always left the light on inside.

"What are yours about?" I asked quietly.

I felt like shit when he answered.

"Memories mostly," he said. "My friend I told you guys about— Bishop? He got beat real bad when he first showed up. I stepped in, but he was pretty messed up before I ended it. I relive that sometimes."

"Oh," I said softly.

"It doesn't happen a lot," he said, giving me a squeeze. "Just once in a while."

"I can hear you two talking," Charlie called from outside the door, startling me. "You awake?"

"Do you think if we don't answer, she'll leave?" Draco whispered.

"Not likely," I whispered back.

"I can still hear you," Charlie called. "We've got dinner at my sister's house, remember? Get up and put some clothes on!"

"How do you know we don't have clothes on?" I called back.

Charlie turned the handle on the door and pushed it open an inch.

"Shut the door!" me and Draco yelled at the same time.

"Knew it," Charlie said, slamming the door closed again. "Get dressed, lovebirds."

"You want to go over to Lily's with us?" I asked, sitting up in bed. I stretched my arms above my head. Even with the nightmare, I felt completely rested. I'd needed the nap.

"Yeah, I'll go with ya," Draco said, leaning back, his arms crossed behind his head.

"Are you going to get dressed?" I asked as I stood and reached for my clothes.

"Just enjoying the show first," he teased.

I grinned as I pulled on my underwear. "You know, with you laying like that, I want to tickle you so bad."

"Don't even try it," he warned.

When I gave a small lunge for the bed, his arms shot down to his sides. I couldn't help but laugh. He got me back a few minutes later when he pinched my ass while I was putting my tank top on.

It felt good, being there with him. I'd forgotten how light he made me feel. Like I was on a permanent vacation or something. I ignored the little niggling thought in the back of my mind that it couldn't last. I was walking a tightrope and I knew it, but I just...couldn't stop myself. Now that the dam had broken, I couldn't stop the water.

"I'm ready," I said, turning toward Draco as I brushed out my hair. "You ready?"

"Damn, that was quick," he said as he opened my bedroom door. "Used to take you hours."

"I grew up," I said with a shrug as I led him out of the bedroom.

"She stopped wearing makeup," Charlie clarified, standing right outside my door.

"Jesus," I said, jerking to a stop. "I need to put a bell on you or something. Eavesdropper."

"And she doesn't do shit with her hair," Charlie continued, ignoring me. "And she's got a fucking *capsule wardrobe*. Don't ask me what that is, because I don't have a fucking clue."

"It means all my clothes go together," I said in exasperation, following her down the hall. "So I don't have a bunch of shit that doesn't match. It makes things easy."

"Makes things boring as fuck, you mean," Charlie shot back.

"Draco, how many pairs of jeans do you have?" I asked, turning to look at him. He looked like a deer caught in the headlights.

"Uh, five or six," he answered slowly.

"Shirts?" I continued.

"Ten?"

"I bet they all go together, huh?"

"Uh."

"You can wear any pair of jeans with any of the shirts, right?" I clarified.

"They're jeans and tees," he replied.

"See," I said, turning back to Charlie. "Draco has a capsule wardrobe, too."

"Draco's a dude," Charlie said with a laugh. "He doesn't count."

"We goin' to Leo's?" Draco asked as me and Charlie glared at each other.

"Yeah, let's go," I said, grabbing my wallet and keys. "We can take the Jeep."

"I'm drivin'," Draco said as he led us out of the apartment.

I immediately started coughing. Shit, I'd forgotten my mask.

"Dammit," Draco grumbled as he hurried us toward the Jeep.

I tossed him the keys as we reached it and climbed into the front seat as soon as it was unlocked.

"I can't believe you're letting him drive," Charlie said with a chuckle. "Twenty-four hours and you're already the old lady."

"Shut it," I shot back. "New rule—if you're in the back, you don't get to talk."

"You guys always fight like this?" Draco asked with a laugh as he started the Jeep.

"No," I said.

"Yes," Charlie said at the same time.

"Good to know," he said under his breath.

"She's doing it on purpose," I said as we got on the road. "Just to irritate me."

"Now why would I do that?" Charlie asked.

"Back seat," I said, turning to point at her. "No talking."

"You better put that finger away," she shot back.

"Whatcha gonna do about it?" I asked, wiggling my pointer finger.

"Jesus," Draco said, turning his head to look at me. "You two are like an old married couple."

"We spend too much time together," I said with a huff, turning back toward the front.

I locked my fingers together and put them in my lap. Normally, I didn't let Charlie get to me. She had always been the one to push everyone's buttons-it was just her personality and I actually kind of loved her for it. She said things that no one else would and didn't give a single fuck about the consequences. It was hilarious most of the time. But I was anxious after the dream I'd had, and the longer Draco and I were together outside my little bedroom, the more nervous I became that some outside force was going to bring everything to the surface.

We were safe alone inside my room. It was the outside world that scared me. Going over to Lily's, where everyone was bound to show up, was making me nervous.

"You alright?" Draco asked, setting his hand down on my thigh. "You got quiet."

"I'm okay," I lied, putting my hand on top of his.

When we got to Lily's, there were already a few cars parked in the driveway and on the street. Both my and Charlie's parents were there, and so were Amy and Poet. Amy's little hybrid looked so funny surrounded by big SUVs and motorcycles, but she refused to get rid of it. I loved it. Especially the little decals on the back window, the outlines of a curvy naked woman and a grizzled old man with a walking stick.

"Lily better have made something good," Charlie said as we parked. "I'm hungry."

"Your sister always makes good food," I replied. "Better than anything we could've gotten at home."

"We should probably get some lessons or something," Charlie joked as we got out of the car. "Eventually, we're gonna be old enough that they expect us to cook."

"Bite your tongue," I joked as we hurried for the front door. "I don't want people coming over. You can never get them to leave."

"Amen, sister," Charlie said, throwing open the front door. "We're here!"

"Aunt Charlie! Draco!" Gray shouted, throwing his arms up in the air. He tipped the tiny lawn chair he was sitting in and lost his balance, landing flat on his back. "I'm okay!"

"Grayson, get out of your sister's chair!" Lily called from across the house. "That's the third time you've tipped it over today."

"Come here, you little hellion," Charlie said, grinning.

"What am I, chopped liver?" I asked in disgust as Gray ignored me completely.

"Someone's got a crush," Lily said conspiratorially as she came over to us. She hugged me hello, holding me for an extra second longer than anyone else would have. I relaxed. This was why Lily was everyone's favorite.

"He better not try to steal my girl," Draco joked, accepting his own hug from Lily. "How ya doin,' Auntie?"

"Better than you," she said, leaning back to look at him. "Yikes."

"Barely even hurts," Draco lied.

"I didn't invite your parents or Curt," Lily said, rolling her eyes. "You're welcome."

"You're the best."

"I can't promise they won't just show up, though," Lily said with a shrug. "You think you can keep your cool?"

My stomach clenched.

"I can for you," Draco said charmingly.

"You're full of shit," Lily replied, laughing. She got distracted by someone calling her name and strode off, so Draco and I made the rounds, saying hello to everyone.

"Let me look at you," Draco's great grandma, Amy, said, lifting her hands to cup my cheeks. "You look happy."

I smiled.

"And scared," she said softly. She rubbed her thumb over the apple of my cheek.

"I'm okay," I replied.

"And a liar," she said with a small smile, lifting an eyebrow. "Just remember that anything worth having is a little scary."

"Let go of the lass," Draco's great grandpa, Poet, said from his seat. "I want a turn."

Amy huffed, but smiled as she let me go.

"Hey, Poet," I said, leaning down to give the old man a hug.

"Hello, darlin'," he said, patting my back. "How you doin'?"

"I'm good," I replied as I pulled away. "Ready for these fires to get under control, though."

"You and me both," he said with a chuckle. "This smoke is hell on these old lungs."

"You're not old," I teased. "You're seasoned."

Poet laughed. "Seasoned. I like that."

"Are you flirting with my great gramps?" Draco joked. "With my nan right there? Bold."

"She wants him, she can have him," Amy said with a chuckle.

"You be careful," Poet said to me. "She talks a good game, but she's a possessive one."

"I'll keep that in mind," I replied.

"You get it handled?" Poet asked Draco.

"All good, Gramps," Draco replied, wrapping his arm around my shoulders.

"Good boy," Poet said with a wink.

"Did he just wink at you?" I asked as Draco led me toward the kitchen.

"Don't you worry about that," Draco replied dismissively. I elbowed him in the side, making him laugh.

"There's my baby girl," Farrah called out as we reached the kitchen.

"I'm pretty sure that one's mine," Rose corrected dryly.

"Tomato, tomahto," Farrah said with a wave of her hand. "They're both mine and they're both yours."

Rose chuckled. "I guess that's fair." She leaned over and gave Charlie, who'd beaten us to the kitchen, a loud kiss on the side of her head.

"They've got a head start," Charlie said to me, nodding toward the drinks on the table.

"I see that," I replied.

"Pick your poison," Farrah said to me. "We've got everything except Jaeger."

"The guys are in the garage," Lily told Draco as she passed us. "Escape while you can."

"I'll stick to soda for now," I told Farrah. She and Rose complained in unison as Draco leaned down to whisper in my ear.

"I'll be back in a bit," he said, kissing the spot below my ear as I nodded.

"They're cute," Farrah announced as Draco walked away. "Aren't they cute?"

"Adorable," Charlie said dryly, pouring vodka over ice.

"Yeah, yeah," I said, pulling out a chair so I could sit with them.

"It's weird," Rose said, looking at me while she wrinkled her nose. "Am I supposed to give you boy advice or something?"

"I think that ship has sailed," Farrah said with a cackle.

"Well, she's never really dated or anything," Rose said. She looked at me. "You know where babies come from, right?"

"Oh, God," I muttered.

"When two people love each other very much—" Rose said.

"They don't have to love each other," Lily pointed out, cutting her off.

"Right," Rose said, nodding as she pointed to her best friend. "You're right."

"If I didn't already know where babies come from, living with Charlie would've educated me," I said dryly, making the entire table roar with laughter.

"How the fuck did you manage to drag me into this?" Charlie exclaimed, throwing her hands up in the air.

"You're being safe, right?" Farrah asked, looking surprisingly serious.

"Jesus, Farrah," Charlie said, throwing back her drink.

"*Mom*," Farrah corrected, looking at Charlie expectantly.

"Yes, I'm safe," Charlie shot back. "I thought we were talking about how cute Kara and Draco are?"

"Oh, they are," Farrah said, dropping her chin onto her hands as she looked at me dreamily.

"I change my mind on the drink," I said, getting up from the table to grab a soda out of the fridge. "I'll take some whiskey in my coke."

"Atta girl," Farrah said.

Lily rubbed my back as I passed her.

"Where did all the kids go?" I asked.

"I sent them out to the garage with the guys," she said with sneaky smile. "They can deal with them for a while."

"Leo will probably have them cleaning engine parts, assembly line-style," I said as she handed me a glass with ice in it.

"Whatever keeps them occupied," she replied with a shrug.

I sat down at the table and settled in. The longer we were at Lily's, the calmer I became, but every time the front door opened, I braced for impact. Rose's parents showed up, and Grandma Callie came right to Farrah and got herself a drink, like she'd been there the whole time. She and Farrah had been best friends since the beginning of time, even before Farrah had married Grandma Callie's brother.

As I looked around the table, I realized that we were all sitting there with our best friends. Callie and Farrah. Lily and Rose. Me and Charlie. Three generations, almost. Technically, since Charlie and Lily were sisters, Charlie was in the second generation. There was such an age gap, though, that she fit in better with me and the twins.

As I watched the women around me, I also realized that the dynamics were pretty similar with each of us. Farrah was the crazy to Callie's calm, just like Charlie was to me. Rose was way wilder and more outspoken than Lily, too. For some reason, whether proximity or necessity, we'd been drawn to each other.

"You're having too much fun in here," Amy teased over the chatter as she came into the room. "I'm going to have to ask you to keep it down."

Everyone laughed.

"You want a drink?" Lily asked, rising from her seat.

"I'll get one if I want one," Amy said, waving her off. "You don't have to wait on me, honey."

She came and sat in the chair next to me. Leaning over, she said, "It's a good thing they have such a big table."

"I think they buy them in bulk," I replied. "They all have massive kitchen tables."

"It's so we can do this," Grandma Callie said, gesturing toward the table. "Room for everyone."

"Our table isn't that big," Lily protested, looking around. "We just bought extra chairs."

"You know, now that you said that, I am feeling a little cramped," Charlie said, pushing her elbows out to the sides, jabbing me with one of them.

"Knock it off," I said with a laugh.

"Stop needling your sister," Farrah ordered.

"I'm not needling her," Charlie replied. She looked at Lily. "I thought I was promised food? Where's dinner?"

"Shit!" Lily said, popping out of her seat. "The lasagna!"

"If you burned my dinner—" Charlie said ominously, stopping to laugh when Farrah threw a piece of ice at her.

"It's fine," Lily called when she got to the oven. "It has five more minutes."

Lily's little kitchen became a hive of activity as we all pitched in to finish up dinner, taking a few seconds here and there to finish off and make new drinks. As I helped Charlie assemble a green salad, she looked at me, tilting her head to the side.

"She made frozen lasagna," Charlie said with a scoff. "Hell, even I could make that."

I laughed so hard, my stomach muscles started to ache.

"What?" Charlie asked, disgruntled. "I could."

"I know," I gasped. "Me, too."

"Well, I don't know about you," Charlie said, almost knocking me over as she bumped me with her hip. "You suck in the kitchen."

"*I* suck? Weren't you the one I walked in on—" my words were cut off as Charlie slapped a hand over my mouth.

"Finish that sentence and I will end you," she said, glancing over her shoulder. "My *mother* is here."

"Oh, *now* she's your mother," I asked, my words completely muffled by her hand. "I thought she was Farrah?"

"Hey," Lily said, yelling at us. "Be careful with those knives."

"No emergency room visits tonight," Rose ordered, coming over to take the knives from the counter in front of us.

"I wouldn't have actually resorted to violence," Charlie said with a whine, dropping her hand from my face.

"She knows I could take her," I announced to the group, just as the guys started filtering in from the garage.

"Looks like you've been havin' a good time in here," my dad said with a grin, catching Rose by the hips as she passed him. He leaned down and kissed her. "You taste like booze."

"You taste like smoke," Rose replied.

"Weird," I called out over the noise. "All I can taste is vomit. In my mouth."

Charlie snickered beside me. "Good one."

"So disgusting," I said with a laugh. "They could at least try to act like adults."

"They'll forever be horny teenagers," Farrah said, swatting my ass as she passed me. "All the good relationships are."

"My parents are the same," Charlie said, fake dry heaving. "And they're older than yours."

"Filthy," I said quietly, making her laugh. My eyes met Draco's across the room.

He was smiling.

I blew him a kiss.

"Knock that shit off," Charlie said, pinching my side.

"Ow," I complained, pinching her back.

"Give me a minute to catch up before you guys start being all cute-sy," she ordered sternly, but she was smiling.

"Youah heah," my little brother Jamison said as the kids came inside. He ran to me and wrapped his arms around my hips. "I missed you."

"I just saw you, monkey," I reminded him, lifting him into my arms with a grunt. Both of my little brothers were built solidly, and I had a feeling they'd be as big as my dad eventually, maybe bigger.

"Brody fahted in the cah," he said, his little arms circling my neck. "It stunk so bad."

"Gross," I replied, the correct amount of awe in my voice. "Did you roll the windows down?"

"Mom wouldn't let us," he said in a mixture of delight and disgust. "It's too smoky outside."

"That's gnarly," I replied.

"Gnawly," he agreed. Then he squirmed to be let down.

"You should get him back," I said, leaning down to put him on his feet. "Fart on the way home."

"I'm gonna twy," he said gleefully.

He ran off with the other kids, and as I stood back up, Draco was there.

"Did you just tell your brother to hot box your parents' car with his ass?" he asked conversationally.

I could feel my face begin to heat. "That was a conversation between siblings," I muttered as he leaned down to give me a quick peck on the lips.

"Kara farts like a wildebeest," Brody announced from across the counter, making my jaw drop open in horror. Draco laughed loudly.

"I'm going to kill you," I said, pulling away from Draco to chase him.

"Help!" Brody screamed, running from the room.

"You better run," I yelled at his retreating back. "You're the wilde-beest!"

"Siblings are the worst," Charlie said. "You're not a wildebeest, Kara." She looked at Draco, who was still laughing. "Kara doesn't fart. Ever."

"You're making it worse," I told her through gritted teeth. "Shut up."

"Everyone farts, honey," Grandma Callie said as she passed me a plate with a serving of lasagna.

"I'm sorry," I told Draco. "I can never see you again."

He smiled, but I knew it was the wrong thing to say. Unfortunately, there was no way to backtrack or salvage the situation because suddenly, the food was ready and everyone was around us, dishing up their plates.

Things calmed down, at least as calm as they could be in that particular crowd. The kids were settled around the coffee table in the living room with their plates, and the adults spread out around any possible surface in the kitchen and dining room to eat.

Liquor, beer, and way too much soda for the kids flowed as we visited and argued and generally had a good time. It was always like that when we got together. Family dinners were loud, but it was relaxing to be surrounded by people you knew loved you. You could argue or bitch and you knew that no one would judge, they'd join right in, the arguments forgotten within minutes and the complaints added to until you weren't sure where the conversation had even started.

"We should go out," Lily said, happily, looking over at Leo. "We haven't been out in forever and I actually did my hair today. I look *good*."

"You always look good, dandelion," he replied, grinning.

"Is that a no?" she asked.

"We can go out," he said. "Where you wanna go?"

"A bar," Rose said, smacking the table.

"Uh, you're forgetting something," Charlie called from across the room. "I'm not staying home to watch the kids."

"Like we'd leave your drunk ass with the kids," Rose scoffed.

"We can keep them," Amy said cheerfully.

"That sounds like a disaster waiting to happen," Farrah said with a grimace.

"Please," Amy said dismissively. "They're angels for us."

Poet laughed.

"Gray and Brody are old enough to help us with the littles," Amy continued, ignoring her husband. "We'll just stay here with them until you get home."

"Are you sure?" Lily asked doubtfully.

"Don't talk them out of it," Rose said, widening her eyes at Lily. "We can go to one of the bars where I used to work."

"Are any bars even open?" Grandma Callie asked.

It looked like even the oldies were planning on going out. I looked over at Grandpa Grease, Casper, and my dad, who'd finished their plates and were discussing God knew what at the edge of the group. None of them looked like they cared whether we went out or went home to sleep, they were just along for the ride.

"They'd never close down," Rose assured her mom. "Everything else shut down, so it's the perfect time for a bar to stay open."

"You wanna go?" Draco asked me, grabbing my empty plate and stacking it on top of his.

"Do you?" I asked.

"Might be fun," he said with a shrug.

I knew he'd do whatever I wanted to do, but I wondered how often he'd had a night like this since he'd been out. From what I'd seen, he'd stayed pretty close to home for the most part. There'd been parties at the club—there were always parties at the club—but he and Curtis hadn't really maintained any friendships with people we'd known as kids. Had he even gone out since he'd been old enough to do it?

"Sure, we can go," I told him.

I was too relaxed to feel any apprehension, even though normally I would've avoided going to a bar in town.

I didn't even see it coming.

# CHAPTER 12

# DRACO

R OSE WAS RIGHT—THE bar was open and packed to capacity when we got there. Lucky for them, I was sure the fire marshals had enough on their hands and wouldn't be stopping by.

I laughed as Rose strode up to the bar like she owned the place, and a few minutes later, a couple of tables near the back magically opened up for us. I'd been out a few times with my brother, but it wasn't nearly the experience that going out with this group was. The women were loud and rowdy as we ordered drinks, but the guys weren't. If anything, they seemed hyper alert to our surroundings.

Huh. It wasn't just me that felt a little boxed in.

"You'll get used to it," Grease said, handing me a beer. He hadn't waited for the waitress to take our orders, just gone up and got a round of beers himself.

"Yeah?" I asked. I couldn't imagine getting used to the amount of people we had surrounding us.

"Once you realize that none of these people even want to acknowledge our existence—" he paused with a beer halfway to his mouth as a woman walked by, looking him up and down. His eyes shot to Callie, who was oblivious. "The men don't, at least," he finished with amusement.

"It's easier at the club," I replied, taking a drink of my own beer. I hadn't had anything at Lily's but I was allowing myself one at the bar. I wasn't about to get pulled over for some reason and end up back in jail for a DUI when I was still on parole.

"Hell," Grease said with a grin. "Everythin' is easier at home."

"You grab me one?" Gramps Casper asked, taking one of the beers from Grease. "I doubt we'll be here long. Farrah already looks ready to pass out."

"Good, she needed to let off some steam. Just make sure she pukes before you bring her in the house," Grease ordered.

"I'll smoke with her on the porch when we get back," Gramps replied. "It'll keep her from pukin'."

"No shit?" I asked.

"Works every time," Gramps said with a grin. "Pot settles her stomach and her head. Falls right asleep."

"Good to know," I replied.

"Don't see Kara partyin' that hard," Grease said in amusement, looking over at her.

Kara was laughing at something someone had said, but compared to the other women at the table, she looked almost sober.

"Hell, I meant for me," I joked, making them both laugh.

"You think about prospectin'?" Grease asked after a few minutes. "You've been cagey."

"Not sure yet," I said cautiously. I wasn't sure it was even possible to burn bridges with this crowd—I was considered part of the family—but I didn't want to make it harder on myself if I did decide to become a prospect. If I said I didn't want to and then changed my mind, they'd never let me live it down.

"What's holdin' you back?" my gramps asked.

"Bein' a prospect after Curt gets his patch," I muttered.

Grease laughed.

"That's not all it is," Gramps said, watching me closely. "What else?"

I shrugged. "Not sure workin' on cars is what I wanna do," I said quietly. It was the equivalent of telling them I wasn't interested in the family business, and it was the first time I'd actually said it out loud.

"That's all?" Gramps said in surprise.

"That's not enough?" I asked.

"Hell, bud," Grease said, shaking his head. "You don't gotta work in the garage."

"I barely do," Gramps pointed out. "Pitch in here and there, but I mostly do the books with your ma."

"Only so many jobs—"

"You'll find your place," Grease said, slapping me on the back as we moved to the side so the waitress could carry her tray to the table. "You come see me on Monday. We'll talk to Dragon and figure shit out."

"I wanna go to college," I blurted out.

Was it just me or had the bar suddenly quieted, making my voice carry?

Gramps laughed. "So, go. Nobody's stoppin' ya."

The conversation turned, and I stood there for a few minutes, bewildered at the fact that we'd had the discussion I'd been dreading for months, in the middle of a crowded bar, and it was suddenly settled. I looked over and made eye contact with Kara and jerked my head toward the bathrooms. I needed a minute.

After she nodded in understanding, I strode away. My skin crawled as I brushed shoulders with people, fighting my way through the crowd. Thankfully, there wasn't a line when I got there and I stepped right inside and locked the door behind me.

I stared at my fucked up face in the cracked mirror.

Did I want to prospect and ultimately patch in with the Aces MC?

If I was honest with myself, I'd just been delaying the inevitable. I was a convicted felon. There wasn't a lot of options for me anymore, no matter how I spun it. I had to consider that.

But more than anything, did I really think that I wouldn't become a member eventually? Grease was right. The club was home. I'd grown up on that property, camping in the big field out back, playing pranks in the garage and learning to ride my bike on the gravel in the forecourt. Hell, you could see the club from the front porch of my childhood home.

As I washed my hands, something inside me settled and the decision was clear.

Walking back out into the crowded bar, I was surprised to find that Kara wasn't at our table, but halfway to the restrooms. She didn't see me as I got closer to her, and I realized why when I was only a couple feet away.

"You're lookin' real good," the guy in front of her said, instantly pissing me off. "Where you been?"

"I've been around," Kara replied.

The words were fine, like they were having a friendly conversation, but I'd never heard Kara use that tone before in my life. While Kara had never been one for confrontation, I would've never in a million years have called her *timid*.

"Couple of the guys are home from school," the douchebag said, reaching for her arm.

I couldn't get there fast enough.

Kara jerked her arm down to her side, avoiding the touch.

"You should come say hi," the douche continued, like she wasn't giving off get-the-fuck-away-from-me vibes.

"I'm here with some people," Kara said, taking a step back just as I reached her. She startled as she hit the front of me. As she turned to apologize, I got a look at her face.

"You need somethin'?" I asked the douche. I recognized him from school, but I didn't remember his name.

"Nope," he said, grinning. "Me and Kara were just catching up."

"Seems like she doesn't wanna catch up," I said, putting a hand on her shoulder. She was shaking and I hadn't noticed it until I touched her.

My anger kicked up a notch. What the fuck?

"She always played hard to get," the guy said, still grinning.

I took a deep breath, trying to control the urge to clock him right in his smug smile as Kara's trembling got worse. Something wasn't right.

"Let's go," Kara said, turning toward me to push at my belly. "Come on, let's just go."

"I'll see you around," the guy said to Kara, making her entire body jerk in response.

"The fuck?" I asked, looking at her and then back at him.

"Hey, I remember you," the guy said, realization dawning. "I didn't at first. Your face is super fucked up, bro."

"I want to go now," Kara said, shoving at me. "Go, Draco."

"That's right," douche said, snapping his fingers. "Draco."

"Go back to the fucking table," Kara said, her fingers digging into my stomach. "Go."

I held the motherfucker's gaze until he laughed and turned, making his way back through the crowd.

"What the fuck was that?" I asked Kara as she shoved at me.

"Nothing," she said, glancing over her shoulder. She still looked freaked the fuck out, even with me standing right in front of her.

"It sure as hell wasn't nothin'," I shot back as she moved around me, hurrying toward our group. I clenched my jaw and followed her, instead of yelling her name like I wanted to.

By the time I reached the table, Kara had convinced Charlie that it was time to go and they were grabbing their stuff.

"You guys out of here?" Leo asked in surprise. "Thought you'd make it longer than us old folks."

"Looks like they're ready to go," I replied through my teeth. Something was seriously wrong, and if Kara thought I was going to let it go, she was in for a rude awakening.

"Everythin' alright?" Mack asked me, getting up from his spot next to Rose.

"Guess Kara wants to leave," I replied, watching her get drunken hugs from all the women.

"Thought she was havin' a good time," Mack said curiously. "First time she's ever wanted to go out with us."

"What?" I asked, turning to look at him.

"Yep." He shrugged. "Doesn't happen often, but we always invite the girls when we go out. Charlie usually shows at some point, but Kara never has."

"Never?"

"Think this is her first time in a bar," he said seriously, watching his daughter. He looked over at me. "That's weird, right? Kids still go out and party with their friends, it's not *uncool* or some shit?"

"You're askin' the wrong person," I replied. "Haven't exactly been partyin' for the last few years."

He nodded in acknowledgement as Kara and Charlie reached us.

"We're heading out," Kara said to her dad, giving him a half-hug as she held on to Charlie's drunk ass. "I'm sure we'll see you tomorrow."

"My parents' house burned to the fuckin' ground," Charlie said to me, fisting her hands up by her face and then spreading her fingers wide. "Poof! Gone."

"Yeah," I said, pulling her away from Kara to help Charlie walk toward the entrance. If Charlie went down, I wasn't sure what Kara thought she'd be able to do about it. They'd both end up on the dirty floor.

I kept one eye on Kara as we made our way through the crowd, and I was so focused on her that I almost didn't catch Charlie as she lurched away from me.

"I know you," she said, pointing at a table. "I know all of you."

The table laughed.

"Don't laugh," she said, sounding surprisingly sober for a moment. "You're all a bunch of little prick douche canoes."

"Shut up, Charlie," Kara said, pushing us toward the door.

"Fucking creeps," Charlie yelled over her shoulder. "You peaked in high school, dickheads, and that's not saying much!"

Out of the corner of my eye, I saw one guy rise from the table, but his friends forced him back into his seat.

"Yeah, sit back down," Charlie yelled just as my gramps came up behind us. "I'll beat your ass again, just like when we were in school!"

"Jesus," Gramps spat. He stepped around me and bent at the waist, throwing Charlie over his shoulder—a move I'd seen him pull on my Gram a hundred times. "I'm gettin' too old for this shit."

We followed him out of the bar as Charlie struggled to straighten up long enough to yell more insults at the table.

"Knock it off," Gramps said, giving her a shake.

"Those assholes," Charlie bitched. "I shouldn't have said anything. I should've just started swinging."

Kara was suspiciously silent.

"You want me to fight with those young fuckers?" Gramps asked easily, setting her on her feet. "You start that fight and I'm gonna have to end it."

"You could take them," Charlie replied, scowling back at the bar.

A couple of people standing outside to smoke were laughing.

"You got it from here?" Gramps asked me, shaking his head.

"Yeah, I'll get 'em home," I replied.

He walked back into the bar as I ushered Kara and Charlie to the Jeep. I didn't even laugh when Charlie bumped her head trying to climb inside, even though it was funny as hell. All my attention was on Kara, who had gone completely silent.

She was like a ghost as she quietly climbed into the front seat, gently closing the door behind her. I rounded the hood as she buckled herself in. As soon as I'd gotten into my seat, she locked the doors.

"Those motherfuckers," Charlie was mumbling, leaning forward to wrap her arms around Kara from behind. "I'll kill 'em."

"Drop it, Charles," Kara ordered softly.

"Fuck that," Charlie said as we drove toward the apartments.

And as luck would have it, halfway there, lights lit up behind me. I was being pulled over.

I tried to control my breathing as I pulled over and reached for my wallet to get my driver's license.

"You got insurance and registration?" I asked Kara as she rummaged through the glove compartment.

"Here," she said nervously, handing them over.

"Keep your mouth shut, Charlie," I ordered as I rolled down my window.

"License and registration," a voice in the darkness ordered. I couldn't see his face because of the flashlight he was pointing at mine.

"Here you go," I said, handing them over before putting both hands on the wheel. I wasn't about to give him any reason to hassle me.

"You been drinking tonight?"

"No, sir," I said.

"You came from a bar," he replied.

"I'm the designated driver," I replied. "I only had one beer."

"So you have been drinking."

"Just a beer—"

"Step out of the vehicle, please."

I took a second to breathe in through my nose and out through my mouth.

"I need to unbuckle my seatbelt," I told him.

"Go ahead."

As I unbuckled my seatbelt, his flashlight moved through the car, pausing on Kara before sweeping over Charlie in the back seat.

He stepped back as I opened the door, and as soon as I was outside, I saw who the cop was. Officer Asshole. Just my fucking luck.

I didn't even ask why he'd pulled me over. I wasn't about to rile him when even the slightest bullshit could fuck with my parole.

"Move to the front of the vehicle," he ordered.

My entire body burned with humiliation as I followed directions, doing a field sobriety test, even though I'd only had half a beer. I could feel Kara and Charlie's eyes on me as I did what I was told like a fucking puppet.

"You're free to go," Officer Dickhead said, handing me my license and Kara's paperwork.

"Thanks," I said, the words nearly choking me.

I got back into the Jeep and buckled myself in, waiting for him to leave. When he didn't, I started the Jeep and pulled back onto the road.

"What the fuck was that?" Charlie asked.

"Not now," I ordered, glancing in the rearview mirror.

He followed us until we pulled into the apartment complex.

"Why the hell did he pull us over?" Charlie asked as we parked.

"He didn't say," I replied, climbing out of the Jeep.

"Well, why didn't you ask?" Charlie sputtered. "He can't just—"

"He can do whatever the fuck he wants," I said, cutting her off. "And there wasn't shit I could do about it. I'm on parole, Charlie."

"You still have rights," she argued as we walked toward their door. "The fucking constitution—"

"Just stop, Charlie," Kara ordered, her voice wobbling. "Jesus, just stop."

Charlie's mouth snapped shut as I unlocked the front door and opened it wide so they could go inside.

"It's been a long day," Kara said as I walked in behind them. She barely looked at me. "I'm just going to go to bed."

"You kickin' me out?" I asked in disbelief. "You want me to go?"

"Of fucking course she is," Charlie snapped, throwing her hands in the air. She stomped back to her bedroom.

"Kara?"

"This is moving really fast," she sidestepped, still not looking at me. "Maybe we should just—"

"You've gotta be fuckin' kiddin' me," I ground out, reaching up to press at the headache forming between my eyes. Adrenalin was still racing through my veins, making my skin feel tight after that shit at the bar and then the run-in with the cop. I didn't have the patience to deal with Kara's bullshit, too.

I just wanted to fuck and fall asleep with her wrapped around me and process it all in the morning. If that made me an asshole, I guess I was an asshole.

"It's been a long night," Kara replied.

"Yeah, you said that," I said. "Any reason why we can't end it together?"

"I just think we should maybe take a little break—" she said, pausing when I scoffed. "Just a short break. Really short. Just—"

"You just think if I leave tonight," I said, the adrenalin turning into anger in a heartbeat, "that tomorrow when you let me back in there, I'll be so happy about it, I won't ask you what that shit in the bar was all about."

"No," she said, shaking her head. She smoothed her hand over the back of the couch. "That's not—no."

"Then why don't you tell me now?" I asked. "Who was that guy?"

"Just some kid from school," she said, trying to play it off.

"Old friend?" I asked sarcastically.

Her eyes met mine.

"No?"

"He's just an asshole we went to school with," she said through her teeth.

"Seemed like a bit more than that," I replied. I wanted to pace, to move and get some of the energy out, but she'd stopped me near the door and there was nowhere to go.

"It wasn't," she replied stubbornly.

"Oh, for fuck's sake, just tell him," Charlie yelled from her bedroom.

"Fuck this," I said, shaking my head. "You tell me why you were fuckin' shakin' and white as a ghost, or I'm outta here."

Kara just stared at me. Her silence was like a punch to the gut.

Instead of heading toward the door, I strode past her down the hallway. Charlie met me at her bedroom door.

"Tell me," I ordered.

Charlie glanced around me at Kara in indecision. Then, probably because she was drunk, answered me.

"I caught those guys—"

"Shut the fuck up, Charles," Kara yelled.

"They had Kara cornered," Charlie said quietly. "You know that little nook by the locker rooms?"

I nodded, nausea pooling in my gut.

"They caught her on her way out—"

"Charlie," Kara snapped.

"Her hair was still wet," Charlie said, swallowing hard. "They weren't doing anything. They just, you know, were crowded around her. They wouldn't let her leave and—"

"If you say another fucking word—" Kara screeched from behind me.

"They were saying a bunch of shit," Charlie said, ignoring Kara as she straightened her shoulders. "Sexual shit. All the stuff they wanted to do with her."

For a second, my sight darkened at the edges, rage like I'd only felt once before tightening every single muscle in my body.

"I took care of it," Charlie said, reaching for me before dropping her hand. "I waded in and just started throwing punches. For a couple minutes, it was a mess, but I think they didn't hit me back because I'm a girl." She looked at her feet. "I did my best, though. I got a couple good ones in, and they left." She huffed out a small laugh. "I have a feeling one of them won't be fathering children."

"Thank you," I rasped out as Charlie looked past me, her eyes filling with tears.

"Sorry," she said to Kara.

"Fuck you," Kara hissed back. "Why can't you ever mind your own fucking business?"

"Sounds like it was a good thing she didn't," I said, turning back toward the woman I had been in love with since I was old enough to know what that meant.

The implications of Charlie's story were almost too much for me to wade through. The fact that Kara had been harassed in school, even though everyone had said she was being left alone, that my brother had left her for the wolves, knowing how life in a small town worked and how she'd be targeted, the way Kara had changed from the bubbly, outgoing girl she'd been to the woman who'd never even been in a bar until earlier that night, and when confronted with those assholes from school had gone white as a ghost—all of it beat at me like a sledgehammer. For the first time in my life, I was at a complete loss at what to do. Where did I go first? Back to the bar? Down to my apartment, hoping my brother would be there? Did I walk back to Kara and make her tell me everything?

By the looks of her, she wasn't about to tell me a goddamn thing.

"That's not all of it, is it?" I asked, not moving from my spot in Charlie's doorway.

Kara refused to reply. She turned on her heel and walked out of sight.

Charlie's door closed quietly behind me as I followed Kara. I found her in the kitchen, cleaning the already pristine countertop.

"You gonna answer me?" I asked.

"Just let it go," she replied angrily, swiping at her cheeks as she turned to face me. At any other time, the tears in her eyes would've swayed me. I would've done anything to stop them. This time, though, I knew the answers she wasn't giving were important.

"That a no?" I asked.

"It's none of your fucking business, either," Kara shot back. "I had a life after you were locked up, okay? Everyone did. Sorry that's hard for you to take."

My head jerked back in surprise.

"I'll let you get back to it then," I said.

I turned and walked away from her, even though it killed me. She was hiding shit and I wasn't about to get blindsided with it later. I was an open book for her and I deserved the same in return.

"Where are you going?" Kara called, following me.

"None of your fuckin' business," I replied tiredly, throwing her words back at her.

I let myself out of the apartment and stood outside the door, unsure about where I should go. Eventually, I just walked back to my own place. Driving somewhere and taking the chance of being pulled over again for some bullshit reason didn't hold a lot of appeal.

The apartment was quiet when I got there and at first, I didn't think Curtis was home.

"Thought you'd be stayin' at Kara's," he said, stepping out of his bedroom into the dark hallway.

It was the wrong thing to say.

The events of the night had amped me up so high that I wasn't even sure I could speak to him. For my entire life, I'd looked at him and seen myself. My mirror image. But when I looked at him now, all I saw was a damn stranger.

"We're done," I ground out, forcing myself to stay put, when all I wanted to do was finish what I'd started outside Callie and Grease's.

"The fuck is your problem?" Curtis snapped. "You act like I fuckin' killed your dog or somethin'."

"I asked you to do one fuckin' thing," I roared.

"She was fine," Curtis yelled back. "Sorry if I didn't want to hold your girlfriend's hand for four years while you were locked up."

"All you had to do was watch her back, Curt," I replied. "What? Were you too busy chasin' tail? You couldn't watch out for her because you were too busy gettin' your dick wet?"

"I did watch out for her," he shot back.

"The fuck you did."

"I *did*," he said, taking a couple steps forward. "I made it known that no one was allowed to fuck with her."

"Well, apparently nobody gave a flyin' fuck what you *made known*."

"What are you talking about?" Curt asked. "I thought you were pissed because I didn't hang out with her after you were gone. What the fuck are you talking about?"

"I'm talkin' about a group of jocks harrassin' her at school and God knows what else—"

"I never heard anythin' about that," he replied, throwing his hands up in the air. "If I had, I woulda done somethin'."

"Sure you would've," I spat.

"I didn't want to be around her," Curtis said, dropping his arms. "But I still watched out for her."

"Why the fuck wouldn't you want to be around her?" I asked. "We've been best friends our entire lives."

Curtis didn't respond, he just stood there staring at me, his jaw clenched. The longer he stayed quiet, the clearer the picture became.

"You have a thing for Kara?" I asked in disbelief. "Bullshit."

"Had," Curtis ground out. "Always did."

"You never said a fuckin' word," I replied, still confused as fuck.

"Course I didn't," he replied with a laugh. "You fuckin' loved her, man. I just wanted to see her naked."

I took an involuntary step forward.

"Not sayin' I do now—I don't," he said, lifting a hand to stop me. "I think it probably had somethin' to do with the way she wanted me."

He wasn't doing himself any favors.

"This is comin' out wrong," he said in frustration. "It was nice knowin' I had her waitin' in the wings, ya know? So when she wasn't—" Curt shrugged. "It was weird. I got confused for a bit."

"Confused," I said flatly.

"Yeah," he snapped. "Confused. Suddenly, you two are sneakin' off and she's not lookin' at me anymore. She's lookin' at you."

"You sayin' you were jealous?"

"I'm sayin' that I was a fuckin' teenager, man," he replied. "And part of me was wonderin' if I'd done what you'd done, if she'd still be lookin' at me like I was the best thing since sliced bread."

I stared at him. Dumbfounded.

"Obviously, that's not the case. I'm not a fuckin' kid anymore and neither are you. It was always supposed to be you and her and I knew it back then. I just got bent outta shape when it all changed."

"You got bent outta shape because she chose me," I said bluntly.

"I got bent outta shape because everythin' fuckin' changed, brother. You and her started sneakin' off together when it had always been the five of us and right after that you went inside and it was just fuckin' *me*," he said, pointing to himself with his thumb. "Stupid? Yeah. I was a fuckin' idiot back then. But I figured my shit out and I watched out for her."

"You told her you wouldn't go to jail for her just because she wanted to suck your dick," I replied in disgust.

The look of surprise on Curtis' face wasn't fake.

"No, I didn't," he said. "I'd never fuckin' say that. Jesus."

"You did," I replied.

"Draco," he said, leaning forward a little. "I'd *never* fuckin' say that, especially not to Kara."

"You callin' her a liar?"

"Kara told you that?" he asked in confusion.

"Where else would I have heard it?"

"Ask Charlie," Curtis said. "You ask Charlie if that ever happened."

"She wasn't there."

"I'm tellin' you, I've got no idea what the fuck Kara's talkin' about," Curtis replied.

"She said you were drunk," I said, watching his expression for any sign of recollection.

"Fuck," he said, reaching up to run his fingers through his hair. "Fuck."

"All comin' back to you now?" I asked sarcastically.

"No," he replied shortly. "I was black out drunk more times than I can remember after you got locked up."

"Right," I bit out.

"I still wouldn't have left her ass out to dry," Curtis said. "I never did. I kept an eye out."

"You did a shitty fuckin' job," I shot back. "Because what I saw tonight—"

"What the fuck happened tonight?" Curtis said, standing up straight.

"We ran into some guys from school," I said, trying and failing to remember their names. "Kara freaked out."

"Freaked out?"

"Went pale as a fuckin' ghost when one of 'em started talkin' to her," I said tiredly. "Charlie saw 'em and started yellin', Gramps had to throw her ass over his shoulder and carry her out before she started a bar fight."

"Damn," Curtis said. "Wish I woulda seen that."

I glared at him.

"They tell you what it was about?" he asked, leaning against the wall.

"Charlie said back in high school, she caught them hasslin' Kara," I replied. "Wouldn't let her leave and were detailin' all the shit they wanted to do to her when Charlie found 'em and started swingin'."

"Why didn't they tell me?" he asked in frustration.

I thought about the expression on Charlie's face as she'd told me what happened while Kara yelled at her to shut up. The puzzle pieces were beginning to fit.

"I'm bettin' Kara made her promise not to," I said with a sigh. "I'm also pretty fuckin' sure that wasn't the only time they fucked with her. Goddamnit."

"Jesus, Draco," Curt said. "I swear, I had no clue."

"I'm guessin' no one did," I said quietly. "Why the fuck would she keep that shit a secret?"

Curt opened his mouth to answer, then snapped it shut again when someone knocked on our front door.

"Who the fuck is that?" I asked rhetorically as I turned and walked toward the door. "I'm not in the fuckin' mood to—"

"I come in peace," Charlie said as I opened the door, her face swollen and nose stuffed up from crying.

"Get in here," I said, opening the door wider so she could move past me.

She looked in between me and Curtis. "No blood," she said conversationally. "That's good, at least."

I looked over at my brother as he scoffed and realized my anger at him had cooled somewhat. I was still pissed at him, but the urge to beat him to a pulp was mostly gone.

"She won't talk to me," Charlie said, crossing her arms over her chest as she sniffled. "She's so pissed I wouldn't be surprised if she'd moved out by the time I got home."

"She's not gonna move out," I replied. "You guys have fought before."

"Not like this," Charlie said, shaking her head as she bit the inside of her cheek. "Even when she's mad, she usually argues. She doesn't pretend that I don't exist."

"I'll talk to her," I said as Charlie dropped down onto the couch.

"I don't think she'll talk to you either," she replied. "She's completely shut down."

"She'll talk to me."

"You don't fucking understand," Charlie snapped. "You don't know how she gets. She got into an argument with her parents one time and didn't talk to them for a month. Her *parents*."

"Stay here," I ordered. I was going to talk to Kara whether she wanted me to or not. I'd been fighting with my brother, and now Charlie was crying on my couch because Kara wouldn't pull her head out of her ass. That stopped now.

As I stomped toward her apartment, something out of the corner of my eye made me pause. Officer Asshole's cruiser was parked near the entrance of the parking lot. What the fuck was that guy's deal?

Ignoring him, I kept moving. I'd deal with that shit later.

I knocked and reached for the doorknob, cursing when it turned easily and I could let myself in. Charlie had been too upset to lock the door behind her when she left.

"Kara," I called, moving through the apartment.

"What are you doing here?" she asked as I reached her bedroom. Her door was open, but the lights were out and she was curled up under the covers facing the wall.

"Your door wasn't locked," I said.

"Oops," she replied emotionlessly.

"You know better."

"Are you here to bitch about leaving the door unlocked?"

"I'm here to ask why you never said a fuckin' word about gettin' fucked with," I replied through my teeth. "You made it seem like Curt left your ass swingin', but he didn't even know that you were havin' problems."

"I wasn't having problems," she replied, still not turning to face me. "And you asked me what Curt said. You forced me to tell you when I asked you to let it go. So don't act like I came crying to you about it. I *didn't*."

I was so frustrated by what she was saying and the tone of her voice that I wanted to rip her out of bed. What the hell had she gone through, and why the fuck was she still trying to hide it? It didn't make any sense. Had we gotten nowhere over the past couple of days? Because it felt like we'd been slowly moving forward, but now it was back to the same purgatory I'd been in for the last nine months and I was so sick of it I could punch something.

I moved into the room and rounded the bed so I could see her face. She was backlit when I reached her and it took a moment for my eyes to adjust, but once I did, I just stared. Her voice may have been emotion-less but her expression wasn't. Her eyes were filled with a mixture of desperation and sadness.

"Baby, what the hell?"

"I just want to go to bed," she replied, closing her eyes. "Go home."

"I'm not goin' home," I replied, sitting down on the edge of the bed. "Not 'til you tell me what I'm missin' here."

# CHAPTER 13

# KARA

*L*EAVE. *JUST LEAVE. Go. Go. Go.* I whispered inside my head as Draco put his hand on my hip. I needed him to just leave me alone. I didn't want to discuss anything. I didn't want to rehash old wounds. I didn't want to explain to him that I would've cut off my own arm before I went to anyone for help.

"What are you hidin'?" he asked softly. "It's me. You can tell me anythin'."

"I'm tired," I answered robotically. "Lock the door on your way out."

Brick by brick, I built a wall between us.

"Goddamn it, Kara," he said in frustration, getting to his feet. He walked over and smacked the light switch, filling the room with light. "You don't get to do this shit to me. Not after all I've gone through *for you.*"

Ah, the truth. Finally.

As much as I wanted to keep my distance, a bigger part of me burned with vindication. We both knew that I was the reason he'd spent four years in jail, and no matter how he tried to spin it, when it came right down to it, it was always something that would be there in the background.

"You went through it for me, huh?" I said, opening my eyes. "Did I ask you to do that?"

"Apparently, you're incapable of asking for anything," he shot back.

"How about this, I'm asking you to get the fuck out of my apartment."

"So you can curl up in a ball and feel sorry for yourself?" he scoffed. "Sorry, no can do."

"Why the fuck are you even here?" I asked, sitting up. "I thought *you were leaving* if I didn't answer you earlier. So, go. Don't let the door hit ya where the good lord split ya." I never thought I'd use that phrase in my life, but it had practically poured from my mouth. Thanks, Nana, for that particular gem.

"Jesus Christ," he spat. "I never thought you'd be the one causin' all sorts of drama, but here you are, doin' it."

"I'm causing drama?" I hissed, getting out of bed. "You're in my apartment!"

"After Charlie came down cryin' because you ran her out of it."

"Charlie needs to learn to keep her fucking mouth shut," I yelled.

"Oh, like you do?" he asked with a laugh. "How's that workin' out for ya? You're fightin' with your man *and* your best friend."

"My man?" I asked with a nasty laugh. "I thought you were leaving?"

"For fuck's sake," he growled, running his fingers through his hair. "You're a fuckin' nightmare."

"No, I'm just trying to get my life back," I snapped. "There was no drama before you showed back up."

"There was nothin' before I showed up," he roared, glaring at me. "You'd never even been to a bar."

"What the hell does that have to do with anything?" I asked in confusion.

"What kind of twenty-one year old doesn't go to the bar?"

"The smart kind?" I replied, but he continued like he didn't even hear me.

"Where's your make-up, Kara? Where's the clothes you used to wear? The jewelry? Where's your fuckin' tits?"

"Excuse me?" I sputtered.

"Where'd it all go? Huh? Where'd your fuckin' personality go?"

"Please explain to me how my breasts have anything to do with my personality," I said flatly. "I'll wait."

"You fuckin' disappeared," he said, bending a little at the waist so we were eye to eye. "I left and you faded away."

"That's bullshit," I said dismissively. "I grew up."

"No," he replied. "When the fuck did you turn into a little mouse?"

"Fuck you."

"Not even if you paid me," he replied.

I wouldn't have been more surprised if he'd slapped me. It probably would've hurt less. Taking a step backward, I lifted a hand to my chest, rubbing the ache there.

"I think we're done here," I said quietly. My fight was gone. What little he'd pulled out of me seemed to have vanished, and I just really *really* didn't want to be standing there arguing with him.

"We're not done."

"It was easier," I said, meeting his eyes. "If I didn't wear make-up and I cut my hair and I ran until I could sleep at night, it was easier to blend in." I shrugged. "They were talking about my boobs non-stop. It was always something. So when I realized that I seemed to slim down the more I ran, I kept doing it."

"Sweetheart," he said softly. He reached for me and I dodged him. I didn't want him to touch me.

"I didn't feel like putting earrings on. Eventually, I didn't feel like putting make-up on. I liked the way I looked without it. I wasn't calling attention to myself and that felt *better*," I said, backing up until I hit the wall next to the bed. He reached for me again. "*Not even if I paid you,* remember?"

"I'm not tryin' to have sex with you," he bit out. "I just wanna hold you."

"No, thank you," I replied immediately.

"What did they do?" he asked, the vein in his cheek throbbing as he clenched his jaw.

"Nothing," I said with a humorless laugh. "They didn't do anything. Did you think I was attacked? I wasn't."

"Somethin' happened."

"*Everything* happened," I replied, throwing my hands up in the air in frustration. "Some jackass took photos and video of me nearly dying at a school dance and all anyone at school saw were my breasts. Then you beat the shit out of him and got sent to prison and then Curtis didn't want anything to do with me."

"I talked to him, he—"

"I don't want to hear it," I said, stopping him. "It doesn't matter what your brother said."

"It sure as fuck does."

"No," I insisted. "It doesn't. I don't blame him, okay? I don't. I'd feel the same if the situation was reversed. You want to know why I changed? Because all of this, all of it happened because of the way I looked and because I wanted to go to fucking prom."

"That's bullshit," he scoffed.

"Is it?" I asked. "Like you just said, you went through all of that *for me*."

"Don't twist it," he ordered through his teeth.

"I'm not twisting it," I insisted. "*You* are. And if you thought I'd ever tell a single person that boys at school were scaring me, you're crazy. I went to school afraid every day for two years. I wasn't about to get another person in trouble because of me."

His eyes widened in understanding.

"And if you have a problem with what I look like or how I dress, you can go straight to hell," I finished. "Because I changed to feel comfortable in my own skin, and I'm okay with that."

"You didn't have to change a fuckin' thing, baby," he said softly. "You were perfect."

"And now I'm happy," I replied with a shrug. "I'll take happy over perfect."

"You're not happy," he replied sadly. "You're hidin'."

"Says you," I retorted.

"I would spend my life in prison before I ever let you be scared—"

"Exactly," I replied tiredly. "You're still not getting it."

"Not gettin' what?" he asked.

"*I would never want you to.*" My hands curled into fists. "Do you have any idea what it's like knowing you're the reason someone's life was ruined?"

"My life wasn't ruined," he replied. "I just lost a few years."

"You're not listening to me."

"I'm listening, you're just not makin' sense."

"Just go," I said, dropping down onto the bed. "We're never going to see eye to eye on this."

"You're tellin' me to go because I wouldn't let you be hurt if I could stop it?"

"I'm telling you to go because you feel like not being able to control yourself is some kind of badge of honor because you love me," I said seriously.

"What?" he said in disbelief.

"I don't want to be loved like that," I told him with a sigh.

"I don't know any other way to love you," he bit out. "It's the way I'm built."

I looked at him, desperate to make him understand, and realized that the argument was pointless. I couldn't see any compromise that would leave either of us happy.

"Did you know my mom killed herself?" I said finally.

"Yeah," he said softly. "'Course I knew that."

"You know why she did?" I asked, just as soft. He shook his head. "Because she thought I'd be better off if she was gone."

"Baby, this isn't the same as that."

"No?" I asked, tilting my head to the side. "Because it feels remarkably similar."

"Don't," I ordered when he stepped toward me. "I need you to go now."

"I'm not goin' anywhere—"

"I'm not telling you to," I said, meeting his eyes. "I'm asking you to. Please."

"We'll talk more in the morning?" he asked with a sigh, searching my face.

"Sure," I replied. "In the morning."

He stood there for a few more moments before nodding. Then he quietly left the room. As soon as I heard the front door close behind him, I pulled out my phone and used what little savings I had to buy a plane ticket. I grabbed my still-packed bag and some toiletries from the bathroom and within minutes, I was turning off all the lights in the apartment and letting myself out.

It was only a couple hours to Portland and as soon as I got there, I was going to take the next flight out.

I was dragging ass the next morning when I climbed out of my rideshare at the little RV park outside of Missoula, Montana. My hair was pulled back in a ragged ponytail, I'd spilled coffee down the front of my sweatshirt, and I'd realized on the flight that the only shoes I had were the ratty pair of Birkenstocks that I'd slid on in my mad dash out of the apartment.

None of that mattered as I knocked on the side door of the familiar RV and waited.

"Kara," my grandpa said in surprise, his mouth gaping. "What the hell are you doing here?"

"Gee, thanks," I said, mildly offended.

"Lou," he called into the RV as he let me inside. "Kara's here, put some pants on!"

"Ew," I said, elbowing him in the side.

"Kara's what?" she said, coming out of the tiny bathroom. "Kara's here!"

"That's what I said," Grandpa replied.

"Hey, Nana," I said, letting Grandpa take my bag. "Surprise!"

"Best surprise I've had all year," she said, hurrying toward me. She kissed my cheek as she pulled me into a hug. "What are you doing here?"

"I thought it was time for a visit," I said, grimacing when she gave me an unbelieving stare. "I'm off work for at least a few days because of the fires, so I hopped on a plane."

"Only half of that is true," she said knowingly. "But you can explain the rest later. You hungry?"

"Starving, actually," I replied sheepishly. "I almost got something to eat at the airport, but I figured you'd be cooking."

"You figured right," she said with a laugh as she started puttering around the little kitchen area.

"Your folks know you're here?" Grandpa asked suspiciously.

"You know I'm twenty-one, right?" I asked dryly.

"That doesn't answer my question," he replied.

"Howie, leave her be," Nana said with a wave of her hand. She pulled bacon and a carton of eggs from the fridge. "Put this bacon on the smoker, would you?"

Grandpa harrumphed, but grabbed the bacon out of Nana's hands and carried it outside. As he made his way down the steps, he reached up and patted the breast pocket of his t-shirt, confirming that his phone was inside. My lips twitched. He'd be on the phone with my dad the minute he got that bacon on the grill.

"So," Nana said. "Tell me everything that's been happening. Those fires are scary as hell. We've been keeping an eye on the news."

"It's gnarly," I said, sitting down at the little kitchen table. "You want some help?"

"Not enough room, sweetheart," she said with a smile. "You just sit and relax."

"Yeah, the fires are pretty bad," I continued. "Casper and Farrah's house burned down—"

"Oh no," she said quietly. "That family's had enough heartbreak for a lifetime already."

"No kidding," I replied. "Rose wasn't sad to see it go."

"She'd had a lot of history there," Nana said, glancing at me. "Not all of it good."

"I know."

"Still, sad to lose the family house like that. Charlie must be so upset."

"She is," I said, remembering the look in Charlie's eyes when we'd driven over to her parents' property and she'd seen the carnage for the first time. "Our apartment was in the red zone for a while, but the wind must have shifted or something, so we were able to go home yesterday."

"Well, that's good, at least," Nana said, clicking her tongue a couple times. "You smell like a campfire."

I laughed. "Everything smells like a campfire in Oregon right now."

"Your dad was saying that their house is fine?"

"Yeah," I said, pulling off my sweatshirt. "They're inside the city limits, away from all of it. The smoke is bad everywhere, though. You can't really escape it."

"Unless you hightail it to Montana," she said knowingly.

"Right," I said with a laugh.

"What else are you here to escape?" she asked nonchalantly.

"Boy problems," I replied.

"Boy problems?" she repeated in surprise. "I'll be damned, I never thought I'd see the day."

"Hey," I said in mock irritation.

"Must be Draco," she said, glancing out the window at my grandpa.

"Why must it be Draco?" I asked.

"Because he's the only one you'd leave the state to escape," she said with a laugh. "Not to mention the fact that you've never even looked at anyone else."

"That's not true," I argued. She shot me a look of disbelief. "It's not! I've looked. I've just never seen anything else I've liked," I grumbled.

"Well, if you're escaping Draco then the two of you must've broken that little stand-off you've been having for damn near a year." She laughed at my look of surprise. "I've got eyes everywhere, honey. Don't you forget it."

"Jesus, is everyone talking about us? It seems like they'd find something better to gossip about."

"You know you're my favorite topic," she replied, pointing a spatula at me.

"It's no big deal," I said, throwing my hands up. "I just needed a little space."

Nana hummed noncommittally.

"I'm not sure I want the same things he wants," I said. "Or at least not the same way."

"Well, I've got no idea what that means," she said, cracking eggs onto the skillet with one hand. "Unless you mean in bed, and in that case, you should probably discuss this with Charlie... or Rose."

"Ew," I said, balling up a napkin on the table to toss at her.

Nana laughed. "What do you mean you might want different things?" she asked. "You want babies and he doesn't?"

"No." I shook my head. "We haven't even talked about babies. God."

"Then what? You want to travel and he doesn't?"

I shook my head.

"You want to live in Timbuktu and he'd rather stay in Eugene?"

"Timbuktu?" I asked in amusement.

"Well, hell," she said with a shrug. "Back in my day, you either wanted to get married or you didn't. You worked out the rest later."

"I set the timer," Grandpa said as he came back in.

"Kara's runnin' from Draco," Nana told him.

"Ah," Grandpa said in understanding. "Why?"

"Just trying to figure that out now," Nana replied.

"I'm sitting right here," I said, pointing to myself. "And I'm not running from Draco. I said I needed some *space*."

"Sounds like runnin' to me," Grandpa said. Nana hummed in agreement.

"I'm not running," I said in exasperation.

"So what's the story, kiddo?" he asked as he sat across from me with a grunt. "Not that I'm not happy to see ya. You're welcome here anytime."

"I think there might be too much history there," I said vaguely.

"Boy went to prison for you," Grandpa said gruffly. "Some resentment there?"

"No," I said, shaking my head. I couldn't let him have that impression of Draco. "No, he says he'd do it again. A thousand times."

"Good boy," Nana said to herself.

"You do somethin' while he was gone he can't get over?" Grandpa asked, clearly the next logical explanation in his mind.

"No," I said, mildly insulted. "Nothing like that."

"Well, then, what is it?" he asked. "You've loved that boy for years. He clearly loves you. Simple math here, sweetheart."

"It's not always that simple," I retorted.

"It is unless you're lookin' for a reason for it not to be."

"He says he'd do it again, Grandpa," I said, leaning forward on my elbows. "That he'd go to prison again if it meant that he was protecting me."

Grandpa stared at me uncomprehendingly.

"That's a bad thing," Nana said from her place at the stove. The words were almost a question, but not quite.

Grandpa's phone timer went off.

"Be right back," he said, heaving himself off the seat. "Shouldn't have sat my ass down."

"Is he okay?" I asked Nana after he'd left the RV.

"He's just old, honey," she said with a chuckle. "Standing up takes a little doing these days."

I didn't like to think about my grandparents getting older, especially when we didn't see them as often as I liked. I wondered if they'd settle in somewhere eventually, hopefully somewhere near Eugene where I could drive to visit.

"Ten more minutes," Grandpa said as he climbed the stairs again. "Now, back to what you were sayin'. It's a bad thing that he wants to protect ya?" he sounded completely confused.

"Yes, it's a bad thing," I replied in exasperation.

"You're gonna have to break it down for me, darlin'," Grandpa said, leaning his hip against the back of the kitchen bench seat. "Because I wouldn't want a man anywhere near ya that didn't feel that way."

"I don't want some self sacrificing bullshit," I said angrily. "Love me enough to stay out of trouble, how about that? Control yourself enough to stay out of trouble. Maybe have my back, but let me figure shit out on my own?"

"Huh," he said, reaching up to rub his jaw. He looked at Nana, who shrugged like she had no idea what to say.

"What?" I asked. "Spit it out."

"Any man raised right is gonna be willin' to step into the gates of hell and fight off the devil for his woman and kids," Grandpa said, his voice low. "Not sure what to tell ya if ya think that's a bad thing."

"Not sure where you *learned* it was a bad thing," Nana added. "Your grandpa and Dad are those types of men."

"My mom—"

Grandpa raised his hand to stop me. "Please do not try and compare a man's choice to protect his family and a sick woman's psychosis. That's doin' a disservice to both."

"You don't see the similarities—"

"I do not," Grandpa said firmly. "And you shouldn't either, Kara. Your mama was sick and she didn't have the help she needed. Her death didn't have anythin' to do with sacrificin' to keep her family safe. She killed herself because *she was sick*, honey."

"I don't want Draco to go back to prison for me," I said, frustration making my voice crack.

"Why do you think he will, Kara?" Nana asked curiously.

"I don't know," I replied. "Because I told him about how terrible high school was for me. Those same guys who had passed my photos around back then hassled me for two more years."

"The hell you say," my Grandpa replied angrily.

"It was terrifying to go to school every day just wondering if they'd stop with the innuendos and finally do something," I said, staring at the table. "And they'd be easy enough to find now. So, what, Draco just beats all of them up? How will that change anything except to get him into trouble and leave me alone for four more years?"

"Okay," Nana said, taking the skillet off the stove. "We'll get into the fact that you never told anyone you were having problems in a minute." She came and sat across from me. "You told Draco that?"

"Yes," I said, crossing my arms over my chest.

"And did he run out and start looking for those boys?"

"No," I replied.

"So, he didn't go off half-cocked looking to bash some heads in?"

"No," I replied. I knew where she was going with this.

"Then why do you think he would?"

"Just because he didn't then, doesn't mean he wouldn't the next time we saw one of them in the grocery store or something," I shot back. I was getting so sick of having to defend how I felt, especially to my own grandparents. Weren't they supposed to be on my side?

"You're paintin' him with a brush you bought when you were fifteen years old," Grandpa said. "He was what, sixteen or seventeen when he beat up that boy? He's grown up since then, the same way you have. He given you any indication that he can't control his temper?"

I thought back to the night before in the bar, the way he'd stared down that prick Jayden Parker. He'd put his hand on my shoulder to reassure me, but he hadn't been aggressive. He'd been watchful. Protective, but cool as a cucumber.

"He beat up his brother," I said, feeling vindicated.

"Put him in the hospital?" Grandpa asked.

"No," I ground out.

"Why'd he beat Curtis up?" Nana asked.

"Because of me," I said, not exactly clear on that. I hadn't told him what Curtis had said to me until after they'd fought. "I think because Curtis didn't look out for me."

"Sounds like you didn't tell anyone what was goin' on," my Grandpa chastised. "How was the boy supposed to look out for you?"

The words hit with the power of a sledgehammer. Maybe Draco was right and I was the cause of all the drama. He hadn't known what his brother had said to me, but he'd somehow convinced himself anyway that Curtis had let me down—when the truth was, I wouldn't have told Curtis a damn thing anyway. Shit.

"Go on and check your bacon," Nana said to Grandpa, reaching back to pat his hip as his timer went off again. "Let's eat."

As he left the RV with a clean plate, I sat there, my mind picking through the events of the past couple of days. So much had happened that I felt overwhelmed with it all. Someone could argue that Draco and I's new relationship wasn't new at all, considering the history we had—but it still felt new. New, but not fragile.

Being with Draco was new because there was still so much to figure out, because our day to day lives hadn't meshed yet and the situation was completely different from anything we'd had before, because I was afraid that at any moment he'd be gone. But it also felt solid. Like we'd been together for years. I knew his personality, his likes and dislikes, how he felt about his family and how he interacted with them, the way he treated his friends, the things that were most important to him and the things he didn't give a shit about. I knew him inside and out and he knew me.

Bottom line, I needed some time.

"Can I stay with you guys for a few days?" I asked as my grandpa came back inside.

"You can stay as long as you want, baby doll," he said gruffly. "You know that."

"Your grandpa's gonna have to stop walking around in his under-wear," Nana said as she set a platter of fried eggs down on the table. "But we'll make do."

"Aw, hell," he joked, smacking the table lightly. "I didn't even think of that. You'll have to go."

"Thanks," I said, smiling.

"Eat," Nana said, giving my shoulder a squeeze. "And then I'll take you out on my favorite hiking trail."

"I might need to borrow some shoes," I replied, sticking my foot out from under the table.

"What the hell are those ugly things?" my grandpa asked.

I laughed and relaxed into my seat.

# CHAPTER 14

# DRACO

"**S**HE'S GONE," CHARLIE said glumly, swinging her front door open. "I told you she was going to move out."

"What do you mean she's gone?" I asked, looking down at Kara's pile of crap by the front door. "Her stuff's still here."

"She took off," Charlie replied with a shrug. "She wasn't here when I got home this morning. Her bag's gone and she took her bathroom stuff."

I didn't quite believe what she was saying as I strode past her toward Kara's bedroom. Where the hell had she gone? I'd left her apartment late as hell the night before and she'd already been in bed.

"She's not here," Charlie said, standing at the end of the hallway. "But you can check under the bed if you want."

"I told her I was comin' over this mornin'," I said in disbelief. "She called you?"

"Yeah, right," Charlie replied. "I'm persona non grata, remember? She hates me."

"She doesn't hate you."

"Well, she's super pissed, at least," Charlie said, leading me into the kitchen. "You want coffee?"

"Sure," I replied, leaning against the counter. "Where the fuck would she have gone?"

"Her parents' place, maybe?" Charlie said, getting a couple of mugs out of the cabinet. "It's not like she's got a ton of friends."

"I should've known she'd take off," I said in frustration. "I shouldn't have left last night."

"How'd it go?" Charlie asked, handing me a cup of coffee. "I was asleep before you got back."

"More like passed out," I replied, making her shrug. "It went fine."

"Really?" she asked sarcastically. "Doesn't seem like it."

"We'll figure it out," I said determinedly.

Charlie sighed. "I love you both, D, you know that." She paused. "But is there really anything worth figuring out at this point?"

I looked at her in surprise.

"Hear me out," she said, leaning against the counter next to me. "You've been fighting for a long time for something that Kara seems incapable of giving you for whatever reason."

"You're saying I should just walk away?" I asked quietly.

"I'm saying," Charlie said tiredly, "maybe you should just weigh the cost and benefits of chasing after Kara anymore. If she hasn't told you she's all in by now, are you just going to stay on this shitty ass carnival ride forever?"

"Can't believe this is comin' from you," I replied.

"Honestly," she grumbled, "I can't either. I love her like she's my sister, but she's being a jackass and I haven't seen any sign that's going to end. Have you?"

I'd been thinking the same thing all night, but I wasn't ready to tell Charlie that. When it came right down to it, I was starting to wonder if I was in love with Kara because of the past or because of the present. Was I just holding onto something with her because it made things feel normal again and I was desperate for things to go back to how they'd been before?

"Just think about it," Charlie said, bumping my arm with her shoulder. "It's not like I'm some relationship expert. My longest relationship was in high school."

"Two months with what's her name—"

"Aurora McCann," Charlie said with a shit eating grin. "And oh, what a glorious two months those were."

"Why'd you break up?" I asked with a laugh.

"Some boy asked her to a dance and she said yes," Charlie said with a snort. "And it wasn't an invitation for a three-way. I could've been into that."

I coughed, choking on my coffee and my eyes burned as it nearly came out my nose. Charlie chuckled.

"You're such a prude," she said, watching me struggle. She reached for her phone. "Looks like the parents are calling. I don't care how shitty Farrah feels, I'm not bringing her coffee in bed. Hello?"

I finally turned and spit the coffee into the sink, reaching for a paper towel to mop up my face.

"Yeah, Draco's here. Want us to pick up Curtis?" She paused. "Alright. See you there."

She stuffed her phone back in her pocket and looked at me. "I guess the fire marshal said we can go back to the house and see what's left."

"Little late for that," I replied.

Charlie shrugged. "But they don't know that. The 'rents want to see if there's anything left to salvage. You wanna come help?"

"Sure," I said, rinsing out my mug.

"I doubt we'll find anything," Charlie replied glumly. "It was pretty much just ash and stank coming from the pile. Who knew burned down houses smelled so bad?"

I raised my hand and laughed when she punched me. "What?" I asked, laughing. "Don't you remember our place after it burned?"

"Vaguely," she said, walking away. "Text Curtis and tell him to get his ass up. He's coming with us."

I texted my brother, checked the fire map for the thousandth time in the last week, and cleaned up Charlie's coffee cup while I waited for the two of them to get ready to go. Where the hell was Kara? No matter how mad she was, it was pretty shitty of her to be gone when her best friend was going to see what was left of her house. Frankly, it was out of character. The two of them had been there for each other during every big event in their lives.

I got my phone back out and texted Kara.

*Where are you? Headed over to my grandparents place with C and C to see if there's anything left. Meet us there?*

I watched to see if she'd reply, but got nothing.

"I texted her, too," Charlie said, coming back into the room in jeans and a flannel. "I figured long pants and sleeves were the way to go."

"Good call," I agreed.

"You have any work gloves?" she asked as she piled her keys, a mask, and her wallet on the table. "I don't really want to ruin my riding gloves."

"I've got plenty in the truck somewhere," I replied as Curtis came through the front door without knocking. "They'll probably be way too big, but they'll work."

"Everything always hurts worse on the second day," he groaned, stretching his arms gingerly above his head. "How you feelin', brother?"

"I feel fine," I lied.

"Right," Charlie scoffed. "Let's go, Tyson and Holyfield."

"Which one is which?" Curtis asked as we followed her out of the apartment. "Am I the biter?"

"You're definitely Tyson," I confirmed.

"Oh, I don't know," Charlie replied, glancing at me. "You definitely looked like you'd resort to biting if you needed to."

"I wouldn't need to," I said easily. "We takin' my truck?"

"I'll follow you in my car," Charlie replied. "Just in case you want to leave before I do."

"I'll ride with you," Curt told Charlie, following her as we went separate ways.

"Chicken," she said, squawking like one.

I didn't hear what Curtis said back to her because I'd reached my truck and was too busy pulling the seat forward to look for the gloves I knew were there somewhere. It took a few minutes to find them because behind the seat was the one place I left completely trashed. I was always stuffing shit back there that I knew I'd need later. I sorted through jumper cables, a folded up tarp, an extra jacket, a small toolbox, a beanie, two baseball caps, a pair of socks, a stack of mail, and a couple of water bottles until I found the grocery bag that held five or six pairs of work gloves. By the time I'd thrown them on the passengers seat and climbed into the truck, Charlie and Curtis were already gone. I guessed I was following them.

The ride was uneventful and I pulled up to my grandparents' place right behind my parents. It looked like it was all hands on deck. Both sets of grandparents were already there. So were Callie and Grease, Lily and Leo, Will and Molly—I searched through the group and smiled.

"You're here," Reb called as she hurried toward me. "This is so sad! Poor Farrah and Casper."

"Hey, sweetheart," I said as she hit, her arms wrapping around my torso in a bear hug. "You came out to help?"

"Yeah," she said, still holding on. "But Dad said I need to be really careful because there's probably all sorts of sharp shit and chemicals."

"Truth," I agreed. "You want a pair of gloves to protect your hands?"

"You got some?" she asked, finally letting go.

"Yeah, I do," I said, leading her around the truck to get the bag of gloves. "They'll probably be too big, though."

"That's alright," she said easily. "The ones at work are always too big, too, but I wear 'em anyway."

"You still likin' that job?" I asked as I handed her a pair.

"I really do," she replied, grinning. "Everyone is so nice."

"They better be nice to you," I said, throwing my arm over her shoulder as we made our way over to the group. "You let me know if anyone gives you a hard time."

Rebel laughed. "That's what my dad and Uncle Tommy said, too."

I grinned, giving her a squeeze. Rebel was one of my favorite people on the entire planet. She'd grown up with us, and more often than not, there had been five kids running wild together. As we got older, though, things changed a bit. Reb had Down Syndrome, so while we would've gladly had her along for every single adventure, we'd grown in some ways that she hadn't. She still needed stability and predictability in a way that we didn't.

She'd had a really hard time when I'd gone to prison.

"Damn," her dad, Will, said as we reached him and her mom, Molly. "Nice face."

"It's not polite to comment on people's faces," Reb told him seriously. "Even if you're curious."

"I was wonderin' why you didn't mention it," I told her honestly. I should've known.

"Are you okay?" she asked, clearly believing that the normal rules didn't apply since her dad had broken the seal.

"Yeah," I told her. "I'm alright. But you should go ask Curtis why he looks so much worse than me."

Rebel grinned. "Did you beat him up?"

"Hell yeah, I did."

She laughed and walked toward my brother.

"Heard about your little scuffle," Will said as we watched her go. "You get it out of your system?"

"Mostly," I replied.

"You should get your eye looked at if it's not better in a few days," Molly said with a grimace. "It looks gnarly."

"Is that your professional opinion?" I asked. Molly was a nurse.

"Hey, I'm off the clock," she said jokingly. "But you should never mess with something that could affect your eyesight long term."

"Noted," I replied.

"Wish I could've seen it," Will said with a small grin. "Looks like you went all out."

"You could say that," I replied. "Where have you guys been?"

"We've kept Reb home, mostly," Molly said. "She's still been working and stuff, but you know how she gets when shit is crazy. We didn't want to overwhelm her if we didn't have to."

"Fires are pretty fuckin' scary for anyone," I replied in acknowledgement.

"She wanted to come out and help today, though," Will said.

"Of course she did," I said with a nod.

I looked over as another vehicle pulled into the driveway, recognizing Rose's SUV. My stomach clenched. Hopefully, Kara had come to support Charlie even if she ignored me the entire day. I could live with that. I'd be pissed as hell, but I'd live with it.

Only Rose and Mack climbed out of the SUV, though.

"Kara watchin' the boys?" I asked as they reached us.

"No," Rose said in confusion. "Isn't she here with Charlie?"

My stomach twisted.

"No," I said slowly. "She wasn't home this morning."

"What?" Mack said, frowning.

"Charlie stayed the night at our place and when she got home, Kara wasn't there," I replied. "I thought she must've went to your place."

"She didn't," Rose said with a shrug. She looked through the crowd again. "I wonder where she is."

"I'll call her," Mack said, pulling out his phone.

"We left the boys at Tommy's," Rose told me as Mack called Kara. "Tommy said he'd follow us over once he knew Heather wasn't going to completely lose her shit with that many kids."

"Please," Molly said with a wave of her hand, "she's a pro. She watched Reb all the time. She's like a mohawked Mary Poppins."

Rose laughed. "With the vocabulary of a sailor."

"Beggars can't be choosers," Molly replied with a chuckle.

"She's not answerin'," Mack said, putting his phone away. "Went straight to voicemail."

"Did she turn it off?" Rose asked.

"How the hell would I know?" Mack replied. "Don't even know where the fuck she is."

"I'm sure she's fine, babe," Rose said, sliding her arm around his waist. "She's an adult. She can handle herself."

It took everything inside me not to make a comment about how well Kara had been handling herself for the last five years, but it wasn't the place or the time for that kind of conversation.

"I left a message to call me back," Mack said.

"Let me know when you hear from her?" I asked, trying to keep the worry from my voice. Where the fuck was she?

"You know somethin' I don't?" Mack asked, staring at me.

"Got into an argument last night," I replied.

"And?"

"And she was pissed at me, but she was fine."

"What was the argument about?" Mack pressed.

"Jacob Mackenzie," Rose scolded, slapping his stomach. "That's none of your business."

"Like hell it isn't," he said, glaring down at her.

"Ignore him," Rose told me. "He still thinks she's twelve."

I didn't respond. There really wasn't any good way to extract myself from the situation without pissing off Kara's dad. And I really didn't want to piss him off, but it would be a cold day in hell before I told him what me and Kara discussed privately.

"Come on," Rose said, pulling at Mack. "Let's go see where we can help."

"Don't you want to know what they argued about?" he asked her in disbelief as they walked away.

"Of course," she said. "But I'll find out how I always do—by waiting and eavesdropping. Have you learned nothing from me?"

"Gotta admit," Will said as we watched them go, "I don't envy you dating my niece. Rose is going to be the mother-in law from hell."

"Don't say that about your sister," Molly scolded. She looked at me. "But he's right. You're kind of screwed in that department," she said sympathetically.

"At least you'll always have a babysitter?" Will said, making me pale. "You know, when you guys are ready and shit. A long, long time from now."

"Good lord," Molly said under her breath, glaring at me. "If you get that girl pregnant, I'll castrate you."

My hands went involuntarily to my crotch.

"Do you have those gloves?" Charlie asked as she came jogging toward us. "And why are you holding your junk, ya fucking weirdo."

I dropped my hands and handed Charlie the bag.

"We're just going to start at the outside and work our way in," she said as she grabbed a pair. "Did Kara stay at Rose and Mack's?"

"She was never there," I replied quietly. "No one knows where the fuck she is."

"As if we didn't have enough shit to deal with," Charlie said. "Mack seemed worried?"

"No, just pissed that her phone went straight to voicemail," I replied.

"That's good, at least," Charlie said with a shrug. "If there was something to worry about, they'd be in a huddle commanding the troops."

"You think it has somethin' to do with the club?" I asked in alarm. I hadn't even let my mind wander in that direction.

"Nope," Charlie said firmly. "I think she's being an asshole and making everyone worry for no reason."

I didn't bother responding. What could I say to that? Kara had been all over the place lately, pulling me in and pushing me away over and over until I wasn't sure where we were at. I hated to think it, but it had been a hell of a lot easier when she'd just been avoiding me—at least then I'd known what to expect.

We got to work on the rubble, picking through pieces of the house—most of it unrecognizable. My grandparents were going to have to rent a dumpster or two in order to get the property cleaned up, there was no way around it.

"I'll be damned," my Gramps Casper said from a few feet away. "Hey, Cam, you remember these?"

"Is that my coin collection?" my dad asked, picking his way toward us. "I thought I lost that!"

"You must have hidden it somewhere—" my gramps looked around "—in the kitchen or your old bedroom. Think that's where I'm standin', anyway."

My dad laughed as Gramps handed him the small metal box.

"Well, fuck," he said as he rifled through it. "Now I'll never know where it was."

"In the kitchen or your room," Gramps replied. "Hell, I just told ya."

"I wonder if any of these are worth money," Dad said, picking up a dirty coin and rubbing it clean with his shirt.

"Yeah, right," my gram called. "I doubt a dime from 1982 is worth anything more than ten cents, honey. Sorry to burst your bubble."

"I had older ones than that," my dad shot back defensively, holding the box to his chest.

"If the only thing we find is that damn coin collection, I'm gonna be super pissed," Gram said.

We continued to sift through the rubble, but we didn't find much worth saving. Some dishes made it, but they were mostly broken and unusable. We also found some wire coat hangers, metal knobs from dressers and most of an inversion table that Gram had bought to help Gramps' back and he'd refused to ever use, saying he wasn't going to hang upside down like a fucking bat. Eventually, we all just kind of gave up. There wasn't much worth saving.

"Hey," Mack said, striding toward me. "Got a call from my pop. She's in Montana."

"The fuck?" I asked, jerking my head back in surprise.

"Guess she flew up this morning and just got there," Mack replied. "So, she's safe, if you were worryin' about that."

"She plannin' on stayin' there?" I asked, anger making my movements jerky as I tore off my gloves. My arms were black all the way to my elbows, but from the wrist down, they looked clean, almost like a fucked up suntan.

"No idea," Mack said with a shrug. "But she's with my parents and she's fine. Doubt she'll be there very long, though. They live in a damn RV. You can't turn around without bumping elbows with someone."

"Thanks for lettin' me know," I replied.

"No problem." He turned to go and then paused. "Not sure what's goin' on with you and my daughter," he said, meeting my eyes. "But I know her. She was just killin' time until you got out. Girl don't wait that long if she's not invested—you know what I'm sayin'?"

"I hear you," I mumbled.

"You've got shit all over your face," he said as he walked away. "Probably should clean it up before those scratches get infected and you look even worse."

"Thanks," I muttered under my breath.

She'd left the fucking state. She'd actually got on a plane and left the fucking *state* to get away from me. Mack could say whatever he wanted and I was sure that he thought he knew what he was talking about, but Kara sure as fuck wasn't invested in shit.

"I'm in need of some rest and relaxation," Charlie said tiredly as she met me next to my truck with Reb. "You in for pizza, beer, and a movie?"

"And enough snacks to make us sick?" Reb added.

I looked at Charlie's sad eyes and Reb's hopeful expression. "Sure," I replied, even though I really didn't want to hang out with anyone. "I need a shower first."

"That's fine," Charlie said. "We'll grab the supplies and meet you back at my apartment."

"Where's Kara?" Rebel asked.

"In Montana with her grandparents," I replied. "You'll just have to make do with us."

"She what?" Charlie spat.

"Yup," I replied shortly.

"I'm ridin' with you," Curt announced as he reached us.

"Movie and beer at my place," Charlie told him, shooting me a look that said we'd talk later. "Be there or be square." She grimaced. "I'm turning into my mother."

"That's okay," Rebel told her seriously. "Your mom's cool."

"You're my best friend in the entire world, Reb," Charlie said with a smile, reaching for Reb's hand. "Swear to God. You know that?"

"Of course," Reb answered as they walked toward Charlie's car holding hands. "We're all best friends. The best friends ever."

"Did you say that Kara went to Montana?" Curt asked me as we climbed into the truck. "What the fuck is she doin' there?"

"Escapin' the smoke," I said sarcastically. The air was still shitty as hell and everyone had been wearing masks or bandanas over their faces on and off all day.

"She seriously took off?" Curt said, leaning back in his seat. "Jesus, what a time to do it."

"No shit," I spat as I started the truck. "Her best friend's family home just fuckin' burned to the ground and she took off without tellin' anyone."

Curt looked at me, but I ignored him.

My anger grew with each passing minute. How fucked up did you have to be to leave your best friend when she was dealing with something like that?

"And you," Curt said, looking out the windshield. "She left you without a word, too."

"I'm fine."

"You're pissed," he corrected. "Totally justified, man. Don't just make it about Charlie—you got a right to be pissed."

"Just leave it," I replied. I wasn't about to get into that discussion with Curt. We were on shaky ground as it was, and I didn't want to break the fragile truce we'd come to because he said something stupid.

"Fine," he said.

We rode into town in silence.

"I'm just sayin'," he started, the minute we pulled into the parking lot.

"Don't."

He ignored me. "You've been givin' her space or whatever all year. So, what? You're just gonna keep doin' that? I hate to say it, brother, but grow a pair."

"Say what?" I snapped as I parked and Curtis immediately hopped out of the truck. I followed him out. "Did you just tell me to grow a pair?"

Curtis shrugged, facing me across the hood. "You need to figure that shit out unless you want to be moonin' over some chick for the rest of your life—" He lifted his hand to stop me when I opened my mouth to tell him to shut the fuck up. "—even if that chick is Kara. It's gotta end at some point."

"So, I should be like you," I said flatly. "Fuckin' my way through every legal *chick* in Eugene."

"Did I say to fuck someone else?" Curtis asked, looking around at his non-existent audience. "I said to figure this shit out with Kara—she's either in or she's out, man."

"You worry about you," I ordered. "I'll worry about me."

"Right," he said, giving me a thumbs up like a jackass. "Soon as you figure out how to do that, let me know."

I stomped toward our apartment without another word. For fuck's sake, everyone had an opinion about me and Kara. It wasn't surprising, they'd been discussing it since the day I got out—but it was a lot easier to deal with their comments when they were telling me that it would all work out.

As I showered and got ready to head back over to Charlie and Kara's apartment, I tried not to dwell on how pissed I was that Kara had taken off, but it was impossible. I couldn't think about anything else. She'd agreed that we'd talk this morning and then she'd disappeared without a word instead. It was such a shitty thing to do to someone, especially someone you supposedly cared about.

It wasn't just that we'd had plans and she'd blown me off, it was the fact that we'd been having a serious conversation that she'd put a stop to with the agreement we'd continue it the next morning. She'd run. Again. And I was getting the feeling that wasn't something that was going to change.

Did I really want to be with someone who refused to work shit out and bailed when she wasn't comfortable with whatever we were discussing?

I got to Charlie's just in time to help her and Rebel carry everything from her car into the apartment.

"You didn't tell me you were grocery shoppin'," I complained as I loaded bags onto my arms. "Jesus."

"He's new here," Charlie said to Reb, making her laugh.

"That's just snacks," Reb told me, following me inside with a couple of pizza boxes. "We got popcorn and seven different kinds of candy and soda and hot cocoa, just in case we got the urge, and Gatorade to keep us hydrated and—"

"Don't tell him all our secrets," Charlie teased. "He'll want it all for himself."

"The strawberry soda is mine," Reb said seriously. She looked at me. "But I can share if you really want some."

"It's all good," I replied. "I'll drink somethin' else."

"Good," she said as she started unloading the bags.

A couple minutes later, Curtis showed up.

"I'm sorry Draco beat you up," Reb said with a grimace, giving him a hug. "I should have told you that earlier."

Curt's offended eyes met mine. "Who told you Draco beat me up?" he asked, hugging her back tightly.

"He confessed," she said, her head on Curtis' chest. "But he didn't seem very sorry about it."

"Ha!" I said, laughing. "You asked if I had, you bloodthirsty little thing."

"Was it like a UFC fight?" Rebel asked as she pulled away from Curt. "Sometimes those guys get really hurt, but that's not what they're trying to do. They're just trying to win, you know?"

"Yeah, Reb," Charlie said, shooting a look at me and then Curtis. "That's exactly what it was like."

"You still like watching UFC fights?" I asked. She'd written to me every week while I was inside, and at least half of those letters had talked about what fights she'd seen. She could practically describe them move by move and did so regularly.

"Oh yeah," Reb answered. "Me and Dad buy them on TV. We usually get snacks and everything."

"Hell, I need to come over to your place," Curtis said.

"I'll call you," Reb said easily.

"Okay, who's ready to eat?" Charlie asked. "Get yo pizza and yo beer—or strawberry soda."

We settled in with our snacks and I smiled as Reb chose the movie. *The Princess Bride.* She always chose *The Princess Bride.* When we were little, she'd been too afraid of the big rats in the movie, but sometime around middle school, she'd started to love it. We had to have seen it at least three hundred times already. It didn't even occur to her that we'd rather watch something else, because why would we when *The Princess Bride* was clearly the best movie ever?

"I can quote this movie word for word," Curtis told me, taking a drink of his beer.

"Don't," Rebel ordered, looking over her shoulder at him. "You'll ruin it."

Curtis laughed. "Fine. But I might not be able to help myself during the good parts."

"Try," she said flatly, turning back toward the TV.

"Try," I said to him, my lips twitching. "You ingrate."

From then on, the movie wasn't the entertainment. Any time Curtis even silently mouthed a line from the movie, I swear Reb knew, and she shot him a glare over her shoulder to shut him up. Every five minutes, I was holding back laughter as Reb stared over her shoulder and Curtis maintained the most innocent expression I'd ever seen. He looked back at her like he had absolutely no idea why she kept looking at him, and not only that, he was hurt that she would even imagine he'd do such a thing. By the time the end credits were rolling, Reb was seated between us on the couch so she could make sure that Curtis kept his mouth shut.

"Should we watch another one?" Reb asked quietly, glancing over at Charlie, who'd fallen asleep on the floor.

"As you wish," Curtis said, laughing when Reb's head snapped to the side to look at him.

"You can pick the next one," Reb told me, turning her back completely on Curtis. "Just nothing scary, okay?"

"Of course not," I replied. I grabbed the remote and started searching for something else.

"Aw, Buttercup," Curtis said, hugging Rebel from behind, his arms pinning hers to her sides. "Don't be mad at me!"

"I'm not mad at you," she said stiffly.

"You sound mad."

"I'm peeved," she corrected. "That's not the same as mad. Peeved is more like *irritated.*"

"Don't be irritated at me either," Curtis said, resting his cheek on the top of her head. "I don't like it when my favorite girl is irritated with me."

"I'm a woman, thank you very much," she said, squirming to get away.

"Okay, you're my favorite woman, then," he said, letting her go. "But don't tell my mom, or she'll be *peeved.*"

"You need a girlfriend," Rebel said with a huff, leaning back against the couch. "I'm spoken for."

"Say what?" I said, turning my head to look at her. "You're spoken for?"

"I have a boyfriend," she replied proudly.

"What's his name?" Curtis asked, his expression losing the bit of teasing it held.

"Wesley," Rebel replied.

"Wesley?" Curtis asked incredulously, relaxing.

"Yes," Rebel said in exasperation. "But he likes to be called Wes, so don't say Wesley. Only I can use that name."

"Wait, this guy is real?" Curtis blurted.

I didn't have to see Reb's face to know that he'd just dealt a pretty hefty blow. Her shoulders slumped.

"Fuck, Reb," he said, backpedaling. "I know he's *real*. I just—have your parents met this guy?"

"Yeah, they met him," she said, crossing her arms over her chest and leaning a little bit toward my side of the couch. "He comes over and he took me to dinner four times. And he's helped my dad work on his bike and I taught him how to change the oil in his car."

"Whoa," I said, bumping her with my elbow. "Sounds pretty serious."

"I'm too young for anything serious," she said, sending me a small smile. "But he's nice."

"He sounds nice," I said softly. "What's he look like?"

"He has red hair," she replied. "And brown eyes like me. And he's taller than me but he's shorter than you. And he wears jeans a lot. He likes t-shirts but he said t-shirts are causal attire only, so he wears shirts that button down the front when he takes me to dinner."

"Good man," I replied.

"And he has a dimple, right here," she pointed to her cheek. "Only on one side. You can see it when he smiles and when he presses his lips together when he's mad."

"He get mad a lot?"

"No, he *smiles* a lot," she replied, grinning. "He only gets mad when other drivers don't follow the rules of the road because it's unsafe."

"I'm likin' the sound of this guy," I said. "And your parents like him?"

"Yes," she said firmly. "They like him."

"That's awesome, Reb," I said, loving the way she lit up as she talked about him. I realized then that I hadn't been present for her like I should've been. The fact that I didn't even know about this guy was proof of that.

"Where'd you meet him?" Curtis asked, trying to hide his suspicion under a smile.

"At work," Reb said with an annoyed sigh. "He's a cook."

"Hey," he said, frowning. "You can't expect me to not be protective when I haven't even met the guy."

"Maybe next time you can invite him over for a movie night," I said, shooting Curt a look to cool it.

"Okay," Reb replied. "But you'll have to pick him up because he doesn't drive after dark."

"I can do that," I agreed.

"Have you picked which movie you want to watch?" she asked, glancing at the TV.

"Not yet," I replied, going back to it.

"It's too bad Kara isn't here," Reb said as I scrolled through the options. "She's good at picking movies."

I didn't respond. It *was* too bad. She should've been there with us, hanging out like old times. I realized that it had been just this way since I'd gotten out of prison. If the group was all together, there was always a reason that Kara bowed out. She had to go to her parents' house, she was too tired, she had other plans, but she never had time to spend with us. I knew that she, Charlie and Reb had spent plenty of time together, but whenever Curt and I were there, she wasn't.

I'd given her excuses before, knowing that she was dodging me for some reason and we'd eventually figure it out, but I couldn't find an excuse for her this time. She'd bailed at exactly the wrong moment.

As I started another movie and the three of us relaxed into the couch, I knew that whatever Kara's problem was—I couldn't let it be mine anymore. I'd given her nothing but support and acceptance and honest to God adoration for years—and I hadn't gotten that shit back. Enough was enough. Curtis was right, it was time I grew a pair.

Oddly, I felt lighter after I'd made the decision.

# CHAPTER 15

# KARA

"**A**RE YOU SURE you don't want to ride back with us?" Nana asked as we pulled up outside the airport. "It'll only take a couple more days."

"I'm sure," I replied, leaning forward to hug her over the seat. "Now that the fires are mostly contained, I need to get back to work."

"You need money?" Grandpa asked gruffly.

"Keep your money, old man," I said with a laugh, leaning over to give him a hug, too. "I do alright when I'm actually working—especially with tips."

"It's not one of those bikini coffee shops, is it?" he asked suspiciously.

"What the hell do you know about bikini coffee shops?" Nana asked, smacking him with the back of her hand.

Grandpa sputtered.

"I'll see you guys in a couple of days," I said. "Love you."

"Love you, too, honey," Nana replied. "You call when you get home."

"I will," I promised as I hopped out of the truck.

I waved, walking backward a few steps, and then turned and headed inside. The airport wasn't super busy, and I made my way through security quickly, which left me with another hour before my flight. I wasn't happy about it.

I'd spent the last six days doing anything and everything to not have extra time on my hands. The second I slowed down, thoughts of Draco filled my mind. I missed him. I missed him more than I thought I would.

After all the years of him being gone, I thought I would've been used to being away from him, but I wasn't. Even when I'd been avoiding him as much as possible, I'd still known that he was close, just minutes away, if I needed him.

Plopping down onto a seat near my gate, I pulled out my phone. For being gone almost a week, I had a pretty pathetic amount of messages. Two from Charlie, a few from both my parents, a couple from my boss letting me know they were opening the coffee cart back up, and only one from Draco.

I hadn't turned my phone on during the first few days I'd been away, preferring to stay completely disconnected while I tried to figure out what I was going to do. I'd expected to have a whole slew of messages when I'd finally turned it on, but I didn't. After the first message he'd sent the day I flew to Montana, it had been radio silence. I wasn't sure how to interpret that.

All I knew was that I was probably walking back into a complete shit show. I wasn't sure that I was ready to get into another argument with Draco while I was still reeling from the last one, but I knew he deserved more answers than I'd given him. Nana had told me I needed to just lay it all out on the table, what I was afraid of, what I needed from him, and what I was capable of giving. At first, I'd argued, but eventually, I'd realized that she was right.

Nothing between Draco and I would work if both of us were going into things blindly. Love only took a person so far.

I held my thumbs over the keypad, arguing with myself over whether or not I should text him back before I was home. After I'd left without a word like a coward, texting him seemed equally as cowardly. I texted Charlie instead.

*On my way home. Looks like the shop is open again?*

Less than a minute later, she texted me back.

*Yeah. Worked a shift this morning. Air is clearing up a little so it was busy as hell. You need me to pick you up from the airport?*

I smiled a little at her response. She'd answered like the fight between us had never happened. I was more than a little relieved.

*I left my car in long-term parking, but thanks. I'll be home around 4.*

My phone rang just as Charlie sent a thumbs-up.

"Hello?" I answered, watching a family struggle by with three kids and about ten bags.

"Hey, kiddo," my dad replied. "You on your way yet?"

"Yep. I'm at the airport," I said, grinning at a toddler staring at me, her thumb in her mouth, while her mom struggled to keep her walking forward. "But I'm guessing you talked to Nana and already knew that."

"Guilty," he said. "She called when they dropped you off."

"I figured she would," I replied. "Did she tell you her and Grandpa are packing up and heading back home?"

"Yeah, she said she'd be there in a few days. She was hoping you'd just drive back with them."

"I thought about it," I said. "But I already had the ticket—"

"And you didn't want to listen to them bitch about each other's driving for the next two days?" he asked jokingly.

"Pretty much," I confessed. "How are things back there?"

"They're alright," he said with a sigh. I could picture him settling in somewhere, his feet crossed at the ankles while we talked. "The club came through unscathed, so we're back at work."

"The coffee shop is back open, too," I replied. "So it's back to the daily grind for me tomorrow."

"Daily grind," he snickered. "Nice."

"You like that?" I asked, smiling.

"Well done," he said with mock seriousness. Then his tone

changed. "You and me need to talk when you get home."

My smile disappeared. "Grandpa," I muttered.

"You know they can't keep secrets for shit," my dad replied. "Which is why, I'm guessin', you told them."

"I hadn't thought that much about it."

"You've been keepin' secrets for a long ass time, princess," he said. "Time to fess up."

"There's a difference between handling things on my own and keeping them a secret," I argued.

"In this case," he replied, "no, there isn't. We knew somethin' was goin' on with you and we asked you about it—repeatedly—and you told us shit was fine."

"I was handling it," I said.

"You shouldn't have had to," he shot back. He let out an audible breath. "We can discuss all this once you're home."

"Looking forward to it," I replied sarcastically.

"Don't be shitty with me," he warned. "I haven't done shit except support you the only way you'd fuckin' let me—"

"I know," I said quickly, instantly regretting my tone. "I know."

We were quiet for a few moments.

"Rose is pissed," Dad said finally. "Fair warning."

We got off the phone a few minutes later and I had just enough time to run to the restroom before they started boarding my flight. As soon as I'd found my seat, nervous anticipation hit me at the thought of being back home.

Instead of dreading the conversation I needed to have with Draco, the closer I got to Oregon, the more ready I became to lay everything out on the table. Nana had convinced me during the long ass walks she'd dragged me on that he was going to find out no matter what I did and the long runs I'd gone on by myself had helped me come to terms with that fact. Secrets always had a way of coming out into the open and wouldn't I rather he heard them from me? I needed to trust him with everything. The anxiety of making sure that he didn't find out had turned into anticipation of unloading it all at once and getting it over with. Once it was out in the open, I could deal with the fallout—at least that's what I told myself.

By the time I'd reached my car in the long-term parking, I was practically humming with nervous energy. It would still be hours before I was back in Eugene, but I planned on using the drive to work out everything I wanted to say. I was equal parts dread and anticipation. I couldn't wait to see Draco, to be able to look in his eyes and smell him and know that he was close enough to touch, but that was mixed with a sense of foreboding. I wasn't sure how he would react to all of the things I needed to tell him. At least I knew, once it was out in the open, we could move forward. The miserable limbo I'd been in for years would finally be over.

When I finally pulled into town, I checked the clock, and realizing that Draco would still be at work, I decided not to go home first. The club would be neutral ground, just as much my place as his—at least until he patched in—and if things went south, there would be other people there to stop him from doing something stupid.

I rolled my window down as I reached the gates and groaned as I realized who was standing guard.

"Oh, great," Curtis said flatly. "You're home."

"Nice to see you, too," I replied in the same tone. "Would you open the gate?"

He stared at me for a long moment and then took his sweet time rolling the gate backward just wide enough for my car to fit through. Lucky for him, my dad had taught me to drive instead of Rose, or there was a good chance I would have run over his feet as I threaded through the space.

I flipped him off as I drove down the gravel driveway, not bothering to look back and see if he'd noticed.

I was on a mission and he wasn't the Harrison brother I'd come to see.

As I reached the forecourt, I realized that I was cutting it pretty close timing-wise. Most of the guys were milling around, the big garage doors already closed for the night. Draco's truck was easy to spot, though, surrounded by a sea of Harleys, so I knew he hadn't left yet.

"How was Montana?" Grandpa Grease called from where he was smoking on one of the picnic tables near the front entrance. He leaned forward, bracing his elbows on his knees as he flicked the ash of his cigarette.

"It was good," I replied, lifting my arms out to the sides. "I got a tan."

"I see that."

"Did you miss the smoke?" I asked, waving my hand in front of me as I got closer. "Decided to fill the air back up with it?"

"Funny," he said, emotionlessly. "Guessin' you didn't come to see me. He's inside."

"I'm actually looking for Draco," I said, fidgeting a little.

"He's inside," he repeated with a nod.

I lifted my eyebrows in surprise. "You didn't think I was looking for my dad?"

Grandpa Grease laughed. "Nah," he said shaking his head. "Only one reason a girl comes stomping toward the clubhouse, and it ain't because she's lookin' for her pop."

I grimaced, slowing my steps.

"Go get him," he said, his eyes twinkling as he jerked his head toward the door.

The expression on his face bolstered me a little and I straightened my shoulders.

"Love you, kid," he called out once I'd passed him.

"Love you, too, old man," I replied.

The club was always sort of dark no matter how many lights were on and it took a minute for my eyes to adjust when I walked inside. It was relatively quiet as I looked around the main room, which was a little jarring. I was used to the sound system cranked up to eleven and the noise of up to a hundred people laughing and arguing and stomping around.

"Look who's back," Charlie's dad, Casper, said, coming out of the room behind the bar. Habit made me glance through the doorway before he shut it behind him. I wasn't allowed in that room. Ever.

"Hey," I said, smiling at him. I couldn't see Draco anywhere and I was losing my sense of purpose with every minute it took to find him.

"You have a good time with your grandparents?" he asked, coming over to give me a hug.

"Yeah," I said hugging him back.

"Good," he said as he patted my back. "How're Howie and Louise?"

"They're good," I replied, pulling away. "On their way here, actually."

"You tell them to stop by the club and we'll give that RV of theirs a quick once over," he said easily. "Change the oil and shit."

"I'll let them know," I said, half distracted as I looked around the room again.

Poet was at his place by the bar with Rocky, another member of the club. Uncle Tommy was sitting by himself on a couch in the back corner nursing a beer—his usual place for exactly a half-an-hour after work. He said that giving himself that half-an-hour of quiet before going to the chaos at home was the only reason his marriage worked. Leo and Draco's dad, Cam, were at a table discussing something that I couldn't hear, their voices low. My dad was nowhere to be found, but I could hear Dragon's voice somewhere in the back hallway. Bikes fired up in the forecourt and the familiar noise told me that most everyone else was headed home for the night.

No Draco, though.

"Think he's cleanin' up," Casper said knowingly. "He'll be out in a minute if you wanna wait."

"Jesus, am I that transparent?" I asked in exasperation.

"These walls have seen more women comin' in here lookin' for their men than you could even comprehend," he replied with a chuckle. "You ain't the first, doll."

"Maybe, I should just—" my words stumbled to a stop as Draco walked through the archway that led to the back hallway wearing a cut.

I don't know why the sight of that leather vest on his broad chest hit me so hard, but it did. A mixture of pride, arousal and fear swirled around in my belly as I gaped at him.

"You're back," he said, striding toward me as Casper made a quiet exit. "You have a good time?"

"I—uh, yeah," I replied, my heart starting to pound. He wasn't happy to see me. I could tell by the set of his shoulders and the lack of welcome in his expression. He was being polite, but the familiar warmth was gone. I pressed forward anyway. "Can we talk? I mean," I grimaced and clenched my hands together in front of me for courage. "I mean, I can talk. I'd like to uh, tell you some stuff." I spoke so quickly that my words started rolling together like one long run-on sentence. "Some stuff about while you were gone and the things I haven't told you and you deserved to know them and I know that now and I just really think that maybe if I told you—"

"Not necessary," he said easily. He even smiled a little, like he was letting me off the hook.

"I know that things got a little heated before I left," I said, fully aware that most of the men in the room had their eyes on us and I was making an absolute ass of myself. I figured I deserved it, though, and kept going. "And we both said some things that we shouldn't have."

"I'm sorry about that," he said sincerely. He'd stopped a few feet from me and I was reminded of what he'd said to me in front of my parents' house. He was done chasing me. If I wanted him, I had to go to him.

Gathering up what little courage I had left, I took a few steps forward until our bodies were nearly touching and I raised my face toward his. That's where the courage ended. I couldn't force myself to touch him or to lean up onto my toes.

And thank God for small mercies that I hadn't, because the moment I got close to him, he took a step backward.

It was the harshest rebuff that he'd ever given me. Even when we'd argued, he'd never moved away from me. Never, in our entire lives. Our bodies, before we'd even been aware of it, had always gravitated toward each other.

The air in my lungs left in a whoosh as I stared at him in incomprehension. It actually took me a full second to realize what had just happened.

"Oh," I said softly, my hands starting to shake.

"I'm glad you had a good time," he said quietly. "Really."

"Thank you," I replied, swallowing, swallowing, swallowing, as I willed my eyes not to water. I could feel my nose start to sting and I dug my nails into my palms to try and distract myself. "I see you finally decided to prospect," I said, trying like hell to act like things were normal and failing miserably as my voice wobbled.

"Look, you wanna go outside?" he asked sympathetically, glancing around the room.

That made the urge to cry even worse. I held back a sob by sheer force of will, pressing my lips together hard. As soon as I knew that I wouldn't bawl like a baby, I shook my head. "No," I said, letting out a little huff of air. "No, that's okay." I laughed then, the sound watery and pathetic. "I mean, they've all been watching this play out, right? It's not like they won't be discussing it later anyway."

"Kara," he said softly.

"No, it's cool," I said stepping backward. "No worries. This is fine. It's good, right? This is better. No need to rehash old shit." I swung my arm out awkwardly, still walking backward, and accidentally slammed the top of my hand against the bar. Another uncomfortable laugh escaped me as I pulled my throbbing hand against my chest. "I'll, um, I'll see you around. I mean, it's not like we won't see each other."

He stood there and watched me go.

As I spun and pushed the door open, Tommy's voice carried from across the room.

"That was fuckin' brutal," he said, his voice holding both sympathy and condemnation. I wasn't sure which one of those was for me and which one was for Draco.

The moment the door swung shut behind me, the sob I'd been swallowing back came tearing out of my throat. It was quiet, and painful, and it came from deep in my belly. I blindly took three steps to my car, tripping over my own feet as I hurried, when a pair of strong arms wrapped around me and suddenly I was airborne.

"You're alright, darlin'," Grandpa Grease's voice said quietly in my ear as he carried me across the forecourt. "It's gonna be alright. Let's find your pop."

"I'm okay," I said, my voice coming out in shuddering gasps. "I'm okay. You can put me down."

"Well, now that I've got ya up here," he said, striding toward the door at the edge of the garage as I covered my face with my hands, "I may as well finish the job."

He somehow opened the door, still holding me, and the scent of oil and metal surrounded us as he walked inside.

"The fuck happened?" my dad asked, his familiar footsteps hurrying toward us.

"Came here looking for Draco," Grandpa Grease said, handing me to my dad like a sack of potatoes. "Figured she shouldn't be drivin' like this."

"I'm fine," I insisted, clearly not fine.

"Shh," my dad replied. He pressed my head against his shoulder and without thought to who could be there witnessing my drama, I lost it. My chest heaved and my stomach tightened as I bawled, my arms wrapped tightly around my dad's neck. And even though the pain was vivid and overwhelming, it was almost a relief to be able to pour it out on my dad. It had been so long since I'd allowed myself to let him comfort me.

"You got this?" Grandpa Grease asked quietly.

"Yeah," my dad said. "Thanks for grabbin' her."

Grandpa Grease circled around the back of my dad and smoothed the hair away from my face so his eyes could meet mine.

"You'll be alright," he said. He tapped one finger against my cheek. "Chin up, eyes forward, yeah?"

"Yeah," I whispered back.

I hiccupped as I tried to get myself under control, and after a few minutes, the tears finally stopped and I let out a huge sigh. By then, we'd made our way back to the couch in the back office and I was sitting hip to hip with my dad, his arm slung around my shoulders and my head on his chest.

"Didn't go well, huh?" he finally said.

I huffed out a breath. "You could say that," I rasped. My throat ached and a headache pounded behind my eyes.

"It'll all work out in the end," he said, rubbing my back. "Probably don't feel like it now, but I promise you it will."

"I fucked up," I whispered, staring at the wall.

"Then try to make it right," he said simply.

"I did," I said, scoffing. "That's why I'm here."

Dad was quiet for a moment. "Well, that's all you can do, princess."

"He didn't want to hear it," I replied.

"And that's on him. You can't control other people. You just make sure you're doin' right by them. If they don't want to see it, that's their issue. Not yours."

"I thought I was doing right by him," I said softly. "That's why I was keeping my distance."

"Why the hell didn't you tell me you were dealin' with shit back then?" he asked, tipping his head down to look at me. "I woulda taken care of it."

"That's what I was afraid of," I replied glumly. "When those photos and videos came out, Draco ended up going to prison."

Dad laughed. "Kara, we woulda switched you to a different school or homeschooled you or somethin.'"

"I couldn't take the risk," I replied.

"I know you've been dealt a shit hand," Dad said, kissing the top of my head. "First your mom and then all that shit with me and Rose, and then Draco. I get it, sweetheart. But you gotta learn to trust people."

"I do trust you," I protested.

"You didn't trust that I wouldn't fly off the handle and beat some little high schoolers to death," he replied dryly.

"When you say it like that, it sounds stupid," I muttered.

"Ya think?" he asked jokingly. "I woulda helped ya, princess. You didn't have to go through that shit alone."

"I'm sorry," I said with a sigh.

"Yeah, me too, kid," he replied, kissing my head again. "Why don't you come home with me? You can have dinner with us and let Rose fuss over ya."

"Okay," I said.

"Yeah?" he asked in surprise. "Alright. Come on, I'm pretty sure Molly left her helmet over in Will's bay the other day. You can borrow that and I'll bring it back in the mornin'."

"You want me to ride with you?" I asked, laughing as he towed me through the garage.

"Just what the doctor ordered," he said, shooting me a grin. "The wind in your face and the open road."

# CHAPTER 16

# DRACO

"**M**IND YOUR OWN business," I snapped at Tommy as he strolled over to where I was standing, frozen, after I'd watched Kara leave.

It was for the best, for both of us. There had been too much back and forth, not knowing where we stood. I didn't want to do that shit anymore and Kara couldn't be enjoying it, either. Who would? I'd come to the realization while she was gone that she'd obviously been having a hell of a time keeping me at a distance, but she wasn't any better at keeping me close. I was sick of it and I didn't want that for her, either. Both of us deserved a little stability.

"Man, she came in here lookin' for you," Tommy said, setting his empty beer bottle on the bar. "And you blew it."

"Seriously, Tommy," I said through my teeth. "Drop it."

I wondered if she'd made it to her car yet. I could still stop her if I hurried.

"*She came in here lookin' for you,*" he said again, staring at me. "She ever do that before?"

"You know she hasn't," I snapped. "Everyone gossips in this fuckin' place."

"She came in here, knowin' that we'd all be here," he continued. "Knowin' that she might not get the reception she was hopin' for—"

"Jesus Christ," I muttered in annoyance.

"What else did ya want, kid?" he asked in disgust. "For her to get up

230

on the bar and shout her everlastin' love?"

"Stay out of it, Tommy," I replied.

"You're a fuckin' moron," he said, shaking his head as he turned to leave. "And in the future, you better watch how you fuckin' talk to me, *prospect.*"

I stood in that same place even after he'd left. My boots seemed glued to the floor. I'd been waiting all week for her to come back so that I could finally put an end to our cat and mouse shit, and now that it had happened, I wasn't sure what to do with myself. Part of me still wondered if I could catch her and tell her that I did want to hear whatever it was she wanted to tell me, that we'd figure it out and it wasn't too late. The other part of me remembered how it felt when she'd stopped coming to see me, how she'd dodged me for months, how she'd kept secrets and—

"You alright, boyo?" Great Gramps Poet called quietly from the end of the bar.

"Yeah," I replied, snapping out of it. I'd done the right thing. We could move forward now. Maybe, eventually, we'd even be friends again.

"You sure?" he asked as I turned to talk to him. "You sure this is the road you'd like to take?"

"What do you mean?" I asked as I walked closer to him.

"You got two roads in front of you," he said seriously. "One you walk down alone, and the other you walk down holdin' on like hell to the woman you love."

"You sayin' I won't ever find anyone else?" I joked.

"You will," he said easily, lifting his coffee mug to his lips. "But take it from me, they won't ever be her."

The truth of that hit me like a stack of bricks.

"Fuck," I said.

"Better hurry, boyo," Gramps said, jerking his chin toward the door.

"Fuck," I said again, spinning on my heel.

I didn't run, but it was a close thing. Seconds later, I was outside scanning the parking lot. Relief hit fast as I spotted Kara's Jeep parked over toward the picnic tables. I didn't even see Grease until his fist was planted in my belly, knocking the air out of me.

"What?" I gasped as soon as I could pull air into my lungs again. I looked at him in confusion.

"You deserved that," he said easily, moving around me toward the clubhouse. "You're welcome for not fuckin' up your face. Again."

I coughed, sure that what I'd had for lunch was going to make an appearance. Holy hell, that old fucker's fists were like goddamn wrecking balls. I was bent over, my hands on my knees, trying not to puke when a bike started up at the far end of the building. Keeping my eyes on Kara's car, I took a minute to learn how to breathe again.

By the time I straightened up, I realized that Kara wasn't *in* her car. I glanced over, just as Mack pulled out of the forecourt with Kara on the back of his bike.

"Shit," I spat, watching them go.

She didn't look back once.

"Shit," I said again, bracing my hands on my hips.

I considered going back inside. Kara had to come back for her car at some point, right? But the idea of going back inside and getting a second helping of Grease's particular brand of conversation didn't sound all that appealing. After a few moments, I headed for my truck. I'd wait for Kara back at the apartments. Maybe Charlie would have some pity on me and let me wait at their place.

Curt was just switching places with another prospect on the gate as I reached it and he walked up to my window before I could pull out onto the road.

"I'm guessin' it didn't go well," he said, searching my face.

"What?" I asked, playing dumb.

"I let Kara through the gate," he replied, looking at me like I was an idiot. "And she just left on the back of her dad's bike, so—"

"She seem okay?" I asked.

Curt laughed. "She was wearin' a full helmet," he replied. "She looked like a fuckin' robot. What happened?"

"Nothin'."

"Sure," he said, giving my doorframe a couple taps. "That seems likely. I'll see you at home."

I didn't respond as he walked away. My mind raced as I drove home and I tried like hell not to worry. Me and Kara had history, right? One conversation wasn't going to be the end of everything, and psyching myself out that it was wouldn't help anything. As soon as she came home, I'd tell her that I wanted to have that conversation she'd mentioned. It didn't matter that I hadn't been able to catch her at the club. I knew where she lived. Hell, her car was parked in front of my job. I just needed to wait a few hours, at most.

I was still telling myself that as I climbed out of my truck and walked toward Kara and Charlie's apartment.

"Harrison," a voice called from down the sidewalk.

I jerked to a stop and turned toward it, a wide smile pulling at my lips.

"Lover Boy," I called as I walked toward him, laughing when he grimaced. We met in the middle with a back slapping hug. "When the hell did you get out?" I asked.

"Yesterday," he said, pushing me away by the shoulders. "Just Bishop now. Gus works, too. You look good, man. The outside's treatin' ya right."

"You'll always be Lover Boy to me," I replied.

Bishop laughed. "People are gonna get the wrong idea about us, you keep callin' me that."

"Not around here," I replied, grinning. "Boys at the club'll take one look at your pretty face and know exactly why I'm callin' you that."

Bishop gestured toward my cut. "All in, huh?"

"Always have been," I replied. "Just took me a minute to realize it."

"Ain't that the truth."

"You wanna come in?" I asked. "I'm sure we've got somethin' to drink. If not, the girls probably have somethin'."

Bishop's eyes caught on something over my shoulder. "Please tell me neither of your girls have long blonde hair," he said, staring.

I turned to see what he was looking at and laughed as I caught sight of Charlie carrying a bag of garbage down the stairs.

"Draco," she called. "Good! Carry this shit to the dumpster for me, would you?"

I stepped to the side and I knew the second she saw Bishop.

"Hello there," she said, smiling huge as she strode toward us, her hips swaying. "I don't think we've met. Did you just move in?"

"Charlie," I said, amusement making my lips twitch as she reached out to shake his hand with the one *not* holding a huge bag of trash. "This is my friend Bishop, the one I was telling you about."

"Ah, fuck," she said as they shook hands.

"Nice to meet you, Charlie," Bishop said, still shaking her hand.

"Yeah, you, too," she replied snatching her hand back. She looked at me. "I'm going to kill you."

I laughed as she shoved the bag of garbage at my chest.

"We'll come by in a bit," I said, grabbing the bag before it could fall and bust open all over the ground.

"Door's locked," she said happily, walking away as she flipped me off over her shoulder.

"I've got a key!"

"Bullshit!"

I laughed as I walked across the parking lot to where the dumpster was.

"That was Charlie?" Bishop said, glancing over his shoulder as he walked alongside me.

"That's her," I replied, tossing the garbage. "Can't believe you never met her."

"It wasn't like I had a lot of visitors," Bishop replied. "I don't think I even saw the damn visiting room."

"I shoulda came by," I said as we walked back toward the apartments. Bishop had grown up in the foster system and didn't really have any family. I'd known he was in there without any visitors.

"Fuck that," Bishop said instantly. "I wouldn't have had you approved. You got the fuck out, man, I didn't want you comin' back in to see me."

"Still should've," I said apologetically.

Bishop waved me off. He looked up as Curt's bike pulled into the parking lot.

"Jesus," he said, looking over at me. "Knew you had a twin, but that's weird as fuck."

I laughed. "You'll get used to it."

"Didn't want to ask," he said as Curt walked toward us. "But there a reason both of you look like you got hit by a truck?"

"Small disagreement between brothers," I replied as Curt reached us. "Shoulda seen us the day it happened."

"Curt, this is Bishop—"

"Hey," Curt said, reaching out to shake Bishop's hand. "How's it goin'?"

"Not bad," Bishop replied. "Glad to be breathin' fresh air again."

"If you can call this fresh," Curt said jokingly. The air wasn't as smoky as it had been the week before, but it still stank.

Bishop took a deep breath. "Smells fresh as fuck to me."

We all laughed.

"We got anything to drink?" I asked Curt. I couldn't remember the last time we'd been to the grocery store.

"Nah, but I'm sure Charlie does," he replied. He led us toward the girls' apartment.

"She might not let us in," I told him.

"Why the hell not?" he asked, glancing over at me.

I jerked my head toward Bishop, and Curt's eyebrows rose in surprise.

"What was that all about, anyway?" Bishop asked as we reached the door.

"Tell you later," I said as Curt swung the front door open without knocking.

"Lucy, I'm home," he called, striding inside like he owned the place.

"You have your own fucking apartment," Charlie replied, throwing her hands up in the air.

"We don't have anything to offer our guest," Curt replied easily, going for the fridge.

"Then go to the store," Charlie snapped. She looked past him to where Bishop and I were standing just inside the front door. "Jesus. Fine. Come in, sit down, eat my food and drink my beer. You know you're going to anyway."

"We come here because we feel so welcome," I said, making Bishop laugh.

I left him in the tiny living room and moved toward the kitchen.

"Cool it, would you?" I said quietly to Charlie as I grabbed a couple beers from the fridge.

"You cool it," she snapped, even quieter. "You're the one who brought sexual kryptonite into my apartment!"

"Sexual kryptonite?" I asked with a laugh.

"You won't be laughing when I climb on top of your friend and start stripping," she hissed.

"Please don't do that," I replied seriously.

"If I pictured men while I was masturbating," she said, making me jerk back in disgust, "that is who I would picture."

"Please stop," I pleaded. "Jesus Christ."

"If he has a dimple," she said, pointing at me, "I will not be held accountable for my actions." She leaned closer. "And I bet he's *loud* in bed."

She strode toward the living room and I took a second to scrub that image from my head permanently.

"Mostly construction," Bishop was telling Charlie as I went back into the living room. "But I don't have a job yet."

"What kind of construction?" Curt asked. "Charlie's parents are buildin' a new house. They might need some help with that."

"If I get on with the crew that builds it," Bishop said, nodding in thanks as I handed him a beer. "You know who they're usin'?"

"The insurance company is being a huge heaping pile of shit," Charlie said angrily. "So we might end up doing most of it ourselves to cut down on costs."

"Really?" Bishop said in surprise. "That's tough."

"My dad has enough favors from people that it's possible," she said with a shrug. "Everyone owes him something, even plumbers and electricians."

"Your parents have plans drawn up yet?" Bishop asked, leaning forward to rest his elbows on his knees.

The conversation continued and I contributed, but I wasn't even sure what I'd said. I was happy as fuck to have Bishop hanging out with us, but my attention was fixed firmly on the front door, waiting for Kara to come home. It got later and later and eventually, we ran out of beer and moved on to Charlie's stash of hard liquor.

"He's a good man to have at your back," Bishop said to Curt, toasting me with his Mason jar filled with some concoction Charlie had dreamt up. "Glad he never got as pissed at me as he was at you."

Charlie snorted. "You should have seen them," she said, laughing. "Rolling around on the ground like a couple of four year olds." She bent at the waist, trying to catch her breath. "And I should know. I saw them doing the same thing when we were four."

"We weren't wrestling, for fuck's sake," Curt argued, offended.

"You did go down pretty quick," I said, taking a drink of my whiskey.

"Oh!" Charlie sang. "Burn!"

"We'll go another round anytime you want, brother," Curt said, his voice laced with amusement. "Just let me stop pissin' blood first."

Everyone laughed.

"Not in here," Charlie ordered, getting to her feet. "Don't break my shit." She weaved her way across the room and tripped on Kara's stuff, still packed up near the doorway.

"Well, hell," she said. "Someone should put that away."

I got to my feet as she grunted, lifting a box from the floor.

"I'll get that," I said, taking it from her. I carried the box into Kara's room and set it down at the foot of her bed. I paused. She hadn't even made it before she'd left for Montana.

"I can do it," Charlie grumbled from the living room. "Just—" there was a long pause. "Oh shit."

I strode back out to the living room and found Charlie on the floor, scooping shit toward her drunkenly with her arms. "Don't look," she snapped at Curt, who was trying to help her. "Go."

"I'm tryin' to help your ass," Curt replied.

"Don't," she snapped, leaning over the open backpack and the papers that had fallen out of it, like she was trying to block his view.

I almost didn't go closer, because she was getting seriously panicked that Curt wouldn't take a couple steps back, but then, between her arm and her knee, I spotted a photo I hadn't seen in years.

"D," Charlie said, a warning in her voice that I completely ignored. "Step back."

"Move," I ordered.

Something must have sounded off in my tone, because Bishop stood up from his place on the floor of the living room to see what the fuck was going on.

"It's private," Charlie said, still hovering over the pile. "She wouldn't want you to—"

"Move, Charlotte," I repeated, making her jerk in surprise at the use of her full name.

With a grimace, she leaned back and I got a look at what she'd been hiding.

Hundreds of pieces of notebook paper, folded into little squares littered the floor, mixed with photos and a familiar box of matches. I didn't kneel so much as stumble to my knees.

The photo I'd recognized was one I'd taken of me and Kara the week before my court date. She was standing with her arms wrapped tightly around my belly, her head on my chest, while I held the camera out with one hand and the other hand tangled in her hair. I was smiling. She wasn't. I remembered the exact moment I'd taken it. I'd been trying to get her to smile, making funny faces, tickling her, but nothing had worked. She hadn't smiled much back then.

I swallowed hard and picked it up so I could see it better. The sadness in her eyes would've been enough to knock me on my ass if I hadn't already been on the floor.

"D," Charlie said softly. "Just let me put all this back, okay?"

"Don't touch it," I ordered, reaching for the next closest piece of paper.

When I opened it, my stomach burned.

*If you like chicks, we can make it happen. I'll even let you pick.*

I reached for the next one.

*I want to come all over your tits. Would you be into that?*

I grabbed another.

*Playing hard to get is only cute for a while. It's not like everyone hasn't already seen everything you've got.*

"Holy fuck," Charlie whispered as she read it upside down.

I reached for the next one.

*One of these days we'll have to hang out. I'm real good with my tongue. Are you good with yours?*

My jaw ached with how hard I was grinding my teeth together, but I couldn't stop. I grabbed another and everything stopped. It was in Kara's handwriting.

If you'd just been more like Charlie, none of this would've happened. Stop being such a fucking crybaby.

"No," Charlie said, her voice loud as I stared at that little piece of paper. "No, we need to put this back. Right now."

I looked up and met her eyes. "If you touch a single fuckin' piece of paper, I will physically toss you out."

"It's my fucking apartment," she snapped back.

"Don't give a shit," I replied seriously.

"Charlie," Curt said from somewhere behind me. "Come on."

"No," she argued. "I'm staying right fucking here."

I picked up another piece of paper, this one clearly written by a girl.

*You're such a slut.*

And another.

*You should just quit school. You know you're going to be a prostitute anyway. Why wait? It's not like you need to learn math for that? Can't you count yet?*

I went through the notes one by one. Some of them were filthy, some more mild, all of them bad. The ones Kara had written herself were somehow the worst.

Stay away from Curtis, you idiot. He hates you. You deserve it. Just move on.

"Shit," Curtis said quietly from over my shoulder.

Underneath the letters was a braided bunch of hair with rubber bands at each end. The long hair she'd gotten rid of. A single beaded earring that I remembered, that had gotten twisted up in her hair all the time and we'd have to help her untangle it, but she'd kept wearing anyway because she'd loved them. A daisy chain in a small plastic baggie, withered with time. Another stack of photos, me and her, the five of us—Charlie, Rebel, Curtis, Kara and me—all standing in a line, wearing riding gear and covered in mud, a photo of me jumping off the culvert at our swimming spot, a photo of me laughing, a photo of me mid-sentence talking to someone out of frame, a photo of the two of us smiling with Kara on my shoulders.

I went through every single piece of Kara that had fallen out of the backpack, my heart pounding with each new thing I uncovered. I emptied the rest of the backpack and found the box that had held it all. It was one I'd made in woodshop that I'd carved her name into the top of and given her long before things between us had changed. She'd kept it.

Finally, when the notes were smoothed out in a neat stack and the other little items were set carefully on top of it, I leaned back on my heels.

"I didn't know she was getting those notes," Charlie said softly. "She never said anything."

"Of course she didn't," I replied.

Mack had been right when he said that she'd been biding time until I'd gotten out. She had. But the rest of it was so much messier than I'd realized. Somehow our relationship had gotten mixed in with everything else that had happened to her. The box of stuff was proof of that. She kept it all in a box I'd fucking gave her.

No wonder she'd been pushing my ass away.

I flipped the matchbox through my fingers, remembering the night we'd built a fire with it a few weeks before my court date.

*"Everythin' is gonna be fine," I told her, tightening my arms around her waist. "But if I have to go to jail—"*

*"Don't say that," she whispered, leaning her head back on my shoulder.*

*"If I do," I continued, giving her a squeeze, "Curt will look out for you."*

*She stiffened slightly. "I'll be fine."*

*"I don't want anyone to mess with you," I said, resting my chin on the top of her head.*

*She paused. "They won't. You worry too much."*

I remembered that little pause vividly.

The little notes hadn't started after I'd gone to prison. They'd started before and she hadn't told me. She'd been too afraid of what I'd do.

Kara hadn't been keeping secrets since I got out. She'd been keeping secrets since before I'd left.

# CHAPTER 17

# KARA

"YOU'RE STILL ON my shit list," Rose said as she wrapped her arms around me from behind and rested her chin on my shoulder. "Even if you're doing the dishes for me."

"But this moves me in the right direction?" I asked, only half joking.

"We'll see," she said. "You're just so pathetic right now. Being mad at you kind of feels like kicking a dog or something."

"I'm not sure if I'm more offended about the pathetic part of that or the dog part," I replied, wrinkling my nose.

"I'm sorry Draco's being an asshole," she said, her chin still resting on my shoulder.

I thought about the look on Draco's face. "He was actually really nice about it," I replied.

"Which made it even worse, I bet," she said knowingly.

"Yes," I said, pausing. "If he was an asshole, at least I could've been mad!"

Rose laughed and gave me a squeeze. "I hear that."

"I mean—" I stared at the pan in my hands. "I don't really blame him? I don't know. It just figures that when I was ready to fix shit, he was ready to be done."

"Men are idiots," Rose said.

"I can hear you," my dad called from the table, "and so can your sons."

"My sons won't be idiots because I'm teaching them different," Rose replied snottily.

"Mama!" Jamison yelled at the same time from the living room. "Bwody fahted on me!"

"You were saying?" I asked Rose drolly.

"Okay," Rose said, letting go of me. "Fart jokes are always funny, so that doesn't count."

"Mmhmm," my dad hummed.

"Boys are gross, men are idiots," Rose whispered with a laugh.

"Still hear you," my dad muttered. I looked over my shoulder at him.

Rose turned and put her hands on her hips. "Could you go do something?" she asked him. "Because we're trying to have some girl talk here."

"Do your thing," he said with a wave of his hand.

"He's nosy," Rose said to me.

"*He's* nosy?" I teased.

"Hell," she said with a huff. "I should have been nosier. I should've read your diary or something."

"I didn't have a diary for that very reason," I shot back. "Most of what I wrote down, I burned in the fire pit out back."

"I *knew* you were burning shit back there!" she said, her jaw dropping.

I laughed as I leaned my butt against the counter and dried the last pan from dinner.

"Thanks for doing that," she said, taking the clean pan from me. "It's nice to have the break."

"I help you," my dad protested.

"You're not part of this damn conversation," Rose snapped in irritation. I wouldn't have been surprised if she'd stomped her foot. "And most of the time, you're so tired when you get home that you pass out in your chair."

"I'll give ya that," my dad grumbled.

"As much as I love listening to the two of you bitch at each other—"

"This is friendly sparring," Rose argued.

"I need to get home. I have to work before anyone else in the world is awake."

"Except, you know, the people you're making coffee for," Rose said with a laugh.

"Yeah, except those," I said, tossing the towel at her. "We good?"

Rose caught the towel and looked at me. "We're always good," she said seriously. "You know that. But I'm still pissed that you were getting bullied and terrorized and never said anything when we *asked*."

"That's overstating it a bit," I said quietly.

"That's understating it," she shot back. "You were fucking *stalked* at that school."

"Well, I'm not there anymore," I replied. "So you don't have to worry."

"And they're all adults now," Rose said darkly. "If we run into them—" She shrugged and mimed taking off her earrings and pushing up her sleeves like she was about to fight someone.

"And that's why I didn't tell you," I said, only half joking.

"Pfft," Rose said. "I'm not an idiot who does shit with witnesses, and I'd make sure they got physical first. I'm very provoking."

"Jesus, ain't that the truth," my dad piped up.

"Love you guys," I said with a laugh. "Thanks for dinner. Come by the shop in the morning and I'll make you something good."

"I'll be there," Rose said, snapping me lightly with the towel as I walked away.

"Love you, too, princess," my dad said, getting to his feet to give me a long hug.

"I'm leaving, brothers," I announced as I walked through the living room. They were watching some anime cartoon and barely even looked up to wave at me. "Love you."

"Love you, too," Jamison said, his eyes still on the TV.

I paused behind them.

"Yeah," Brody said with a shooing motion. "Love ya."

"Hey, Rose," I said making my way toward the door. "You're failing with Brody!"

"Hey," my brother called out in protest as I left through the front door.

I'd put on a good show, I'd had years of practice, but as soon as I was outside, my shoulders slumped. I didn't want my parents to worry about me any more than they already were. With our history, and my mom's depression that had eventually ended her life, I knew that my parents had always kept an eye out for any signs that I wasn't dealing well. They probably always would.

I wasn't depressed, though. I never had been, even when shit had been terrible. Sad, yeah. Scared, hell yeah. But I'd never even considered that things wouldn't eventually get better. Amy had told me once that nothing lasts, not good times or bad—so you had to just enjoy the good while it lasted and endure the shit until it was over. I figured that was a good philosophy to live by.

So, I knew that the sting of Draco's dismissal would fade. The overwhelming grief that I felt wouldn't always feel so overwhelming. It was just another thing I'd have to endure.

"I don't have my car," I said, coming to a stop in the driveway.

"Wondered when you'd notice," Rose said from behind me, making me jump.

"Shit!"

"Come on," she said, walking over to her SUV. "I'll run you back to the clubhouse."

"Thanks," I said, hurrying to catch up with her.

"Your dad said he'd take you on the bike," she called over the hood as she got inside. "But he's beat, so I told him to stay with the boys," she said as I climbed into the passenger seat.

"His leg been bothering him?" I asked. When I was a kid, my dad and Rose had been kidnapped and while they were held, my dad had been tortured. We didn't talk about it, or the fact that he still limped when the weather changed, but I always knew when those old wounds were acting up.

"Nah," she said reassuringly. "Climbing under cars all day just isn't as easy as it used to be."

"Gotcha," I said, looking out the windshield.

"How are you doing really, princess?" she asked softly.

The familiar endearment hit me right in the gut. My dad had always used it and still did, but Rose had stopped as I'd gotten older.

"I'm okay," I said. "I'm—Jesus, I'm fucking sad."

"Been there," she said quietly.

"I'm angry and I'm sad and I'm—I don't know what to do with my hands, you know?" I flopped them out in front of me, making her chuckle. I knew she'd understand what I meant.

"When me and your dad split up back in the day," Rose said, "I was exactly the same. Like, what do I do now? How am I supposed to just move on from this like it didn't happen? And yeah, *what am I supposed to do with my hands?* It's like your whole body feels foreign or something. You don't know what to do with yourself."

"Pretty much," I said, twining my fingers together on my lap.

"I can't tell you it gets easier," she said as we paused at the gate to the clubhouse. A different prospect, looking bored out of his mind, was working the gate and he waved us through. "Because your dad and I got back together." She looked at me. "But if you need anything or you just don't want to be alone, or you just want to come home for a few days or a few hours to get away from everything, you know we're always there.

You're my favorite person to hang with."

"Lily's your favorite," I replied dryly.

"Lily's everyone's favorite," we both said at the same time.

"But thanks," I told her as she pulled up next to my car. "Love you, Ma," I said as I opened my door.

"Love you, too," she said softly.

I closed the door between us before we both started crying. There were only a few times in my life when I'd called Rose *Ma*. I referred to her as my mom to other people, because she was—she'd adopted me when I was a teenager. But I'd met her when I was older and I'd just always called her Rose when I was speaking to her. I wasn't sure why, but it had stayed that way. So, when I called her ma, we both felt it. It had somehow become a special thing that we both understood, a private acknowledgement of her place.

She waved, blew me a kiss, and drove off as I got into my car.

I drove home in silence, not bothering to turn on the radio. Any upbeat song would irritate me and I was walking such a tightrope that I knew any breakup song would push me right off and I'd be a sobbing mess by the time I got there. I tensed as I passed a police car, but it must not have been Officer Asshole, because he paid no attention to me.

By the time I'd parked and made my way toward my apartment, my bag slung over my shoulder, all I wanted was to cry in the shower and crawl in bed. Between the flight home, the mess at the clubhouse, and dinner with my parents, it had been a long ass day.

As soon as I opened the front door, I knew it was going to be even longer. Charlie and Draco were sitting on the floor blocking my way inside. Curtis stood behind them with a guy I'd never seen before, probably one of Charlie's admirers. He looked exactly her type. It only took a second for me to take all of that in, but it took a few moments longer to notice the expression on Draco's pale face.

I looked down at the floor where they were sitting, surrounded by the pile of stuff I'd left there, and my ears started to ring.

They'd found the box.

My skin started to tingle as I stared at all the little notes I knew had been folded, now laying open in a neat pile.

"Baby," Draco said softly, his voice holding all the things I'd wished for when I'd gone to the clubhouse earlier that day.

Earlier, when I'd made the decision to tell him everything *on my terms.*

This—this was beyond comprehension.

"How dare you," I breathed, staring at him.

"I'm sorry," Charlie said. I could tell by just her words that she was drunk. "We were just going to bring your stuff into your room."

"And you accidentally unzipped my bag and pulled out the box that was in the very bottom of it?" I asked flatly.

"We—" she shook her head. "Me and Curtis were kind of fighting over it," she said quickly. "The zipper caught and I pulled and the bag fell and—"

"Spare me," I snapped.

"It *was* an accident," she said, her voice pleading. "I swear."

"And then you accidentally went through it?" I asked softly. I took another step back.

"She tried to put it back," Draco said, pulling my attention back to him.

"You made your decision," I replied, my voice barely a whisper. "Why the hell would you do this?"

"I was wrong," he said, getting to his feet. "I went out to find you, but you were already leaving—"

I put my hand up to stop him. The apartment was silent as I reached up and pressed my fingers against my forehead, hiding my face with my hand.

"No," I said, shaking my head. "No. Get the fuck out of my apartment."

"Kara," he said gently, taking a step toward me.

"Get out," I yelled, dropping my hand.

"We need to talk," he replied stubbornly.

"You—" I was so angry I could barely speak. "You went through my things. You read through my private things."

"How could I not?" he asked, his hands out in front of him, palms up.

"I don't even know that guy," I shouted, pointing at the man who clearly wanted to be anywhere but standing inside my apartment while I lost my shit.

"I didn't look at your stuff," he said quickly.

"Great," I snapped. "I feel so much fucking better."

"You didn't say shit," Curtis said, finally breaking his silence as he stared at me. "You were gettin' those and you didn't say shit."

"Oh, fuck you," I replied, sneering at him. "You made it clear you didn't want me anywhere near you. Fuck you and your blame shit."

"I don't even remember it," he said, leaning forward at the waist.

"I don't give a flying fuck," I yelled. "Get out!"

Charlie was still sitting on the floor between us and she flinched when I yelled, then frantically reached for the stack of letters.

"Don't touch them," I snapped. I fell to my knees and practically shoved her out of the way, grabbing fistfuls of the box's contents and stuffing them into the backpack.

I hadn't seen the words in years. I'd stuffed them in the box and put them away and refused to look at them again. But, the minute I saw the familiar handwriting, the same nauseous feeling and skin tingling fear that someone was watching me swept over me from head to toe. I shuddered. My hands started to shake as I zipped the backpack closed.

The room was silent.

"I'm so sorry," Charlie said, putting her hand on my back. She dropped it when I glared at her. Her betrayal was worse. I'd trusted her more than anyone else on the entire planet and she'd let them look through my things.

"You've chosen your side," I said flatly. "Either you move out or I do. Maybe you can move in with Tweedledee and Tweedledum."

Charlie's mouth tightened and her eyes filled with tears.

"That's enough," Draco ordered. He reached for me.

"Don't touch me," I snapped.

My words didn't stop him. He pulled me to my feet and ignored the way I shoved at him as he threw me over his shoulder.

"Clear out," he ordered the rest of the room as he stomped toward the hallway.

I pounded on his back and kicked my legs. When that didn't work, I pinched any skin I could reach as hard as I could.

"Stop it," he ordered, slapping my ass. "Jesus."

When he dropped me onto my bed, I came up swinging and just barely missed him as he jerked backward.

"Get out," I screamed, pointing at my bedroom door.

"I'm not goin' anywhere," he shouted back.

"Yes, you are," I gritted out. "Get out."

"You want to be with me?" he asked, frustration making the words come out hard.

"I don't even want to look at you," I hissed.

"You're mad," he replied. "Fine. You want to be with me?"

"Get out."

"Doesn't matter how many times you say it," he shot back, slamming the door closed. "I'm not goin' anywhere."

"Did you have fun going through my shit?" I asked nastily. "It would make a good drinking game. Take a shot every time my boobs or vagina were mentioned?"

"Jesus," he replied in disgust. "The fuck is wrong with you?"

"Am I just supposed to be okay with you rifling through my stuff?" I asked in disbelief. "Okay." I stood up and walked to my dresser, jerking open the top drawer. "These are my underwear," I said, dropping a pile of them on the floor between us. "Did you get a good look?"

Draco stared at me.

"Oh, these ones," I said, pulling out a ratty stained pair that I'd had for years. They were stretched out and huge, comfortable when I felt like garbage, and no one ever saw them, so I'd kept them. "These are my period underwear," I said, holding them up in all their glory. "Nice, huh?"

"Baby, stop," he said tiredly. "Just stop."

"Why?" I asked, turning back toward the drawer. "I mean, my life's an open book, right? I'm sure I have an even better pair in here somewhere."

"I don't care about your underwear," he said.

"No, those aren't nearly as interesting, huh?" I replied, closing the drawer with my hip so I could lean against the dresser.

"I shouldn't have looked," he said, making me scoff. "But I'm glad I did."

"Great. Good for you."

"There were hundreds of them, Kara," he said softly.

"Really?" I asked easily. "I never counted."

"Can you just—" he paused, growling as he ran his hands through his hair in frustration. "Can you just fucking *talk* to me?"

"Oh, *now* you want to talk?" I said with a derisive laugh. "Funny."

"I thought you were going to tell me all this shit," he replied. "Isn't that why you came to the clubhouse?"

"You lost that chance," I replied.

"I'm here now."

"There's nothing else to say," I said, crossing my arms over my chest.

"Nothing?"

"You read them all," I replied, shaking my head in disbelief. "So, there's not much left. They cornered me—not just the time Charlie saw—all the time. They'd find me when I was alone, which was pretty often because Charlie was basically my only friend. Make comments. Brush up against me in a way they could play off as an accident if I said anything to anyone."

"I shoulda been there," he said softly.

"Yeah," I replied just as quietly. "You should've. But that's not how it all played out, is it?"

"I'm sorry—"

I laughed, the sound grating. "I don't want you to be sorry," I said honestly. "Do you know how guilty that makes me feel? That you feel guilty because you went to prison *for me*? That you feel like it was your job to protect me after you'd already given up so much? Jesus Christ."

"It's always gonna be my job to protect you," Draco said, pointing to himself with his thumb. "That's never gonna stop."

"You pulled away from me today," I replied, my anger morphing into pain. "Today it was *you* who hurt me."

"I was trying to do the right thing," he said, his voice rough. "I was just tryin' to step off this fuckin' merry-go-round we've been on for so long."

"Don't you think I want that, too?" I asked, my voice wobbling.

"You pulled away from me over and over," he shot back. "You went to fuckin' Montana."

"I was scared!"

"I'd never do anything to scare you," he said in disbelief.

"I didn't want you to know," I said through my teeth. "I knew you were going to find out and I never wanted you to know any of this."

"Why?" he said in confusion.

"Because I wasn't sure what you would do," I confessed, the truth falling heavy between us.

"Kara," he said with a sigh, his eyes steady on mine. "We're not kids anymore. Baby, I'm not *ever* leavin' you again."

"I didn't want you to know the things they said to me," I confessed, the truth so embarrassing that my voice wobbled. "It makes me feel dirty. Like, maybe you'd see it and—"

I couldn't even finish the sentence before Draco was across the room, his fingers tangled in my hair and his mouth on mine.

"Fuck them," he said against my mouth, his fingers tightening in my hair. "They're nothin'."

I cried as he kissed me. For all the times I ran until I could sleep at night and all the times I laid in bed wishing that he was with me and all the times I wanted to tell someone, anyone, what was happening. For the fear and the anxiety and the pressure of keeping so many things bottled up inside me. For the relief I felt every day when I'd close my front door behind me, knowing that within a few hours, I'd be watching the clock, dreading the next day when I'd have to do it all over again. I cried for every Sunday that I'd sat at home, knowing it was visiting day and I wasn't seeing Draco. I cried for the time we'd missed. For hurting him every time I'd pulled away, when all I wanted to do was the opposite. I cried in relief, knowing finally that the truth hadn't changed anything.

"You're mine and I'm yours," he said, wiping the tears off my face, our foreheads still pressed together. "Nothin' that happened or ever will happen changes that."

"I missed you so much," I whispered back, my chest heaving as I tried to control my tears.

He closed his eyes and sighed, his body leaning into mine.

The knock at my front door was an unwelcome intrusion.

"Ignore it," he said softly, his eyes still closed.

Another knock. Then a familiar voice.

"Eugene Police!"

Draco's eyes shot open. "What the fuck?"

"Let me handle it," I said, grabbing the bottom of his cut as he turned toward the door.

"Like hell," he spat, dragging me along as he threw open my bedroom door.

"Please," I said desperately. "Please. I'll just send him on his way."

Draco stopped so fast that I smashed into his back.

"You got somethin' else to tell me?" he asked in disbelief.

"He hassles me. He's pulled me over like five times. Stopped me on the street. But that's it, I swear," I replied. Hating that there was more I hadn't said and he was finding it out this way. I'd planned on telling him, but we hadn't gotten to that part yet and now it looked like I was still keeping secrets.

"He makes you uncomfortable," Draco said. It wasn't a question.

I nodded.

"That stops now," he said flatly.

I wiped off my face as we moved toward the door, knowing I wouldn't be able to stop him.

"What's up?" Draco asked as he opened the door. I stopped a few feet back, letting him handle it even though I wanted to physically block him with my body. My hands were clenched into fists as I struggled to trust that he wouldn't let anything bad happen.

"Neighbors heard yelling," Officer Park said, looking past Draco at me. "You alright?"

"I'm fine."

"She's fine."

"Why don't you step outside, miss?" he asked firmly.

I took an involuntary step forward, years of *enduring* had conditioned me to just deal with him and get it over with, but I caught myself before I took another step.

"No, thank you," I said politely.

"You wanna take a step back?" he said to Draco, his hands braced on his hips as his eyes slid over Draco's cut.

"I'm good where I'm at," Draco replied. He was steady as an oak.

Officer Park stood there, staring for a long moment before finally realizing that there wasn't much he could do. He'd been out maneuvered because we weren't playing into his bullshit.

"Keep it down," he ordered, his gaze centered back on me.

The words made it clear that he hadn't shown up to make sure I was okay. I had no doubt that the neighbors had called, we had a few shitty ones and there had been a lot of yelling, but he wasn't there because he thought there'd been some sort of domestic dispute. He'd heard my address and used it as an excuse to fuck with me and we all knew it.

Draco closed the door as Officer Asshole walked away.

"See?" he said through his teeth. "I didn't kill him."

"I saw that," I replied, trying not to laugh in relief.

"I wanted to," he said. "And seventeen year old me would've told him to go fuck himself."

"I know," I said softly.

"It's not in me to ever let you deal with that shit on your own," he warned. "That's not gonna happen."

"I know," I replied, my voice still soft.

"But I'm not gonna fly off the fuckin' handle," he continued. "I'm not fuckin' stupid."

"I know."

"I'm not goin' back to prison."

"I know."

"And I love you," he said almost angrily.

"I know."

"Then why the fuck are you still standing over there?"

A watery laugh escaped me as I ran at him. He caught me and boosted me up until my legs were wrapped around his waist and my face was pressed against his neck.

"I know him from somewhere," he said, walking back toward my room.

"He was there when they arrested you," I mumbled against his throat. "I saw him through the window."

"And he saw you," Draco said, his voice vibrating with anger.

"And he saw me," I confirmed.

"He's not gonna fuck with you again," he said as he laid me on the bed. "No one's gonna fuck with you ever again."

"Don't—" I started to say, stopping when he shot me a look. I needed to trust him, no matter how hard that was.

As he pulled off his cut and his t-shirt, I relaxed into the bed. That was a worry for another day.

"Don't," he ordered when I reached for the button on my shorts. "I'm strippin' you tonight."

# CHAPTER 18

# DRACO

KARA'S EYES LIT up as I stripped. My movements were jerky with leftover adrenalin and my heartbeat was pounding in my ears, but I didn't give a shit. After the revelations of the past few hours, I was dying for her.

Once I was down to just my boxers, I climbed onto the bed, unsure what I wanted to unwrap first.

"Everything okay?" she asked quietly, reaching up to rest her hand on my chest.

"You tell me," I said, meeting her gaze.

"Finally," she said, a small smile tugging at her lips. "Yeah."

"There's nothin' about you I don't wanna know," I said, unbuttoning her shorts. I tugged them down, catching her underwear with my fingers and pulling those down, too. I tossed them off the side of the bed, and bent down, kissing her softly just beneath her belly button. "There's nothin' about you that's ever gonna turn me off."

"Not even the underwear?" she asked, embarrassment making her cheeks pink.

I huffed out a laugh as I slid her t-shirt up, helping her pull it off over her head. "I might not have sisters," I said, "but I got a mom. She didn't hide that shit from us. You wanna wear your granny panties when you're on the rag, go for it."

"On the rag? Panties?" she sputtered. "Ew."

"On your period," I corrected with mock seriousness. "During shark week. When Auntie Flo comes to visit."

"Are you trying to be sexy?" she asked in confusion. "Because you're missing the mark big time."

I dropped my head forward and laughed, the pressure that had built in my chest over the past week finally easing.

"I'm not trying to be sexy," I told her as I pulled her bra off. I was losing my train of thought with all of her bare skin laid out there in front of me like a feast. "I'm just being real with you."

"Uh huh," she replied, unconvinced.

"I'm not squeamish," I said, reaching out to cup her tits in my hands. "That's all I'm sayin'. Wear whatever the fuck you want. Stop shaving your legs and your pits. I don't give a shit. You're still gonna be you. You're still gonna smell like you and feel like you. You're still gonna turn me on more than anyone else I've ever met. I'm gonna want you, no matter what."

"The feeling's mutual," she said, groaning as I leaned forward and pulled one of her nipples into my mouth. "I've never wanted anyone but you."

I paused, tilting my head so I could see her face.

"I've never been with anyone but you," she said, running her fingers down my cheek.

I'd asked her before, and it had killed me that I didn't know if she'd been with anyone else—but that had never been a deal breaker for me. It couldn't be. After all we'd been through, it seemed petty to even wonder. But I couldn't deny the way it felt, knowing that she'd never been down that road with anyone but me. No one else had ever seen her this way, naked and open, both relaxed and thrumming with anticipation. And if things went the way I wanted them to, no one else ever would.

"You're relieved," she said, reading my expression.

"Baby," I said, kissing the space between her breasts. "I'm glad, but knowing that you've never had sex with anyone else is the thing that I'm least relieved about tonight." She smiled.

"Wish you were my first."

"I don't," she said, her eyes twinkling. "I'm glad you knew what you were doing before I got you."

"Lies," I argued.

"Okay, maybe," she said with a shrug. "But it doesn't bother me. Not as long as I'm the only one from now on."

"I can promise you that," I said.

The conversation ended there.

Stretching out beside her, I pulled her against me, letting out a sigh when she gently bit my lower lip. Her hands roamed, her fingers tracing my spine as I pressed my mouth against her throat, her shoulders, her collarbone, lower. As I made my way down her body, she arched, her legs circling my hips.

"Not tonight," she said quietly as I reached her stomach. "I need you inside me."

"We'll get there," I said, pressing my forehead against her belly. She smelled incredible.

"Now Draco," she said, sitting up and pressing at my shoulders. She shoved so hard that I landed on my knees in shock at the foot of the bed.

I didn't even have time to say anything before she was sliding off the bed onto my lap, reaching between us to grip my cock.

"Fuck," I groaned, my head falling back. "Bossy," I said under my breath, making her giggle.

Then we were both holding our breath as I slipped inside her and she ground her hips down, taking me in completely.

I watched Kara, her back arched over the edge of the bed as I lifted her slightly and let her slide back down. She was on top, but I controlled the movement. I nearly lost all control when she reached up and pulled my head down to her nipple, letting out a soft sigh when I followed her direction and wrapped my lips around it. As her little noises grew more frantic, I shifted my hand so my thumb rested on her clit. I didn't even have to move it, our rolling hips did the work, and before long, she was coming hard, her entire body breaking out in goosebumps as she gasped. I watched it hit her until she went boneless and barely had time to pull out before I was coming on both of our stomachs.

We were quiet for a while, catching our breath as her hands ran through my hair.

"Probably should have told you before, I have an IUD," she said, leaning up on her elbows to look at me.

"You do?" I asked.

"I didn't like the hormone stuff," she said as I awkwardly stood, pulling her with me. "And since I knew I didn't want kids for a long time, I figured long-term protection was pretty smart."

"You mean I can stop pullin' out?" I asked for clarification, trying to keep up with the conversation.

"Yeah," she said with a chuckle.

"Thank God," I muttered. "It sucks."

She laughed again.

"Wait," I said as she moved toward the door. "If you weren't with anyone, then why?"

"I guess in the back of my mind," she said sweetly, shrugging, "I knew we'd be here, eventually."

I dropped to the side of the bed as she left the room.

*She'd always known we'd be here eventually.*

Fuck. I was all fucking in. My heart raced. This was finally it.

I sat there, buck ass naked, and stared at the open doorway.

"Marry me," I said the minute she walked back in.

Kara laughed so hard she snorted. "No."

261

"What?" I said in disbelief.

"You have a ring?" she asked, tilting her head as she stepped in between my knees.

"Not on me," I replied sarcastically.

"Our lives have been so—" she shook her head. "I want *that* to be right, you know? Once I'm done with school and we've lived together a while and you know, we're ready for kids and stuff. Then ask me again."

"Am I gonna get a different answer?" I asked suspiciously.

"Depends on how big the ring is," she teased.

"Oh, you're funny," I said, falling backward and dragging her with me so she landed with a thud on my chest.

"Oof," she said, her hair hanging down, creating a curtain around our faces.

"You want kids?" I asked.

"Maybe," she whispered back. "Eventually. You?"

"As many as you'll give me," I replied instantly.

"Okay," she said, a wide grin lighting up her face. "But later. After I'm done with school."

"Me, too," I replied.

"You, too?"

"Wanna be study partners?" I asked sheepishly.

"You're going to school?" she asked, scrambling up to her knees, her ass resting on my stomach.

"Yeah," I said. "You cool with that? We don't have to go to the same place or anything. I might not even get in where you do. I probably won't with just a GED."

"Are you kidding?" she asked excitedly. She threw her hands up in the air and arched her back. "My man's going to college!" she yelled to the ceiling.

"Shh," I said, pulling her back down as I laughed. "You're gonna piss off the neighbors again."

"Me and you," she said, her face joyful in a way I hadn't seen since she was fifteen years old. "We're going to be college sweethearts."

"Works for me," I replied. "Carry your books for you." I wiggled my eyebrows.

"Hell yeah, you will," she said with a giggle.

She dropped down at my side and curled up against me.

"Why didn't you go before?" I asked, rubbing my fingers up and down her back lazily. She stiffened for a moment before relaxing again.

"I didn't want to see anyone I knew," she replied.

I kissed her forehead.

"Hey, who was that guy here earlier?" she asked a few minutes later.

"That was Bishop," I said, realizing that I'd ditched him. I wasn't sorry about it, though, and I doubted he'd cared.

"The friend you were telling us about?" she asked, resting her chin on my chest.

"Yeah. He just got out," I replied.

"That's good. I'm glad he's here."

"Me, too."

"I wasn't glad he was here earlier," she said dryly.

"Yeah, you made that clear," I replied, my lips twitching.

We were quiet for a while as I ran my fingers lightly up and down her spine.

"It was never really Curt, you know," she said after a while, her voice quiet. I froze for a moment, but I didn't want her to stop talking, so I ran my fingers down her back again. "It was," she paused. "It was the fact that he seemed safe." She shrugged and sighed. "He was easy to adore because I knew in the back of my mind that nothing would ever come of it. I liked the romance of it all, but not the reality."

"Oh, yeah?" I said, my voice hoarse. We'd never really talked about it before and I'd told myself it didn't matter. I guess it did, though, because it was always going to be a part of our history and from the tone of Kara's voice, she was holding onto some guilt about it.

"You were such a manwhore," she said with a huff. "I couldn't think of you that way. I couldn't let myself, not when you were with a different girl every week. That would've killed me."

"I was an idiot," I muttered.

"You were a teenage boy," she said, kissing my chest. "You were fun and sweet and smokin' hot, but I wasn't ready for you. Not then."

"I always kind of wondered," I said, kissing the top of her head. "You know, if after it all went down back then whether you were with me because you felt guilty or—" My words broke off with a yelp when she pinched my belly hard.

"I wasn't with you because I felt guilty," she said incredulously. "Why would you even think that?"

"Because you were moonin' after Curt," I said defensively. "And then that just kind of vanished and me and you started hangin' out."

Kara sat up and for a second, I was distracted by the way her tits swayed.

She snapped her fingers in front of my face to get my attention.

"It was never guilt," she said seriously. "But I can't say that it didn't change things."

I just looked at her.

"It was so many things," she said with a small smile. "It was the way you stood up for me and the way you were unapologetic about that."

I let out a huff of air.

"It was the way you looked at me—"

"I always looked at you."

"I finally *saw* you looking," she said softly, running her fingers lightly down my cheek. "And it was the way you always made sure that I was okay. The way you reassured me even though I knew you were scared. You seemed to know me better than anyone else and I could be fully myself with you. Even when I was in a bad mood or upset. It wasn't guilt, baby. Never that." She leaned down and kissed me. "It was like after all the time we spent together, I looked at you and suddenly thought *oh, there he is.*"

"I had that same moment," I said, reaching up to push her hair back from her face. "*Oh, there she is.*"

"You did?"

"Yeah," I whispered. "But I was fifteen years old and you were wearing a little purple bikini."

"I thought you were being serious," she said with a laugh, her eyes lighting up.

"I am serious," I replied. "That bikini almost fuckin' killed me."

Kara rolled her eyes as she sat back up. "I was never with you because I felt guilty, like you deserved to get your mack on because you'd beaten up my bully."

"*Get my mack on?*" I sputtered, trying not to laugh. Kara ignored me.

"The guilt was there, it's still there," she said. "But I was with you then and I'm with you now for a lot of reasons that have nothing to do with guilt. Like the way your ass looks in a pair of jeans. The way you laugh and it changes your entire face." She threw up her hands in frustration. "The way you look like a damn romance hero all dark and broody but your great grandparents are the first people you search for when you show up at a barbeque and you genuinely like hanging out with them."

"They're not gonna be here forever," I said, a little defensively. "I wanna get my time in when I can."

"I know," she said, her eyes soft on mine. "I love that about you."

"You've got nothin' to feel guilty about," I said, pulling her back down so she was snug against my side again. "Nothin' that happened was your fault."

"That's not exactly true," she replied. "But let's not argue about it tonight."

"Alright, sweetheart," I said with a sigh. "But we're gonna discuss it again until you stop carryin' that shit."

We talked for hours, finally turning in the bed so she could pull the sheet over us. She fell asleep with her ass pressed tightly against my crotch, her hand holding mine against her chest.

I was awake for a while though, sifting through everything I'd learned that night. The things I'd never be able to fix for her and the things I could. I'd been serious when I told her that I was never going back to prison, but something had to be done about that cop. I was going to have to take it to the club.

I fell asleep just before Kara's alarm went off.

"Shit," she said, sitting straight up in bed. "I have work!"

"Fuck," I said as she threw off the sheet and got to her feet.

She looked at the clock. "No time to shower," she said, rushing to her dresser.

I laughed as she paused with a drawer open then turned, moved a step in one direction and then the other. "Clothes are in my bag."

"Living room," I said, crossing my arms behind my head so I could watch her.

"Right," she said. She hurried out of view and was back seconds later. She tossed the backpack that had caused so many problems into the closet from across the room, and set her bag of clothes on the bed. "We'll burn that later," she said, gesturing with one hand.

It took her about thirty seconds to get dressed and then she was rushing out of the room. When she came back in her hair was pulled into a ponytail with little hairs hanging down around her ears and neck because they'd already escaped the hair tie.

"You can go back to sleep," she said around the toothbrush in her mouth. "I should be done around eleven."

"I got work, too," I reminded her.

"Right," she said, leaving the room again. When she came back, the toothbrush was gone and she went straight to the closet, kicking the backpack further inside as she pulled a hoodie off the hanger.

"You always like this in the morning?" I asked, chuckling as she got her head stuck in the sweatshirt.

"Only at four am," she said in frustration as she finally got the sweatshirt on.

"Good to know."

"I gotta go," she said, coming over to lean down and kiss me. It took everything I had not to pull her back into bed.

"Love you," she called over her shoulder as she left. Like she hadn't even thought about it. Like she'd been doing it every day for years.

I sat up and pulled on my jeans as she moved around the living room and caught her just as she was about to go out the front door.

"Love you, too," I said.

Kara paused, her hand on the doorknob, and shot me a smile over her shoulder.

She didn't notice that I followed her outside and watched as she got to her Jeep safely. I didn't go back inside until she'd pulled out of the parking lot.

Since there was no way I was going to be able to sleep again, I finished getting dressed and let myself out of the apartment. I figured I might as well get changed and go into work early. It's not like anyone would care if I started earlier and quit earlier—as long as I was getting shit done, I could make whatever hours I wanted.

I was quiet as I let myself into my place, but I couldn't help the startled bark of laughter that left my mouth when I found Charlie and Bishop curled up together on the couch—thankfully, fully clothed.

"What?" Bishop said, waking instantly. He nearly squashed Charlie as he jerked, his eyes searching for the threat.

"Just me, man," I said softly.

"Fuck," he said, relaxing back down against the cushions.

"That gets better," I told him, remembering the first months on the outside. It took a while to get used to waking up without the fear.

"Good to know," he said.

"You look cozy," I joked.

"You care—"

"Nope," I said, cutting him off. "She's an adult."

"Alright," he said, curling his arm tighter around Charlie's shoulders. "Quiet then," he ordered, glancing at her. "Have a feelin' this one wakes up swingin', and I wanna stay where I'm at a while longer."

"Good luck," I said with a grin as I headed to my room. "You'll need it."

"I'm gettin' that," he said quietly, more to himself than me.

The rest of the morning went pretty much like every other morning for the last eight months I'd been working at the garage. I did a tune-up on an older minivan and changed out the transmission on a Tacoma, which was a complete bitch, but by the time everyone else was breaking for lunch, I was done for the day.

As I walked outside, wiping my hands with a rag, I ran into Grease.

My hands shot up in the air, the rag still dangling from one of them.

"You're fine," he grumbled. "You're a fuckin' idiot, but I'm not gonna hit you again." He chuckled as he passed me. "You might wanna steer clear of Mack, though."

"Shit," I muttered, looking around the forecourt. I'd been so in my head about everything that had happened the night before and watching Kara get ready for work that morning that I'd hadn't even thought about how Mack had taken Kara on his bike the night before.

No one knew that we'd fixed things. They'd all seen me reject her the day before and as far as they knew, that was where we still stood.

I figured I'd better find him before he found me.

Mack was at the bar talking to Will when I stepped inside the club-house. It was pretty quiet that time of day, but there were always at least a few people milling around. Grandma Brenna came out of the kitchen as I reached the end of the bar.

"Hey, Grandson," she said, smiling. "You looking for something to eat?"

"That's okay," I said, holding back a grimace when Mack turned to face me. "Thanks, though."

She looked between me and Mack and nodded, walking right back into the kitchen as Will headed in the opposite direction.

"You got balls, prospect," Mack said, not bothering to get up from his stool. "Lookin' for me?"

"Yeah," I said, moving forward even though I wasn't sure it was the smartest choice.

"Ya found me," he said flatly.

"I just wanted—" I started, stopping when he huffed.

"You look about ready to shit yourself."

"I'm not," I said, straightening my shoulders. "I just wanted to let you know that me and Kara are good."

"That right?" he asked, unimpressed.

"We worked shit out last night," I replied.

"Musta been after I had her bawlin' in my arms 'til she damn near hyperventilated," he said, his eyes on me never wavering.

I took that blow, barely flinching.

"I screwed up," I replied. "Fixed it."

"Oh, yeah?"

"Yeah," I gritted out, getting annoyed at his expression.

"Thought you were it," he said. "Trusted that."

"I am," I replied.

"You got no idea what it's like to have a daughter," he said, his hand on the bar curling into a fist. "Daughter like Kara is worse. Keeps shit close to the chest, doesn't come to me for nothin'."

"I know," I said. He ignored me.

"So when she does come to me, I know it's bad."

"I'm tellin' you," I replied. "I fixed it."

"Better hope to hell you did," he said. "'Cause if I find her cryin' like that again, you're a dead man. Member or not, grandson of the president or not, they won't find enough of ya to bury."

"Got it," I replied.

"Then we're done here," he said, turning back to face the bar.

"That's it?" I asked, a little surprised. I'd expected to be hit at least once. I was just hoping if I found him instead of him having to track me down, he'd go a bit easier on me.

"You expectin' me to welcome you into the family?" he asked, his back still to me. "Boy, get the fuck outta here."

I stood there for a second like a fucking moron and then turned on my heel just in time to see Kara come through the door. I forgot Mack even existed.

"I was hoping to catch you before you left," Kara said happily as she walked toward me.

She must have gone home to shower after work because her hair was still damp and wavy around her face. She was in a sundress that I'd never seen before, but she was still wearing the same ratty ass sandals. God, she was fucking gorgeous.

"Just got off," I said as she got closer.

"Good," she replied. With a grin, she jogged the last couple of feet between us. I caught her around the waist as she gave a little hop, wrapping her arms around my neck. "You want to get out of here?"

I barely kept my hands off her ass and I was a fucking saint for it, too, because she smelled incredible and I could tell she didn't have a damn bra on.

"Where you wanna go?" I asked, our faces close together.

Kara's nose wrinkled. "I need to find Charlie," she said.

"She was wrapped around Bishop on my couch this morning," I replied.

"Interesting development," she said, raising her eyebrows.

"No shit."

"Her car wasn't there when I got home," she said. "I'd usually check her parents' house, but—" She shrugged.

Charlie's parents' house was no longer there.

"We'll find her," I said, leaning the last inch to give her a soft kiss.

Tommy started whooping from the corner. Will was fucking applauding.

"Oh, shut up," Kara yelled at them.

"It's just so sweet," Tommy sang, clasping his hands under his chin. "It's like watching a soap opera."

"Like you were any better," Mack said, turning on his stool to face the rest of the room. "We watch your shit play out every damn time your woman is here."

"We're passionate people," Tommy said, dropping his hands.

"You're fuckin' lunatics," Mack shot back, making Will laugh.

"Hey, Daddy," Kara said, smiling at Mack, her feet still dangling half a foot off the floor as she clung to me.

"Hey, princess," he said, his lips twitching.

"Everything's better now," she told him sheepishly.

"That's what I hear," he replied. He looked the two of us up and down. "You look real pretty."

Kara's smile widened even further and she leaned her head on my shoulder.

"Gorgeous," I whispered in her ear. "New dress?"

"I was feeling festive," she told the both of us.

Mack chuckled. "Get the hell out of here," he ordered. "I gotta get back to work."

We left right after he did and after driving around a little while, we found Charlie's car outside of Lily's house.

"I'd tell you that I want to do this on my own," Kara said, glancing at me as we walked toward the house, "but I'm too much of a coward."

"It's gonna be fine," I replied, reaching for her hand. "You guys always figure shit out."

Aunt Lily opened the door at Kara's knock and without a word, took a step back to let us in.

"Nephew," she said to me.

"Auntie."

"She's in the kitchen, Kara," she said, giving Kara's arm a squeeze.

Kara led us in that direction, and when she got to the kitchen, froze.

She and Charlie stared at each other for so long, having a silent conversation, that even I started to get uncomfortable.

"You two had sex," Charlie finally said, standing up so fast that her chair tipped over backward.

"You slept with Bishop!" Kara replied accusingly.

"We were fully dressed."

"Likely story!"

"Did you see his fucking cheekbones?" Charlie asked, throwing her hands in the air. "I deserve a fucking medal."

"Didn't notice his cheekbones," Kara confessed, letting go of my hand. "But I did notice the eyes."

"Blue as the fucking Caribbean," Charlie said in disgust.

"Long lashes."

"Why do guys get the good eyelashes?" Charlie spat in irritation.

They were in each other's arms in less than a second, their words too low for me to hear.

"I knew it wouldn't take long," Lily said from behind my shoulder.

"Shoulda seen them last night," I said as we watched Charlie and

Kara hold each other.

"Friendship like that," Lily said, "it's like a marriage. You say the shittiest things and then you forgive." She looked at me. "There's no other choice."

"Good to know."

"I see you finally figured things out," she said with a smile.

I nodded. I'd figured out more than she could imagine.

We stayed at Lily's for a while, but eventually, I wanted Kara all to myself. We hadn't had enough time that was just the two of us and I knew exactly where I wanted to go.

"Draco," Kara said softly as I parked outside the playground where we'd snuck off so many times as kids.

"Feel like a swing?" I asked.

She answered me by throwing open her door and climbing out of the truck.

"It still looks the same," she said, looking around as she stepped onto the bark chips. She pointed off to the left. "That spider web thing is new."

"Swings are still here," I said.

"My favorite," she replied with a grin. She led me over to them and sat down.

"You never knew this," I said as I gripped the chains and pulled her backward until her feet were dangling in the air. I let her go and she swung forward. "But I liked pushin' you on these things because the seat frames your ass perfectly."

"What?" she asked, looking at me over her shoulder as she swung back toward me.

"Like a fuckin' juicy peach," I confirmed, laughing at her scandalized expression. I caught her by the seat and pressed my thumbs against the cheeks of her ass. "Yum."

I let her swing forward again.

"Pervert," she gasped, laughing.

"Though, this time," I said, walking around her so we were facing each other, "you've got a dress on."

She pointed her toes until they barely brushed my chest, letting her skirt billow up with the wind, giving me a spectacular view.

"You're killin' me," I said, grinning.

She dropped her legs and her eyes met mine.

The next time she swung toward me, I caught the chains and pushed her backward until her face was level with mine.

"You know how much I love you?" I asked.

"Yeah," she said, letting go of the swing to cup my cheek in her hand. "I've always known that."

"You know you don't have to be afraid anymore?" I asked.

"Yes," she replied softly.

"Don't keep shit from me anymore," I ordered.

"I won't."

We stared at each other.

"You know how much I love you?" she asked quietly.

"Yeah," I replied, the words hitting me harder than they should have. "I've always known that."

"You know you don't have to be afraid anymore?" she asked, even quieter.

I leaned my forehead against hers. I should've known she'd seen it. I knew she'd been watching me since I got out. The hypervigilance hadn't gone unnoticed. "Yes," I said, the words leaving me on a sigh.

"You won't ever leave me again?" she asked.

"Not until they put me in the ground," I said, meaning the words more than I'd ever meant anything in my life.

We'd get married later, after we graduated from college, and Kara had started her job as a guidance counselor at the local high school, and we'd bought a tiny house on the outskirts of town.

But the vows we said then weren't half as binding as the ones we told each other in that park.

# EPILOGUE

# DRACO

WE WERE AT the clubhouse for a barbecue to celebrate the fires being one hundred percent contained, but I also had an ulterior motive. During the weeks that had passed, I'd never been in the same place with so many other members of the club at once. During the week, the brothers were in and out constantly. If Grease and my gramps Casper were there, my dad and my grandpa Dragon weren't. If Mack and gramps were there, Grease wasn't. I'd been waiting impatiently and the barbecue had finally rounded them all up.

Kara was in another sundress. It was like her happiness had manifested in a new love of all things flowing and feminine. Of course, she also might've just loved the easy access they gave me as much as I did, because nothing else about her appearance had changed. She'd been serious about preferring not to wear makeup or jewelry and she still didn't do any of that, but there was something noticeably different about her anyway. Like a weight had been lifted off her shoulders. She carried herself differently, smiled more easily, became animated in a way I hadn't seen in years.

Part of that was me, I knew. I probably looked different, too, walking around with a permanent smile on my face. But I thought Kara's changes came more from being unburdened by all the shit she'd been carrying alone. Now that we knew, she simply didn't have to hide anymore.

"Hey," my mom said, stopping us almost the moment we'd climbed off my bike.

Yeah, that was new, too. It felt damn good to be on the back of a bike again.

"Ma," I said, leaning forward to kiss her cheek as Kara's hand slid into mine.

"Jesus," my mom said, looking between us, "this is harder than I thought."

I just looked at her.

"I'm sorry, Kara," she said with a grimace.

"That's okay," Kara replied quickly. She'd been on me for weeks to make up with my mom, but I hadn't. I still couldn't believe she'd treated Kara like shit and I wasn't about to forgive.

"No," my mom said, shaking her head. "No, I fucked up bad."

She glanced at me and then back at Kara.

"I was a fucking mess when Draco was put away. I'm not trying to excuse it. You were a kid and I fucking crushed you and that's on me. Totally on me. I just wanted to tell you how sorry I am. So sorry." She crossed her arms. "I never blamed you for what happened and I shouldn't have said that shit to you. I couldn't be mad at Draco for being such a fucking idiot because I was so goddamn worried about him all the time, and I guess I had to blame someone."

"You're forgiven," Kara said, elbowing me in the side when I didn't speak.

"We're good," I told my mom. I wasn't ready to forgive her yet, but we were closer to it now that she'd owned up and apologized.

"Good," she said with a small smile, letting out a loud breath.

Kara giggled.

"I'll find you guys later," my mom said, smiling at me and then at Kara. "I need to help your grandmothers get the food out."

She walked away and Kara grinned up at me.

"We're not goin' over to dinner or any of that shit yet," I told her as

I led her toward the crowd of people gathered around the picnic tables in the forecourt.

"She apologized," Kara scolded. "I forgave Curt when he apologized."

"You ignored his ass for a week while he followed you like a fucking puppy, groveling," I reminded her.

"I still forgave him," she said, elbowing me again as we reached the table where Curtis, Charlie, Rebel and Charlie's sister Cecilia sat.

"Hey, you have a good time in California?" I asked.

"Yeah, I love it down there," Cecilia said. "It was a nice visit, even though I couldn't wait to get home. Olive's allergies were so bad we had to wait until the smoke cleared—literally."

"Good thing your house didn't burn down," Charlie quipped easily. "It was a close thing."

"I'm aware," Cecilia said dryly. "Should I have stayed and fought the fire singlehandedly so Mom and Dad didn't lose their house?"

Charlie snorted. "I was there."

Kara laughed. "We didn't do shit and you know it," she told Charlie, pointing at her. Charlie swatted her hand down. "All we did was piss off the guys and grab your great Gram's quilts."

"I saved the quilts," Charlie told her sister importantly.

"I saved my kids," Cecilia replied.

"Fine," Charlie sighed, flopping her body onto the table, her arms outstretched. "You win."

"I'm gonna get a beer," I leaned down and told Kara quietly. "You want anything?"

"Water would be good," she replied. "Thanks, baby."

"Thanks, baby," Rebel copied with a little giggle, her eyes on us.

"That's enough out of you," I told her, giving her ponytail a little tug as I walked past her.

"How's Wes doing, Reb?" Kara asked as she sat down at the table.

I didn't hear Reb's answer, but I guessed it was something along the lines of how great Wes was. Honestly, I couldn't really blame her. I actually really liked the guy. He was exactly as she'd described him to us. Jeans and a button down, red hair, and the guy smiled all the fucking time. Like he was just happy to be there, hanging with us. He had Down Syndrome like Reb, so he knew what she went through on a daily basis. It also didn't hurt that he worshiped the ground she walked on. Even Curtis had given his blessing. It was impossible not to.

I looked around as I walked toward the coolers lined up against the building but I couldn't see any of the guys I'd hoped to corral while we were at the clubhouse. Grabbing a beer and a water, I paused by the building, looking through the crowd again. Not a single Aces officer was outside.

"Draco," my great gramps called from the doorway, "your pop needs you and Curtis inside, boyo."

"Alright," I said, turning to get Curt. He must've heard because he was already rising from his seat at the table.

"You know what this is about?" he asked as we made our way into the club.

"Not a clue," I replied. I knew why I wanted to talk to my dad, but I had no fucking clue why he'd need to talk to me.

Gramps was standing behind the bar when we got inside and he opened the door to the small room back there, gesturing with his chin, his eyes crinkling at the corners as he smiled.

I'd never been in that room. Neither of us had. It was closed to non-members, and even though it was mostly a formality, we hadn't patched in yet.

When we reached the doorway, I froze.

The room was packed.

My Grandpa Dragon, Uncle Leo, Grease, Tommy, and Will, Kara's dad Mack, my Gramps Casper, and my dad.

On the table they sat around sat a matching set of rockers.

"Phones," Great Gramps said, holding his hands out. Me and Curt dropped our phones in his hands, stunned.

"Door," Grandpa Dragon said to Great Gramps. He was every inch the President as he stood.

I swallowed hard, glancing between him and the rockers as Great Gramps shut the door, closing us in.

"Usually do this one at a time," Dragon said. I couldn't think of him as Grandpa then. Not when he was talking to us as equals, his back straight and his face as serious as I'd ever seen it. "But seein' as how you two've done everythin' together since you came out of your mama's belly, figured we'd make an exception. Any complaints?"

I jerked my head from side to side as Curt murmured "No," from my left.

"Good," he said. "Cuts," he said, gesturing to the table.

Tommy got up from his spot to our left, and gestured to his spot. He slapped my back as I passed him, but otherwise, the room was silent.

Taking my pocket knife out of my pocket, I stood next to my brother as we laid our cuts face down on the table. It took less than a minute to cut the thread holding my prospect patch off the back, but it felt longer somehow. Like time was passing at the speed of light and as slow as a sunrise at the same time.

Dragon handed us our Aces and Eights MC rockers and as we laid them on our cuts, the room filled with a roar.

The men around us, ones who'd raised us, stomped their feet, yelled, and beat their fists on the table.

I couldn't stop the pride that filled my chest as I glanced around the room. I knew it was a moment I'd remember until I was an old man. When everything else was a vague memory, I would see that moment with absolute clarity.

Grease spoke as soon as the cheers had quieted.

"Curtis, you've paid your dues and shoveled shit for over a year and you've probably seen this comin'."

"Surprised the shit outta me, actually," my brother said, making everyone in the room laugh.

"Draco," Grease said, his tone making everything inside me still, "you haven't been wearin' that prospect cut long."

I nodded.

"But you've been workin' for the good of the club a hell of a lot longer," he said. He paused, and in that moment, I remembered every message I'd passed, every contact I'd made, and every secret I'd brought home to them. "You've earned a rocker ten times over, brother."

I swallowed and nodded again.

"Plenty of men right outside that are waitin' to congratulate you—"

"And a tattoo gun," Will called out jokingly.

Fuck. I pictured the full back tattoo I was going to end up with by the end of the night. Kara was going to have to keep her hands off my back for a few days while I healed. She wasn't going to be happy about that.

"But we've got a few things to discuss first," Grease said.

"I actually had somethin'," I said, making his eyes eyebrows lift in surprise.

"Table's yours," he said curiously.

"There's a cop—"

"Aw, fuck," Tommy muttered.

"He's been fuckin' with Kara," I said, giving him a nod.

"Fuckin' with her how?" Mack asked.

"Pullin' her over for no reason," I answered. "Stoppin' her on the street."

"This cop got a name?" Grandpa Dragon asked.

"Park," I said.

"Shit," Gramps Casper said, drawing the word out. "I know that fucker."

"You do?"

"He remembers fuckin' *everyone*," Tommy said.

"Cousin of the Sholes kid," Gramps Casper said.

"What?" I asked, stunned. Travis Sholes was the whole reason I'd gone to prison.

"I'll take care of it," Gramps said. "Couple words with a friendly sheriff I know."

I opened my mouth to argue and he stopped me with a raised hand.

"Takin' out a cop is a stupid move," Gramps continued. "We don't do that unless there's no other option."

"Scarin' him wouldn't hurt," Mack muttered.

"Give it a week," Gramps said, "and he'll be civilian Randy Park."

"His name is Randy?" Tommy said, laughing. "Parents musta hated him."

"That work?" Gramps asked me. "If he's still a problem, he won't have a badge to hide behind."

"Works for now," I said slowly.

"Doubt he'll do shit once he stops wearin' a badge," Grandpa Dragon said easily.

"No payback, though," Will said with a grimace.

"I've seen the guy," Curtis said quietly. "Doubt he's got much except the uniform. He'll feel it."

"Alright, now we've got that covered—"

A tentative knock made Grandpa Dragon pause.

My great gramps opened the door. "What do ya need, lass?"

"My husband," Callie said, her voice apologetic.

"What's up, Sugar?" Grease said, rounding the table.

"Some guy from Montana," she said in confusion. "How'd he get my number, Asa?"

"I'll take care of it," he said, kissing her as he took her phone from her hand.

Great Gramps closed the door again as Grease lifted the phone to his ear.

"Yeah?" He paused, listening. "You got it," he said before hanging up. He opened the door again and set the phone on the bar before coming back in.

I watched as Grease met Grandpa's eyes, then looked at each of his sons.

"Horsemen are callin' in their marker."

The whole room went electric and I had zero idea what the fuck was happening.

"It's been almost twenty-five years," Will said quietly.

"And we'll give 'em whatever they need," Great Gramps said, his voice low.

Coming in Spring 2022

# CRAVING UNBOUND

A crossover novel by Nicole Jacquelyn and Madeline Sheehan.

# ACKNOWLEDGEMENTS

To the bloggers and readers – thank you so much for your patience and excitement about Kara's story. I know that I've slowed down a lot and don't publish as often as I used to—babies make it tough to sit in front of my laptop no matter how badly I want to write—but you guys never forget the Aces and I'm so grateful for you.

To Mom and Dad – It's weird when your parents are your best friends, right? I love you guys.

To my kiddos – Stop growing! Every day each of you gets bigger and smarter and braver and funnier. I'm so proud of you guys… never move out, okay?

Sister – love you!

Nikki – As always, you're the wind beneath my wings. Thank you a million times for coming with me on this journey, especially Kara's. You showed up for me during a time when I would've fully understood if you bowed out. I can't tell you how much that means to me.

Madeline – Who would've guessed eight years ago that a Facebook message between strangers would've started a friendship like ours? Lucky.

Toni – Peas and Carrots, dude. Always.

Letitia – Thank you for the absolutely fantastic job you do, giving my characters a face that we show to the world.

Michelle, Pam and Beatrice – You guys are lifesavers. Thank you for all of the messages, the time you've put into the reader group keeping everyone engaged and excited about Kara's release, and most of all the friendship. You guys have given me so much peace of mind, holding down the fort while I dealt with life.

Amber and Melissa – thanks for being my first readers again. Love you guys.

Donna – I'll never stop thanking you for reading my first book and then sharing it with the world. You took a chance on an unknown writer and completely changed her life.

Printed in Great Britain
by Amazon

54240191R00161